The Healer's Cross

by

Rich Sestili

PublishAmerica
Baltimore

ISBN: 1-4137-1397-1
PUBLISHED BY PUBLISHAMERICA, LLLP
www.publishamerica.com
Baltimore

Printed in the United States of America

To my very good friend, Bobbi

Other books by Rich Sestili:

FOR YOUR PENANCE

Thank you for encouraging me to join the GA Writers Assoc. Best of luck in Grad school

Spghetti Rich

6-02-04

Dedication

I would like to dedicate this book to my dear cousin Raymond Sestili from Pittsburgh, PA. He is an inspiration to everyone who knows him.

I would also like to dedicate this book to the many men and women of the armed forces who have suffered disabilities, but never complain about them, going about their daily life in the best manner possible. I salute all of you.

Chapter One

The quiet of the church was telling as the worshippers nudged their way into the pews of old St. Mark's. Polite as ever, in this multi-ethnic community in New York City, the parishioners managed to fill small open spaces of each pew waiting for Mass to start. It was a wonderfully warm day in May, 1961, and the early morning sun was streaming through the ornate stained glass windows causing small shafts of light to shine onto the waiting crowd.

There were the typical coughs from the older people and the nodding of the head to each other, but very little talking. Rosary beads dangled from the hands of old twisted arthritic hands, and women in babushkas tightened the knots around their necks. The almost century-old church had tarnished brass fixtures hanging from the stucco ceiling, and what seemed like an endless supply of large white candles burning everywhere. There were statues to the Blessed Mother and St. Joseph and St. Anthony, and one large statue to St. Mark, the patron saint of the parish.

Shuffling in the pews continued as the ushers crammed latecomers into every possible space. Teenagers gave up their seats when they saw older ladies standing in the aisles leaning against the walls. They sat and waited.

Then, promptly at 9 o'clock the brassy sound of the Mass bell rang out and the priest and two altar boys entered onto the red-carpeted floor of the sanctuary from the sacristy.

There was the typical muttering of Latin from him and the altar boys as he started into the first part of the Mass. The congregation waited, heads bowed for their turn at the first response. No choir, no lectern leader, just the automatic short phrase responses in Latin to the priest's messages.

Still they waited for the moment when he would come to the lectern and give his sermon. That's what they were here for. They wanted to hear, "the man" as he was called by this parish. The man who the whole city practically was talking about. The person who was important enough to have his picture and a 2,000-word story about him in the *New York Times*.

They waited and breathed a little heavier as Fr. Dennis Marleski bowed to

7

the altar and went over to the lectern to give his sermon on this Sunday morning. He walked up the three steps to the elegant wood carved pulpit, pushed back his vestments to free his hands, made a cursory glance at his watch, rolled up the edge of his crisp white sleeves, and paused to take in the size of the crowd.

"My dear friends, good morning," he started out. "I am tremendously pleased to be here at St. Mark's as the visiting priest. I shall be here for the whole summer semester as I am teaching classes and giving lectures at Fordham. Many of you have already called the rectory to welcome me and I warmly appreciate it."

Father Marleski fingered the elegant carved lectern and stared straight ahead to the back of the church in what appeared to be his way of letting the congregation know he was anxious to be part of them. His sermon started out plain enough, but the people waited and listened hoping to hear more about him than what was in the good book.

"Yes, it is true," he said, as he was about in the middle of the sermon. "What the Times wrote about me is true. Besides being a priest, I am a teacher, actually a philosophy teacher, which in itself is a tough thing to do. Especially now in these modern times of 1961.

"The article mentioned how I helped uncover years of corruption in the City of Pittsburgh by one of its rogue administrators, and in doing so, helped solve a major crime of that time. Yes, it's all true. However, as a former World War II combat marine, who had to fight with God's calling to be a priest, I must tell you, I do not want to make a career out of crime fighting. I hope you understand?"

Fr. Marleski displayed a big smile on his rugged square-jawed face and motioned to the heavens with his hands.

The audience shifted in their seats and small pockets of laughs could be heard. Smiles began to break out over the faces of the congregation as they focused harder on the man in the green vestments with the handsome, but rugged facial features and a shock of thick white hair.

"One thing that I definitely believe in, as did so many of the teachers in religious history, is that we are here for a purpose. We were given certain talents in order to help others. The question for me was, how best to help my fellow man. I think I was knocked off my horse with a bolt of lightning," Marleski said, a small sardonic smile breaking the seriousness of the tone.

"The Lord showed me that becoming a priest and a teacher was my way of helping. But, as a philosopher, with every answer comes another question.

The big question is, 'how am I going to continue help?' How are you going to help? Yes, you."

Father Marleski pointed to the entire congregation and paused, waiting for some type of a head-shaking response.

The congregation nodded as if on command. The entire crowd, acting as one, took in a deep breath and shifted themselves in their seats, trying to find a more comfortable way to deal with this man's challenge. These were simple people from blue collar or hard-labor backgrounds.

These were the people who shoveled snow off the sidewalks in the bitter cold of the winter, and prepared dinner for the wealthy at the hotels, and who fixed cars and subway trains. Helping other individuals was not exactly a way of life for them. Survival of the fittest was more like it. Yet, all of them stared at Fr. Marleski and then bowed their heads, maybe looked right and left to another parish member without focusing on any one individual, and nodded again with a guarded approval.

The look on the faces of many of the faithful told more about what was going on in their minds. Did they really understand what he meant? Was he a bit too much of an academic for them? Surely these people had enough to do in taking care of their own families, let alone helping one another. Maybe he meant this sermon for the rich folks at St. Patrick's Cathedral, and St. Mark's was just a warm up. How should each of these members get involved helping another?

"But giving of one's self and sharing one's skills is much on the rise today. I am delighted to tell you that many doctors and nurses especially here in the Northeast, are forming small specialized hospitals for those who cannot afford medical care on their own. Patients with rare diseases and illnesses are being taken care of. And I am especially happy to report to you that many poor souls who suffer from mental illness now have a place to turn."

The quizzical looks stayed on their faces as Fr. Marleski continued on.

"Many of you might be called upon to help in these small hospitals or nursing homes someday, and I ask that you be generous in giving of yourself, very much like the Good Samaritan in the scriptures. I call it the Interdisciplinary Compassion of the Christian Soul."

As Father Marleski continued on, he realized he was getting a bit deep for his crowd, but nevertheless, they were here for him, and nothing else. They soaked up every word he had for them. For one of them, something special was going to happen. They knew it; that's just the way it was.

After Mass, Monsignor Brody, the pastor of St. Mark's was sitting in the

9

sacristy waiting for Father Marleski and eager to welcome him after that great sermon.

"Well done, Dennis," the Monsignor said, as Father Marleski came off the altar. He reached out and shook his hand and offered a cherry-faced smile. "I'm sure that all of the college graduates in the church welcomed your celebrated plea for, what was it? 'Interdisciplinary' something?"

Marleski gushed with a snorting type laugh and the monsignor also chuckled as the two of them realized how hard it was for a college professor to speak in ordinary tones to this audience.

"Well, you sure have me convinced, Dennis, that I must do more to help those who need helping," the monsignor said.

"I feel like a tough guy when I ask them for an extra buck in the collection basket at Christmas and Easter, but you? Ohhh, you need to give them philosophy. Fortunately for me we already have a soup kitchen that I started. I hope that counts upstairs."

Father Marleski shook his head more, laughing at himself for not being able to communicate a simple idea in a simple way. He was pulling off his vestments, and still shaking his head.

There was a knock on the sacristy door.

"Come in," the monsignor said.

"Excuse me, Monsignor. Excuse me, Father, but we have something unusual I must tell you about."

The ever-polite sixty-year-old usher dressed in his five-year-old, two sizes too small polyester tan suit, bowed gracefully as he entered with the collection basket in front of him.

"What is it, Mr. Almatti?" the Monsignor asked, as he turned his head.

"In the collection basket today we received something unusual."

"Well, considering that Father Marleski delivered a rather unusual sermon I think it's fitting," he laughed.

"Well, this is really different, Monsignor." The usher reached into the green felt basket and pulled out a gold watch. "It's not cheap and it didn't fall in the basket by accident, Monsignor. It was in a white envelope with this note."

Monsignor Brody dropped the smile from his face, stood up and with a dignified curious look on his wrinkled forehead walked over to Mr. Almatti to see the unlikely gift.

The monsignor fingered the envelope and then the note and read with a soft voice.

"The healer told me to give up my best jewelry."

"Oh boy," Father Marleski chimed in with a chuckle in his throat. "I did no such thing. I asked the people to give themselves to charity, and to these specialized hospitals. I didn't ask them for jewelry."

The monsignor and the usher let out with unholy laughs as they considered Father Marleski's words.

"I wonder if this is a mistake. Tell you what, Mr. Almatti," the monsignor said. "Put it in the safe with the rest of the valuable lost and found items and I'll figure out what to do with it, tomorrow."

"Father Marleski, what do you make of it?"

Marleski went over to the usher, held the watch in his hand and studied it. A woman's wristwatch, obviously appearing to be pure gold to him, with several diamonds around the edges.

"Monsignor, it's a very expensive watch," Father Marleski said, as he folded up his Mass vestments and put them away. "The person who gave it is obviously quite rich. There are those who enjoy giving something of sentimental or personal value to the church. It has a deeper significance for them. Europeans are noted for this type of generosity."

The monsignor stared at the watch again, and then back to Fr. Marleski. "Dennis, there isn't one single solitary soul in this parish who could possibly afford a watch like this, let alone give it away in a collection basket."

"Must be somebody who believes in the healing power of St. Mark," Marleski said, and then repeated the note. "Let's see here, 'the healer told me to give up my best jewelry'. I believe it is a dilemma for you and the parishioners to solve, Monsignor."

The two priests confirmed their suspicions to each other, shrugged their shoulders in agreement that it was an unusual act and laid the subject to rest.

The following Sunday, Father Dennis Marleski again said the 9 o'clock Mass. Again, the good monsignor was present as a courtesy to his guest. Father Marleski could not resist telling the parishioners about the generous gift that was placed in last week's collection basket and tried hard to redefine what he meant by helping one another. He also got into the mystery of the gold watch.

"This is truly an unselfish act of generosity," Father Marleski claimed. "I don't ask that we make a habit of this, but I would personally like to thank that person."

After Mass, the priest and the monsignor again were sitting in the sacristy

11

sharing ideas and drinking coffee when Mr. Almatti entered with a green collection basket in front of him. His entrance and delivery was almost a video replay of the week before. The look on his face was as blank, but as eye-opening as a deer in the headlights.

"Mr. Almatti, come in," the Monsignor said.

"Monsignor, Father, excuse me, please," he said in his obsequious way. "You're not going to believe this, but..."

Monsignor Brody went over to the usher and reached into the green basket without taking his cold-steel, grey eyes off his dutiful parishioner. The Monsignor pulled out a white envelope, opened it and read quietly.

"The healer told me to give up my jewels. Have the good Father Marleski call this number."

Father Marleski stopped his busy chore of putting his vestments into the armoire and walked over to the two men. He took the envelope from the monsignor and handled it with a tender touch. He examined the front and back, and looked at the contents.

There were two inexpensive women's rings: one engagement, one wedding.

"This is not from the same person we had last week," Marleski said. "This person is not rich at all. Last week's donor obviously was quite wealthy. This week's donor is a simple woman, older, too. Look how worn these rings are." Marleski held them in his hand for the two men to examine.

The monsignor and the usher looked at Father Marleski with quiet acknowledgement of his expertise. There were no smiles on their faces, but they continued to watch with quiet praise as Father Marleski repeated the phrase on the note and the phone number.

"Mr. Almatti," Father Marleski said. "Could you get me the note from last week?"

"Of course, Father. It's in the safe with the watch."

The usher left the sacristy running down the steps and headed toward the lost and found room with the urgency of an army private ordered to the front line. He opened the safe with his fumbling hands, took out the envelope containing the watch and the note, and returned to the two priests.

Father Marleski was still standing, pondering the woman's rings when Mr. Almatti handed him the envelope with the watch and the note.

"You see, Monsignor? Different paper, different envelope, different type of gift, different price."

"What do you make of it, Father?" the monsignor asked.

"Very strange," Marleski uttered. "We now have two people who have had favors granted. I guess you'll have to call this number, Monsignor and find the answer?"

The monsignor sat in his black wooden chair, with his one leg crossed over the other, bouncing his foot to an unheard musical rhythm, with his hand resting on his knee. He looked squarely at Father Marleski who had handed him the items and went back to the armoire.

"Excuse me, Dennis," the monsignor intoned with a kind voice. "But honestly, the person asks directly for you. I have been running this parish for ten years and nothing like this ever happened before. It is truly your doing."

Father Marleski finished placing all the vestments in the tall armoire, closed the door with a definite and delayed action, hoping his two guests would disappear, and wrapped his shirt and collar over him.

"Monsignor, I can't get involved," Marleski said as he continued to adjust his clothes. "The last time I answered the call to help I almost got arrested, then had somebody tail me for two months, then almost got killed, ended up in a hospital and didn't have a good night's sleep for about a year."

The monsignor sat in the same position, still bouncing his foot to this simple beat, and never flinched in sympathy.

"Many are called, but few are chosen," the monsignor said. He tried to deliver it as a serious, profound statement, but broke into a quick laugh and gushed a red color in his face.

Father Marleski continued getting dressed, laughing, shifting his collar, tugging on his coat and adjusting his white sleeves.

"Blessed is he who minds his own business," the priest said. "For he shall not get killed."

Both the priest and the monsignor had genuine respect for each other's feelings. Father Marleski was shaking his head, "no", but kept smiling at his host.

"I'll pray about it, Father. I'm sure the light will shine upon you."

The monsignor handed the gentle priest the note with the phone number on it and watched as he squeezed it gently in his hand. The priest changed the dead flat expression on his lips into an upward pointed smile. "I better be careful what I preach, Monsignor. As you have said, 'many are called, but few are chosen'. I wonder what kind of a real mess I'm getting myself into this time?"

After breakfast that morning, Father Marleski returned to the study in the rectory to work on some of his lectures. He felt uneasy and distracted as he repeated the movement of reaching for the note and mouthing the phone number. It bothered him, as he repeated the words to himself... "the healer told me to give up my jewels."

He tried scribbling notes for his lecture on his large yellow pad, but became edgy and paced around the study, then the living room, and then the kitchen. His uneasiness led him to the front door, the porch, the sidewalk, and on his way to a perky walk.

He paced himself in the spring air and drank in the new feeling of contentment with his exercise. Yet, his stomach tightened as he felt an involvement in another wrenching dilemma. He roughed his brow with his fingers and punished his cheeks with his hands to wake up the blood flow in his face.

"How do I get myself into these things?" He exhaled as he livened the pace. He passed several people on the street who looked at him with a wary glance as he talked to himself.

"I'm not going through another one of these situations."

It took Father Marleski two days to face up to the task of making the phone call. He plopped himself down on the living room easy chair, by the fireplace, and dialed out the number. He wished to himself that he would get the unfriendly, "the number you have dialed has been disconnected...." so he could return to his normal life.

What he got instead was a gravely voice on the other end.

"Hello," a man said with a weak, gravely tone.

"Ahhh, hi. I don't know where to start. I got your number...somebody gave me your number... put it in the collection basket."

"I know you priests take Sunday off, but Monday, too?" the voice said in a half joking tone.

"I had things to do," Father Marleski returned. "What exactly can I do for you?"

"I read about you in the paper. Seems you like to get involved and help people."

"I'm not a miracle worker. I'm just a priest. The note talks something about a healer. It's not me," Marleski repeated.

"I know it's not you," the old man said. "Look, can we meet and talk?"

"I will help, but I can't get involved in any long charity things because I have to return to my permanent assignment in Pittsburgh. I'm just here for temporary duty at Fordham."

"I know all about that," the voice said. "It's nothing like that. It's your expertise in the area of intelligence I need. I promise not to take too much of your precious time."

"Where shall we meet?" Marleski asked.

"You like beer?"

"Yes, I do," Marleski said. "But I'm not allowed to admit it."

"We have a lot in common. Meet me at Lucky's Bar and Grille. East Forty-Third, between Second and Third. Say in a couple of hours? It's a quiet little place. We can talk."

"What do you look like?" Father Marleski asked.

"I know what you look like. I'll find you."

Father Marleski closed the line, leaned back in his soft red chair and sighed. "How do I get myself into these things?"

Marleski left the rectory about two hours later and headed for Third Avenue. He thought about grabbing a cab, checked his pocket for money and decided to look for the bus instead. He had no idea how much the beer would cost at Lucky's. After all, this was New York, it wasn't Warinski's deli where he could put a sandwich on the tab if he were short of cash.

His bus ride was uneventful, but he enjoyed people-watching, soaking in the variety of characters that New York gave him. The affluent, he thought, never take the bus or the subway. They take cabs or limos. The real people were on the bus or in the pits. The looks, the clothes, the smells, the cigarette smoke mixed with cheap perfume. The heavy jeans torn at the knees and the slovenly attitude some had toward their fellow passengers.

He jumped from the bus at Forty-Third, along with a small clutch of other passengers, and headed for Lucky's.

He continued to shake his head at the irony that had befallen him. An intelligent priest going to Lucky's Bar and Grille to meet somebody he had no idea what he looked like, except that he liked beer, had a gravely voice and sounded older than fifty.

Father Marleski found the old bar easily enough. A small plate glass window in front with a green plastic lace curtain and a garish looking neon sign: "open, cold beer". The priest hesitated for a second, gathered his thoughts, and pushed on the old wooden door with the crescent shaped glass window. Bravely he went in without first spying through the glass. Boldly he would present himself, the reluctant knight, on a new crusade.

Inside the bar, the atmosphere was what his new friend had promised:

small, quiet, unpretentious, and not too smoky.

Father Marleski figured that Lucky was the heavyset guy behind the bar who squinted at him when he walked in. The priest wandered over to the bar and found a comfortable place in the corner, under the neon White Horse Scotch sign.

Father Marleski shifted a barstool to his liking, placed his black hat on a safe dry spot on the bar, and pulled himself closer to the scraped wooden rail.

"What'll you have, Father?" the barkeep asked as he dried off a beer glass with a suspiciously clean white towel.

"Draft beer, please; small one."

The barkeep in robot-type fashion grabbed a small straight glass from the stack, pushed it under the nozzle, and pulled on the oversized wooden handle until the sudsy small bubbles ran over the side. He looked at the priest without saying a word, and placed the beer on the counter with the certain aplomb of a construction worker handling a concrete sack.

Father Marleski's appearance was stunning under the glow of the sign. His tall frame, high cheekbones, chiseled chin; white hair, broad shoulders and military type posture were stunning. He looked more like a well-preserved older football player in a black suit, than a priest.

Father Marleski laid some money on the bar and hoped that the bartender would just push it away.

"I'll start a tab," the guy said. "Say, Father, you're not here to scare away any of my customers are you? You don't look like the overzealous type."

"Actually I'm here to meet somebody."

"Who?" the barkeep asked, as he rubbed the bar with the same white cloth that he used to dry the glasses.

"Older guy. That's all I know." Father Marleski lifted the cold, wet beer and sipped the foam from the rim. He eyed the barkeep and tried to smile hoping it would make both of them more comfortable.

"Are you Lucky?"

"Hardly," the man said. "Name's Rusty. Lucky died several years ago. Aneurysm. Never knew what hit him."

"Nice to meet you, Rusty, I'm Father Dennis Marleski."

The priest reached over the bar to shake hands with the bartender and the action brought a sudden response in kind from Rusty.

An hour had passed, and Father Marleski tried to keep some sort of dialogue with Rusty who he thought would offer some advice on anyone unusual who frequented the place. Father Marleski thought his contact would

16

have been the older guy sitting in a booth reading a Wall Street Journal. But the patron gave him only a cursory glance, then a top to bottom disapproving look of a priest being in a bar.

The old man left when Father Marleski kept looking his way, taking his briefcase and well-read newspaper with him. There were only a few more customers left in the bar and Father Marleski had already surveyed them and figured that none of their voices fit the person he had talked to on the phone.

Father Marleski kept checking his watch, glancing at the *Daily News* on the bar, and feigning interest in a speech by President Kennedy about the Bay of Pigs on the tinny bar radio. The priest became nauseated with his own activity. He tried in vain to be comfortable, testing several different padded bar stools, shifting, standing, walking around, going to the rest room several times and finally giving into the idea that this entire ordeal was a hoax.

"Rusty, I have to go," the priest said, showing his exasperation. "How much do I owe you?"

The barkeep went over to the priest and fussed with the few dollars and change laying on the bar. The priest made sure he had enough for bus fare back to the college, and left most of the rest of his change as a tip. He placed his black felt hat firmly on his head and started for the door. He stopped as a courtesy to allow another patron to enter:

an older man, about sixty or so.

The man's appearance stunned the priest. He was about five-feet-four, and walked with a shuffling motion of short steps. The man leaned forward, head bent slightly down, wearing a long black coat, long black and gray hair hanging in pais on each side of his face, black and gray beard, black pants and a large black hat on top of his head.

Father Marleski expected a surprised look out of Rusty, but apparently the old Jewish man had been here before. The priest was impressed and curious with the Jewish man and purposely delayed leaving.

Rusty walked over to where the priest had been, picked up the emptied beer glass, the loose change, and rubbed the bar with a damp towel.

"See ya again, Father."

"See you, Rusty," Father Marleski said as he watched the old Rabbi shuffle up to the bar with the ease of an old Oklahoma cowboy.

Rusty turned to his new customer.

"Rabbi, what can I get you?"

"Cold beer, and a large glass. Make it one of those German beers."

Rusty turned back to the stainless steel refrigerator door and pulled out a cold German beer with a long name on it. He popped the cap with a puffing sound and placed it and a cold glass next to the old Rabbi.

"Leaving so soon, Father Marleski," the Rabbi said, as he looked into the bar mirror at the priest.

Father Marleski went into a frozen animation as he stopped his direction at the front door. He eyed the man sitting at the bar by using the same mirror.

"How do you know my name?" Marleski asked as he walked toward him.

"I told you we have a lot in common," the old man said, as he looked straight ahead to the large wall of whiskey bottles on Rusty's side of the bar.

Father Marleski backed up to the bar and sat down on a stool next to the Jewish man.

"Are you a Rabbi?"

"No, but gentiles think that all Hassidic men are Rabbis."

"I guess you have a point."

"Wanna beer?" the old man asked. He scrunched up his cheeks and pushed his gold-rimmed eyeglasses a bit higher on his nose.

"Actually I've had my two-beer limit, thanks."

The pensive Jewish man smiled as he poured the healthy brew down the center of the glass and made a hefty white-creamy collar. He lifted the glass, drank, and then wiped the foam from his heavy black and gray mustache.

Father Marleski felt uneasy that the old man knew so much about him.

"I'm here because you said you needed some help," the priest said, as he placed his elbows on the flat surface of the bar. "Exactly what kind of help?"

The old man drank some more, let out with a rush of an "aaahhhh" as he placed the empty glass down, motioned for Rusty to give him another, and looked with a slight side glance to the priest.

"I didn't know that Hassidic Jews drank beer?"

"It's not a sin. Whiskey's a sin, not wine, not beer."

Father Marleski grew more amused by the older man and broke into an unbelieving smile, shaking his head with a slow side-to-side motion. He paused and pushed the brim of his hat back from his forehead with a heavy thumb.

"Are you going to tell me?" Marleski asked again.

"I have a wonderful thing, and I have terrible thing you might say. I have a lot of pain, but my pain actually heals people."

"Please no riddles," the priest begged.

The holy Jewish man lifted his hands toward the priest in an uncommon presentation.

"Take these gloves off my hands, Padre."

The old man was smiling with his beer-wet lips, and staring directly at the priest.

Marleski looked around the bar and saw that none of the other customers were looking at either of them, not even Rusty who was cleaning up some tables. Father Marleski looked at the old man with an eschewed glance, not knowing exactly where this was going.

"Go ahead," the man begged with a whisper. "I won't bite."

Father Marleski obliged and tugged at the tight-fitting, hardly-used, black leather gloves.

"Why do you wear them? It's not cold out," the priest said.

"You'll see."

Father Marleski gripped with his fingertips and pulled with a careful, continued motion. The final pull exposed the man's hands. They were short, pudgy, and wrapped in white gauze bandages. Father Marleski lifted his eyes briefly and then returned his glance to the bandages.

"Did you get burned?" he asked quietly.

The old man looked around the bar with a heavy suspicion and then began unwrapping the gauze strips with the tremendous, practiced speed of a spinning-wheel making yarn.

Father Marleski stared at the action and wondered what would happen next. The man finished the clinical chore, clenched his fists like a fighter, squeezed his fingers tighter, then relaxed, opened his hands and turned his palms up for the priest's eyes.

"Ever see this before?" the old man said, pushing his hands closer to the priest as he looked over his shoulder to make sure nobody else was watching.

Father Marleski leaned back against the bar and stared down at the man's hands.

"Unbelievable," he said.

He held the Jewish man's hands with the tender practice of a doctor and examined them to make sure this wasn't any trick. There were deep wounds in the center of the man's palms, bloody, but not pulsating. The wounds were real, about an inch long, and a half-inch wide at the center, and about one-quarter inch deep.

"How long have you had this?" Father Marleski asked, as he ran the tip of his thumb near the fresh blood.

"About six months. See, not only do the wounds bleed, but they actually have a diamond shape that a spike would make."

Father Marleski held the man's hands up above the bar, using the reflection of the light bouncing from the wall mirror. His cursory medical exam was interrupted when he heard Rusty coming back toward the cash register, and the old man dropped his hands to his lap.

"Amazing," the priest uttered. "How did you get it?"

"It just happened. I had a nervous breakdown about a year ago. They put me in a special home in Brooklyn to recuperate. I was paranoid, delusionary and all that technical stuff. My psychiatrist, who also is Jewish, told me I had lost my faith, causing my paranoia. While I was committed, I prayed very hard to get my faith back. Two months after I was sent home, this bleeding started."

"Do these wounds bleed everyday?"

"No, but when they do bleed, they hurt severely."

"What's your name?"

"Weinstein. Solomon Weinstein."

"Well, Mr. Weinstein, you're the first person I've ever seen with the stigmata."

"I asked God the question, why me? I'm Jewish, but I have the wounds of Christ."

"Well...." Marleski tried to say something profound.

"Yes, I know, Christ was Jewish is that what you're going to tell me, Marleski? Cute."

"I didn't want to be that corny."

Rusty came over to the two holy men interrupting their steady conversation.

"Can I get you gentlemen another beer?"

The Jewish guy nodded and smiled. Father Marleski waved Rusty off.

"Go ahead, Father," Solomon encouraged. "I'll pay for it."

Father Marleski smiled as he refused, but stared back down to the man's hands.

"So how do you want me to help you?" the priest asked.

"Help me get rid of it. This is not a blessing to me," he said.

"It hurts so bad. I eat aspirins for breakfast. I can't sleep at night. I have no life. I live like a hermit. Can't see my friends. I can't even go to my doctor anymore because he wants to put me away. Says it's neurotic or psychotic."

"Are you married?" Marleski asked.

"My wife went back to Israel when the shrink put me in the hospital. Never saw her again. Took the two boys with her. I miss them so much. I cry every night."

"I'm not a doctor," Father Marleski protested. "I don't know what I can do to help with this ...condition. Do you really heal people?" Father Marleski asked.

"Yes, but only those who really believe."

"How many people have you healed?"

"About five, maybe ten. I don't remember. Maybe more."

"And you tell them to give up their best jewels to the church in Thanksgiving?"

"Why not?"

"Why do you think this happened?"

"I can't think anymore. I just want it to go away. The pain is too great. What can you do to help? I understand you have connections."

"I don't know," Father Marleski said. "I have to think about it. I need to do some research. Ask some experts. I'll keep it as confidential as I can."

"I trust you," Solomon said, as he lifted the full glass of cold beer to his lips again. "I liked your sermon, especially the part about helping each other."

Father Marleski cracked a short smile, stood up to leave the bar, reached his hand out and shook Mister Weinstein's hand, hoping to get some of the man's blood in his own palm.

"You have a lot of faith, Padre. You're not afraid to touch me."

"It's the business, Mister Weinstein. You have to have faith."

The two men forced out a nervous laugh at each other, while Father Marleski examined his hand to make sure he had some of the old man's blood.

"Hey, Father. That Kennedy guy," Solomon said, as he pointed to the pink plastic radio near the cash register.

"You Catholics sure picked a good one. I really like him. Best guy since Roosevelt."

Father Marleski left the bar smiling at his new mysterious friend. He stopped as he walked out through the swinging door to tug on his coat and gain his composure before walking back toward Third Avenue. He looked around to make sure that nobody was following him when he reached for his handkerchief and wiped the evidence of Weinstein's wet blood on it.

He folded the pure white hanky back into perfect squares, protecting the blood on an inside fold, and placed it back into his pocket.

"Well, Mister Weinstein, I wonder what kind of trick you pulled off to make it look real. A Hassidic Jew with a stigmata. How did I get myself into this mess?" Father Marleski mumbled to himself as he walked.

He went toward Third Avenue, shaking his head in a slow and exaggerated movement as he talked and muttered to himself. The cold beer, and late afternoon breezes from the shaded sidewalk, had a refreshing effect on his thoughts.

As he walked along, he eyed a heavy-set young woman wrapped in a worn, brown, trench coat, selling flowers on the corner. Brass and wooden buckets on the ground, filled with carnations, ferns, and skimpy gladiolas. Her composure seemed bothered and uncomfortable as she shifted often on a battered gray steel chair, exposing her deformed, elephant-like legs.

Father Marleski looked at her too obviously, trying to examine her grotesque limbs without being caught. She eyed the priest back with a curious look, absent of a smile, and then guided his focus back to her legs. His immediate thought was to go back to the old man and bring him over to this woman. A good test, he thought. Place your hands on this woman and cure her, Weinstein. His cynical attitude was hurtful.

"Lord help me," he mumbled to himself, over the drone of passing cars and wailing taxis.

What if it worked? What if the old man is telling the truth?

Father Marleski pushed himself away from the scene by taking larger steps, hoping to escape from the thought of responsibility for this woman's plight. His impetuous nature to be a Good Samaritan often got him into trouble.

He headed for the bus stop with a troubled mind, pulled his right hand out of his pocket and examined it. He opened and closed his hand, with a slow repeated motion, imitating what the old man did. The wet blood had wiped off onto the hanky, but it left an unusual stain on the priest's palm.

What if it didn't work? What if the old man really is a psycho-whacko who should still be in the loony bin? How did he pull it off?

Third Avenue closed in, and he stood at the curb with the unruly herd of traffic mocking him, and the gush and smell of the diesel fumes from the aging buses pushing him aside.

Father Marleski wondered one more thing: "Why?"

Chapter Two

Father Marleski enjoyed his brisk walk back to the south end of Central Park. He loved the excitement of the big city and was impressed with its diversity.

When he turned at W-60th street he knew he had to call on his old comrades Father Art and Father Tony Mezzini who were both back at Duquesne. Fortunately the universities had WATS lines, which made it easy and economical to call each other.

Inside his small tight office with institutional green painted shiny walls, Father Marleski reached for his phone and called his old friend in Pittsburgh.

"Father Art here."

"Art you old son of a gun. What are you doing?"

"Praying that I don't hear from you, Dennis. What gives?"

The two priests joked around for a while and caught up on some old chitchat when Father Art pierced the fluff with his sheer communication skills.

"What kind of trouble are you in this time, Dennis?"

"Art, what do you know about the stigmata?"

"Uh-oh, extremely rare. Let's see who had it? Assisi, Saint Theresa the little flower? Anybody else? Ignatius. How about that monk in Italy? You know, what's his name? Oh yeah Padre Pio. I hear that his stigmata is for real."

"Art, what if I told you I saw a guy here in New York City who has it?"

Father Art leaned back in his hard wood swivel chair and put his feet up on his desk. He raised his eyebrows and prepared for a deep pensive mood. As a professor of anatomy he had read many textbooks about physical phenomenon, but the stigmata was a religious manifestation, not just a physical phenomenon.

"I don't have much time to do any checking or research on this, and I don't know anybody here who I can just walk up to and say, 'hey, can you do some unusual research for me?' Somehow, Art, I need to look to my old friends on

23

this one."

"No problem, Dennis. I'll get on it right away."

The two old friends continued their little chat and Dennis began to bore the other priest with all the unusual people he had already met in New York. Father Art yawned and begged off the line, anxious to dig into the historical research.

Father Marleski was excited about his new assignment at Fordham. He liked the spirit of cooperation he received from his new students. Apparently his recent celebrity status helped to get the best and most serious students to sign up for his class. He was surprised that the average age of his students was well above the twenty-two-year-old level. The delivery of his lectures was taken quite seriously, and the questions and discussion groups were creative and thought provoking.

The ethnic diversity of the students was also a great interest to the philosopher priest: Japanese, Chinese, Spanish, African, and Malaysian. He tried his limited knowledge of Japanese with a few sentences and the Japanese students applauded and smiled.

"I'm sorry but I don't know any Malaysian or Chinese," the priest said. "Maybe by the end of the course you can teach me a few words. "

He was winning them over. The relationship with his class was exceptional. His lectures were being held in one of the larger halls that could seat as many as 100; the administration discovered the class was overbooked on the first day of registration. Father Marleski relished the challenge of teaching such a large class and was given an assistant to help.

After a lecture one day, a rather frail older student came up to the podium and opened a rambling dissertation with the priest about the lecture. The apparent Indian accent was hard for Marleski to understand, but he managed to give the student his full attention.

"In my country, there is the strict belief that suffering is the result, and the direct penance for sin. A mother whose child is born dead must believe it was a fault of her sins that caused this action. "

"Of course that's hogwash, " Father Marleski protested as he wiped the blackboard with a vigorous motion. "It is this exact type of mentality that philosophers must overcome. Whether it comes from religious intervention, scientific theory, or tyrannical government intrusion, we must squash these infantile stupidities."

The Indian man was embarrassed by the admonishing tone of the priest.

He was only trying to relay to the teacher what they believed in his country, not what he believed.

Father Marleski realized he was being overly harsh on the student and apologized with a sincere attitude.

The dark complected man, with the heavy accent, smiled broadly and accepted the priest's kind correction. Their conciliatory gesture was interrupted by the loud bang of the two large doors to the entrance of the lecture hall.

It was an older priest from St. Mark's parish who came in to see the teaching priest.

"Excuse me, Father," the older priest said. "But there was a mysterious phone call for you. Sounded important. Some guy called and said Sol Weinstein is in trouble. I asked Monsignor Brody what it meant and he had no idea, but I thought I would come and deliver this message immediately."

"What?" Father Marleski said. "Did they say anything else?"

"Nothing, Father."

"Thanks, Father Michael."

"Is there anything I can do?" the old priest asked, barely catching his breath.

Father Marleski had a sick feeling. Not only was this message disturbing, but it could upset the whole administration at St. Mark's parish. He was the visiting priest and already he was causing trouble.

"Father Michael, please. If there are any other messages just take them, but don't go out of your way to get involved."

The dutiful Father Michael elected discretion as the better part of valor. He was winded from his scurrying efforts to find Father Marleski and was convinced that grabbing his breath was far more important than talking. He nodded his head and wiped his flushed face with the front of his hand several times and headed back out the double doors.

The Indian student spoke up as Father Marleski watched the old priest leave. "Seems New York has found you to be a willing participant for trouble, Doctor Marleski."

"Thank you, Rafaj. I couldn't ask that old priest to help, but I might call on you some time."

The young man's large smile, showing professionally straightened white teeth, ended in a serious straight line, tight-lipped frown.

Father Marleski was anxious to leave class and get to the bottom of the new mysterious phone call. He hustled out of the lecture hall with inquisitive, serious students trailing behind him. They asked more philosophical questions as he turned down the echoing hall toward his office. They stopped at the end of the hall and listened to the priest's last words of the day as he cited certain text references for them to study. Dutifully they acknowledged the mysterious emergency he was experiencing and let him go. Some of them wanted to tag along for curiosity sake, but he brushed them off.

Father Marleski made it back to the sanctuary of his cold office, dropped his books down on his small wooden desk in his room and began mumbling to himself.

"Where do I start? What does it mean? A person I don't even know gets in touch with me, I meet him for a beer, and the next thing I know, he's in trouble, and somebody, I don't know who, calls me and tells me he's in trouble. Lord, how do I get myself into these things?"

Father Marleski checked his desk drawer for any spare cash, found a couple ones and a five, shoved them in his pocket and headed back out the door. His first reaction was to go back to the church to see if there were any other notes or phone calls, but his second hunch pushed him down toward Fifth Ave. He huffed his way south, down to Forty-Third, over to Third Ave and then to Lucky's bar.

He felt like one of the regulars now because this was his second time there.

"Hello, Father, back again?" Rusty said as he wiped the bar glasses with that same damn dirty cloth.

"Wanna beer?"

"Thanks, Rusty, not now. Tell me, about the old man, the Jewish guy who was here the other day, that Mr. Weinstein, what do you know about him?"

"Not much, lives in Brooklyn, comes in, but not on a regular basis."

"Does he always wear those gloves?"

"Didn't notice," Rusty said.

"Does he ever come in here with anybody? Any friends? Does he ever talk to any of the other customers?"

Rusty stopped wiping the glasses.

"Hey, Father. This is New York. I mind my own business."

Father Marleski realized he was being too strong in his approach to find out about the old man. He re-thought his position and backed off. He kept wondering how he became involved.

"Why would a priest worry about some crazy, old Jewish guy?"

Father Marleski turned around slowly to see who was asking the question. It was a burly white man. Tough looking, about six feet tall, maybe two hundred and fifty pounds, pudgy belly, wearing a badly fitted brown suit and oversized felt hat.

"Name's Father Dennis Marleski," the priest said with a cautious tone.

"I know who you are," the man said. "I'm Eldron Burt." He reached inside his suit jacket pocket and produced a worn leather wallet, flipped it open and produced an official looking badge.

"I work at large throughout New York, part of a special squad investigating burglaries, robberies, jewel heists, things like that. What's your deal with Weinstein?" the tough cop asked.

"He's a friend of mine," Father Marleski said, hoping to irritate the pompous police investigator.

"Well if I find him around Midtown again I'm going to put his ass away."

"He's harmless. He's just a gentle old religious Jewish man who's trying to do some good in this world."

Father Marleski tightened his lip as small bits of spit came out of Burt's mouth as he talked.

"He's a crummy Jew, Mister Do-Goody. He'll take you for everything you've got."

Marleski's blood was boiling inside. "I think you're a jerk. I'm a priest, what the hell do I have that the old man could possibly want?"

"I don't know, but your smart mouth could end you up in the slammer."

The tough rogue cop grabbed the priest by his lapels and pulled him in close, giving him a wide-angle lens view of the cop's crusty skin and cigarette breath mouth.

"Hey," Rusty hollered. "Who the hell do you think you are? This is my bar. Cop or no cop, get your ass out of here before I call *il bastardo*."

The cop continued to eyeball Marleski as he released his heavy grip on the priest's coat and let him back off the tips of his toes. The cop looked at Rusty with a nasty look, spit toward the bar, and left; pushing the swinging old wooden doors with disgust.

Father Marleski pulled himself together, grabbed at his coat, straightened himself and his composure and walked toward the bar.

"This New York is giving me one damn big pain in the backside, Rusty. Give me a big draft. No, wait. Give me one of Weinstein's German beers."

"They're two-fifty."

Father Marleski rocked on his heels for a couple of seconds as he grabbed the rounded edge of the wooden bar. "I don't like German beer, anyway, Rusty. Give me one of those big drafts."

27

The priest worked through every thought process he had to cope with the situation. His years of philosophy and psychology pushed him to be rational and force a plan of action.

"I don't like being pushed around," the priest said to Rusty. "Tough cop or no tough cop, I was a linebacker in college, and a marine during the war. I can handle that jerk and I might not even need my years of psychology. But come to think of it. Maybe that would be a lot easier."

Rusty tried to calm himself, but was shaking from the incident. He pulled an extra large draft for the priest, watched as the frothy beer poured over the side of the large glass and slid it down the bar.

"You better stay out of this one, Father. That cop's a mean dude."

"Who's *il bastardo*?" Marleski asked.

"You don't wanna know," Rusty said. "He's the guy we call in when the New York cops give us a tough time. He's kind of like our insurance policy."

"Why do you call him *il bastardo*?" Marleski asked. "That Literally translates to 'the bastard'."

"Well, the Italians and the Puerto Ricans call him *il martello*, or the hammer. But with the cops, we call him by the name that they really recognize. He's the only justice we can get with the gooney birds. The courts don't care, nor does the state nor do the Feds. The only justice is the hammer."

Father Marleski shook his head as he heard Rusty talk. The look on his face became more Neanderthal man than fervent religious cleric. He drank from the tall, cold, wet, glass and stared around the bar to see what other unusual characters he might find. He felt uncomfortable staying here, but he felt worse when he thought about leaving. He nursed his beer, surveyed the bar again, left some money on the counter and went toward the rest room. He knew old Burt was going to be out front waiting for him. He clenched his fists and fought off the reality of the conflict in his own heart: priests don't fight. He needed to avoid this menace and get on with the real task of finding Weinstein.

"Is there another way out of here, Rusty?"

The barkeep motioned with his hand and Marleski headed for the back of the bar near the restrooms. He made his way to a tiny kitchen, past some hanging white aprons and overstuffed garbage cans, and finally found a small exit to the alley.

The adrenaline in his body began pumping as he thought about facing a dumb cop with a quick gun, and a bad temper. He felt relieved as he pushed on the stubborn steel frame door and found his way to a narrow, long, fish-smelling alley. He let out a deep breath, knowing the tough cop would be waiting in a police car out on Forty-Third Street, and not back here in this dingy place. He looked around, being cautious, but not alarmed. He would have time to deal with the tough cop, but not now. He shoved his hands into his pockets and continued down the skinny escape path. His mind wandered as to who he knew at the State or Federal level who could dig up enough evidence on Eldron Burt to bring him to justice. Or who had enough guts to deal with it.

"There it is," Marleski said to himself quietly. "Forty-Fourth Street."

"Yeah, here it is you nosey, holy bastard, a garbage can lid right in your face."

Wham. The priest got hit. Slammed and pummeled by the big cop to the rough stinking pavement. More fists went to his face and ribs. Marleski fought back as blood poured from his nose and mouth. A second cop jumped on Marleski and began punching him in his ribs. He had to fight for his life. A kick to the ribs, by the cop and Marleski grabbed his chest. Marleski grabbed Burt's foot, twisted it and pushed him into the side of a dumpster. Then he rammed him with a shoulder block that buckled the cop's knees. The second cop jumped on Marleski's back and kept hitting him in the face. Marleski didn't quit. The three of them kept fighting, knocking over more metal garbage cans and making one hell of a racket in the echoing alley.

They kept fighting and kicking until all three of them were bloody and bruised. Marleski got in a couple extra rough karate chops to Burt and the second cop. He delivered a roundhouse right on Burt and knocked him silly, staggering the burly monster back into a brick wall. Garbage cans, cats, glass bottles, and wooden lettuce crates went flying and crashing everywhere. Burt reached for his gun in his back pocket and Marleski delivered a knee to his groin. The fighting became more brutal as Burt doubled up from the knee and dropped to the ground.

The second cop kicked the priest in the ribs and knocked him to his knees. The cop slammed Marleski to the side of the head with his pistol and the priest crashed to the concrete.

"Next time we meet up," Burt said grabbing his groin and leaning over for air. "You're going to the hospital and you ain't coming back, wise guy. Priest or no priest."

Father Marleski fought to get up, but couldn't. The detective Burt left the fight holding his groin, bent over and limping out of the alley. Both Burt and his gooney bird assistant were cursing the priest as they left.

29

Marleski put his hand to his jaw and cringed at the pain. It seemed broken to him and blood poured down from his face. His head was throbbing as he fell on his back to the concrete, knocking another metal garbage can full of rotten fruit and stinking meat to the ground with him. The noise brought Rusty and several customers out of the bar and into the alley. Rusty reached down and grabbed the priest and lifted his head up. He wrapped his white apron around the priest's head and started wiping off the blood.

"You're gonna be alright, Father," Rusty said. "We'll see to it."

Rusty and several of the customers looked down the end of the alley and hollered useless threats toward the bully. Old Burt returned their insults with threats and warnings, shaking his fist in return with one hand, and clutching his groin with the other.

"I'll be back, you bastards. You're gonna pay for this," Burt said.

"Don't worry, Father," Rusty said, dropping the tone of his voice to that of a consoling nurse. "He won't hurt you anymore. *Il bastardo* will take care of him.

The priest could barely hear what they were saying. His head was throbbing; his face was a bloody mess.

"Get an ambulance," Rusty hollered to one of the customers. "Tell them to get here right away."

"Should we tell them he got beat up by a cop?" one of the patrons asked.

"Hell no," Rusty shot back. "They'll never come if you tell them that." His face reddened and his jaw clenched. He cradled the priest's head in his arms, still wiping the blood flowing from his face. "We'll take care of that part of it in our own way."

Chapter Three

The response by the police for an ambulance fell on deaf ears. Rusty and two of his customers hailed down a cab and took Father Marleski to the nearest emergency room. They grabbed some ice from the bar, wrapped it into white towels, and put those cold compresses on the priest's head to keep the swelling down.

At first the cabby refused, hollering back something about blood in his car and all that crap, but Rusty insisted, threatening the driver with license revocation.

"It's an emergency, you jerk," Rusty screamed. "He's a priest. It's not like he's a hobo or something."

The cabby relented and helped lift Father Marleski into the back seat. Johnny Sterns and Morty Eckerdt, two of Rusty's customers, jumped in the back seat with the priest, holding his head and dressing his wounds.

"Was it a mugger?" the cabby asked as he floored the gas.

"No, some bastard cop," Morty said. "One of those monsters from the gooney squad."

The cabby shook his head and pressed on, pulling a hard right onto Third Avenue and heading straight for the emergency room.

Johnny and Morty waited with the priest while the doctors sewed him up, gave him a couple shots, and a large bottle of painkillers. Rusty took a cab and headed back to the bar. He left the joint without any backup help; except the Puerto Rican cleanup guy who couldn't speak English, and had no idea how to serve drinks.

Father Marleski was badly bruised and swollen. He had reason to complain, but seemed to be madder at himself than he was at the cop who beat him up. He took fourteen stitches on the right side of his forehead, and both eyes were black and blue. His ribs were terribly sore, and he grunted with a whiffing sound as he slid off the exam table at the hospital.

The priest's two new friends didn't have much to say as they grabbed the

31

bill from the unsympathetic cashier who was only interested in when he would pay.

"He's a priest, lady," Morty said. "Of course they got Blue Cross. But even if they didn't, do you think he's gonna run out on you?"

"Just see to it if he can't pay in thirty days that he calls and tells us what parish to bill it to."

Johnny and Morty mumbled to the old lady who was sitting behind the crusty glass window and went on their way. They grabbed a cab outside the emergency room and headed for Fordham. Father Marleski was grateful for the way these New Yorkers pitched in and helped him. It was opposite of the stereotype he had heard about the city.

He was glad it was getting dark so he could sneak up to his room and not be noticed, but there were students and faculty everywhere. He walked hunched over, protecting his damaged ribs. Even breathing was painful. His head was bandaged with heavy white gauze, protecting the handy work of the attending physician.

"Need a hand?" an older student asked, as the priest walked the steps to his apartment building.

Father Marleski shrugged him off, but grateful that he wanted to help. Once up in his room, Father Marleski took off his torn, black, suit jacket, popped open the bottle of painkillers the doctor gave him, and threw three large horse pills into his mouth. He didn't bother to follow the instructions of the doctor. If he was supposed to take one pill every six hours, then three pills right away had to be that much better. He washed them down with a large glass of water and fell on his bed.

There was a heavy knocking on his door.

"Father, are you going to class this morning?" An older priest from the admin department decided to check on him when he didn't show up for breakfast.

Father Marleski was still groggy and in pain.

"Oh, Lord," he groaned. "It's morning? Can you cancel my classes today, Tom?" Father Marleski asked.

"Not a problem."

Father Tom carefully entered the room and focused on Father Marleski's wounds.

"Say, that looks nasty. I hope you kicked him in the balls."

"I did. But I wish it never happened. Help me up, Tom. I need to get a shower."

Father Marleski was a tough old bull. He ached from head to toe, but kept the complaining to a minimum. After his cold shower and a new change of clothes he headed for the kitchen and made quick work of a cold sandwich and two large glasses of milk. He reached for his painkillers and decided to forego another knockout by the drugs, throwing them into the trash without a second thought.

He had to get his head right for the next round of action. He talked to himself as he poured a cup of coffee, and scribbled circles and notes on a brown bag he found on the kitchen table. He struggled to make sense of the whole thing: the healer, the jewels, Weinstein, Lucky's bar, and the tough stupid cop.

He looked around the kitchen and grabbed another big, brown grocery bag from the pantry. He rumbled through the cook's junk drawers and found a heavy red grease pencil that brought a kind smile to his face. Back to the table where he ripped the bags flat and began drawing flow charts and diagrams. He kept this up for over an hour as he walked around the table acting out different characters in this horrific play, muttering low-pitched sounds and drinking black coffee. He pushed himself hard and accepted nothing less than cutting edge.

About two in the afternoon, he was tempted to look into the trash for the painkillers. He scolded himself for his weakness and headed up to his room for another cold shower. The cold water helped to ease the pain of his head and ribs, but he pushed himself harder. He found the packet of gauze bandage and tape in his suit jacket pocket and re-wrapped his head. He felt clumsy and it looked horrible to him, but he knew that infection in this area was worse than looking like a mummy. He covered his black eyes with a pair of cheap, brown plastic sunglasses.

He dressed with some discomfort and whispered out, "Jesus, help me" about forty times as he put on a pair of faded Levi jeans, white socks, walking shoes, and his favorite navy blue Duquesne sweatshirt. He headed down the stairway, onto the street, and walked as close to Fifth Avenue as he could, trying to hail a cab. The bandaged head must have scared too many of the cabbies away as they passed him by. He went near the Plaza Hotel knowing there would be many cabs around this area. He flagged one down and made it into the back seat, only to exit on the curbside one minute later.

He slammed the door and the cabby drove away screeching wheels.

Father Marleski was visibly upset, and he was an unpleasant sight. He pulled the transit map out of his back pocket and tried to make sense of it all.

"Hey, Father. You need a ride?"

"Who are you," he asked as he peered into the passenger window of the 57 brown Dodge.

"Just a friend trying to help. Where you going?"

"Can't tell you."

"Why did the cabby throw you out?" the stranger asked.

"He said something about his engine was overheating."

"Okay, I'll take you to Brooklyn. I need some excitement."

"How did you know?" Marleski asked.

"C'mon get in. I won't bite."

Father Marleski looked around trying to make sense of it all. He knew getting into a stranger's car was stupid, but he had a sixth sense about this guy.

"How did you know I was a priest?" Father Marleski said as he got in the car.

"Just psychic. Actually, when a cabby tells you he's overheating that means he doesn't want to go to Brooklyn. He's looking for a long fare somewhere else. How did I know you were a priest? Heard one of your lectures about getting involved. Name's Tom Stanley, reporter, *Daily News*."

"Nice to meet you, I'm Dennis Marleski, but I guess you already know that. A very sore and beat up Dennis Marleski."

"Who did it?"

"Some dumb cop."

"One of the gooney birds?"

"You really do know a lot."

"They never picked on a priest before. Mostly they beat up the Jews and Puerto Ricans. Somehow they get away with it. The gooney bird cops shake them down for money."

"What if they don't come up with the money, what then?"

"Last week they found an old Jewish guy floating in the East River. They don't mess around."

"Who investigates this stuff? There has to be somebody: the State the Feds?"

"Not around here, Father. All of the money right now is going into basic city cop services. There isn't enough to go after dirty cops."

"What about the Feds?"

Stanley looked at the priest as he slowed down a bit.

"Father, these guys are so good, there's never any evidence to make an arrest or go for a trial."

Father Marleski took a deep breath and grabbed for his ribs, holding a flat hand against them for support.

"Why Brooklyn, Father?"

"I need to start somewhere. I'm looking for an old Hassidic Jewish guy named Solomon Weinstein. I'm told Brooklyn's got to be the place to start."

"Oh great, you might as well be looking for Smith or Jones."

The reporter drove over the bridge and entered into the Williamsburg neighborhood of Brooklyn. They slowed down as Father Marleski looked at every Hassidic Jew he saw. He kept shaking his head.

"Let's pull over and park. We need to talk to some people," the priest said.

"Park? Like where?"

"There, right there."

"That's a fire hydrant, Father."

"We won't be long."

The reporter obeyed only because the priest was in pain and he didn't want to aggravate the problem. They got out of the car and looked around, exchanging dead flat facial expressions with the local gentry.

"Let's go in here," the priest said, as they eyed the plate glass window with large gold Jewish letters on the front. They opened the door to the ancient kosher butcher shop, and were treated to the unappetizing smell of fresh cut chickens. Three old men wearing yarmulkas, white aprons, and long sleeved white shirts, scuffed around the sawdust covered wooden floor. They froze as the two gentiles came in the door.

"Good afternoon, gentlemen," Father Marleski said, surprising them with his scary appearance. "I'm looking for a friend of mine. His name is Solomon Weinstein. Do you know where I can find him? Short guy, about sixty."

The three butchers standing with their hands on their hips looked at each other in an unbelieving manner. One of them answered trying to be helpful, but emphasized the futility of the question.

"Sol Weinstein on Fifth Street? Sixth Street? Seventh Street? Which one? We only have about two thousand Sol Weinsteins in Brooklyn."

The priest looked at the three butchers, then looked at Tom Stanley, then shrugged his shoulders as they shrugged theirs and politely left the shop.

"Well, that takes care of that," the reporter said, holding back a heavy laugh. "I think you should put an ad in the paper, 'Sol Weinstein, please call me'. Maybe that would help." Stanley said, enjoying every bit of the sarcasm.

The priest put his hand to his bandaged head and started back to the car.

"What kind of work does this guy do, Father?"

"I have no idea."

"He goes to Lucky's bar because he likes the German beer they have there. That's about all I know."

The reporter looked skyward for a moment, then back to the ground in a deep pensive mood. "Hey wait," he said, interrupting his own thought. "Let's get back to Manhattan. I have an idea."

The brown Dodge sedan headed back over the bridge and straight for midtown. The priest said nothing. He didn't know enough about the big city to help. He looked at the *Daily News* on the front seat of Stanley's car and kept reading the headline to himself.

"Bay of Pigs. Did the Kennedys screw up?"

Father Marleski thought about making conversation on the way back to Manhattan, and the Bay of Pigs issue would have been a good one, but he decided to conserve his energy and brainpower. He had more on his plate now than he could handle.

The Dodge made it to Fifth Avenue, then over to West 47th Street, between Fifth and Sixth Avenues. Father Marleski just watched, and grabbed the door handle for support as Stanley pushed the big Dodge through the heavy traffic. He was fearless as he drove, forcing big yellow cabs to give him a piece of the New York asphalt.

"Take a look," Stanley said. "We're coming into the diamond section. Hassidic Jews are big in the diamond business, and this is the heart of it."

There were streams of men dressed in black suits with long jackets, side locks, (pais) beards, and deep serious looks on their faces.

"There he is," Father Marleski said, coming awake as if he were hit with a jolt of electricity. "No wait, there he is. Wait, they all look like him. I'll never find him. Let me get out and ask."

"I can't park here, Father. I'm not one of those big black Lincoln limos."

"Thanks for the ride, Tom," the priest said as he got out of the car and closed the door with his left foot, saving any jarring of his ribs.

"Hey, where will I meet up with you," Stanley said.

"Why?" the priest asked.

"There's a story here. I want to be in on it," Stanley said.

"You'll find me," the priest said. "But I would rather keep my name out of the papers thank you. A guy could get killed like this."

"Father, I think it's a little late for that. You're already involved. The gooneys already have you as a target, and you don't even know why. I think you can use my help."

Father Marleski paused for a moment, bit on his lower lip and waved the reporter off. "Maybe," he said. "Maybe I'll let you know what's happening."

He walked over to a group of men and tapped one of them on the shoulder.

"Excuse me, sir," the priest said, trying to get the attention of a younger Jewish man.

"No hand outs," the guy said checking out Marleski's appearance.

"I'm looking for a Solomon Weinstein, older guy, about this short," he motioned with his hand. "About sixty, walks with quick short steps and he wears gloves all the time."

The Jewish guy laughed. "Sounds like everybody I know except for the gloves."

"Hey, you looking for Weinsteins?" a nebby old man butted in.

"Yes," the priest shot back, turning his head toward the man.

"Weinsteins always go with Spiegelmans. Try the sixth floor of that building there," he motioned with a swinging brief case, toward a granite building blackened with age, that resembled a fortress. "You gotta have a password, though. The guards are really tough. I mean really tough. You try something stupid and they literally throw you out the door."

"Thank you," the plainclothes priest said.

He walked with a determined pace into the lobby, and passed by some burly security cops dressed in light brown uniforms and wearing real guns. They followed the priest with cautious eyes as he wandered through the lobby.

Most of the men visitors to the building were very well dressed in expensive suits or Hassidic clothing. Most of the women were young and gorgeous and wearing perfectly tight, expensive dresses. They seemed to accompany older men who had double chins and thick calfskin wallets.

The ride up the elevator seemed like it took an hour, for the priest. The other riders just eyed him, mostly with untrusting stares, as they fidgeted their hands on their briefcases. Briefcases probably loaded with expensive diamonds. Tall white Polish guys with bandages, wearing casual clothes, wearing dark sunglasses just didn't fit in here.

The bell sounded for the sixth floor, he got off and mingled with the crowd. It was busy and noisy, as the sounds bounced off the scuffed marble floors, and hospital white plaster walls. He made his way through the crowd, being careful not to push anybody around or jar his aching ribs. He tried to look pleasant as he moved through the mix of customers, workers, and the heavy smell of expensive Cuban cigar smoke.

"Spieglemans," he repeated quietly as he walked by each small shop. He found it easily enough as he walked the corridor reading one Jewish name after another. He found it toward the center of the long narrow hall. Two heavy-framed, thick glass doors covered with silver, chicken wire mesh, and a baseball-sized metal grate opening to talk through.

"Help you?" a heavyset black security cop asked, as Marleski got near the window.

"Name's Marleski. I'm here to see a Solomon Weinstein. Does he work here?"

"You got a password?" the cop asked.

"Uhhh password, yes, my password is Lucky's bar."

The black security cop stared a laser hole through the priest's head.

"Mister, I've been here ten years, man. Ain't nobody ever made up anything that dumb, especially a guy wearing bandages on his head, talking about Lucky's bar."

The security cop smiled and bared some crooked yellow teeth surrounded by one perfectly capped gold tooth. He hooked his thumbs into his pistol belt and waited for Father Marleski to say something else.

"Just try it, please," Father Marleski said, toning down his demanding attitude.

"Try it?" the security guard repeated.

"Please. It's really important."

The cop stood there for about a full minute, rolled his eyes, and debated with himself if this was really worth the effort. "I'll be back," the cop said.

The wait seemed like forever as Father Marleski watched the cop go behind some drab wooden partitions. The priest was left standing in the hall, the object of several passersby. He looked up and down pretending to show some interest in some other shops, but was too conspicuous to fit in. The tradesmen on the floor, who talked at ease with each other, eyed him with heavy suspicion, but made no remarks.

Five minutes later the cop came back to the window.

"Nobody knows you," the cop said. "Maybe you have the wrong jeweler. There are lots of Weinsteins."

"Thanks," the priest said, with a slight nodding of the head. His shoulders slumped as he turned and walked away in defeat. He walked with a deliberate slow pace to help him think as he neared the elevator. He toyed with the elevator button and tried to stimulate his interest in anything other than finding this old guy Weinstein. He was standing by the elevator door, still looking down, and feeling dejected, when he heard, "Psssst. Hey, you, Marleski, over here."

He looked around and heard the strange whisper again.

"Pssst."

He saw the heavy dark brown door to the men's room cracked open about three inches.

"In here," the person whispered and showed just his eyes and forehead through the crack in the door.

Father Marleski looked around to make sure nobody was following him and went into the restroom. He met a grey haired Jewish man with a long beard standing behind the door, who quickly locked it behind him. The man held an index finger to his mouth to indicate silence and Father Marleski obliged.

He leaned into Marleski's face and whispered to him. "Solomon is very sick. He needs your help. He needs to get rid of that condition. He's in horrible pain."

"Where is he?" the priest whispered.

The old man's hand was shaking with fear. He pulled a crumpled piece of paper out of his pocket and shoved it into the priest's hand.

"He's hiding."

"From whom?" Marleski whispered.

The old man leaned in closer. "The bastard cops who keep asking us for money for protection. Solomon told them he wouldn't pay anymore and told the rest of us to do the same. He has so much guts for a little guy."

"Who's the bastard cops?"

"You'll see them outside walking around. They dress in plainclothes, but they all have the same kind of hats so they can identify each other."

"Got it," the priest said. "I'm trying to do what I can to help Solomon with his condition, but I can't promise miracles."

"I gotta go. You don't know me," the old man said and unlocked the door with his shaking hands.

Father Marleski waited for a few moments before he left the restroom, just in case anybody else followed the old man. The priest bypassed the elevator, taking the stairs all the way to the lobby, only to pass the suspicious security guards one more time.

"Got anything on you fella?" one of the cops asked as he came over to the priest and put his hands to his chest.

"Like what?" Marleski shot back adjusting his sunglasses.

"Like diamonds you ain't supposed to have?"

Two of the cops corralled him and forced him over to a corner.

"What's your name," one of them asked, as he frisked the priest.

"Marleski. Father Dennis Marleski."

"Hands up, dude. Did you say 'Father'? You don't look like any priest I know."

"I'm teaching here at Fordham," Marleski said, as he raised his hands. "Came to see a friend of mine, but he's not working today."

"That's a good one. A priest has a friend in the diamond business. Gonna buy a three carat for your girlfriend, huh?"

"Look, I can prove who I am. Look at my wallet."

The security guard fetched the wallet out of the jeans and verified the identification.

"Why are you all beat up? And why are you in street clothes?"

"The goon squad, or whatever you call them, beat me up, and priests don't always have to wear black suits. Actually, we don't even wear black pajamas when we sleep."

"He's okay, Jim," one of the guards said after the search. "He's got nothing on him."

"Father, you can go. Sorry about this."

"Thanks," Marleski said. "Worse things have happened to me, but not much worse."

The diligent priest walked out of the fortress-like building refreshed that he was getting closer to finding something out about his new friend Weinstein. Somehow he felt responsible and that he must take action.

He inhaled a large breath of the 47th street air and hoped to clear his head of the heavy cigar smoke from inside. He froze as he noticed Tom Stanley, the reporter, double parked next to the long black limos, and sporting a large yellow sign on the windshield.

NYPD OFFICIAL BUSINESS

Father Marleski was getting terribly upset with the stranglehold the cops had on these Jewish people. He wanted to strike out at the first plainclothes cop he saw. A quick idea flashed into his swollen head when he saw Tom Stanley leaning on the front fender of the car, legs and arms were crossed, and wearing a scary NYPD baseball cap.

"You liar," Marleski said as he read the police sign on Stanley's car, and the baseball cap. "You told me you were a reporter."

Stanley straightened up as the priest started toward him, and shocked Marleski by making funny baseball signs: touching his cap, then his ear, then his nose.

He stopped and backed up a few feet. Stanley's weird behavior shook him. He couldn't put it all together. He backed up further almost to the lobby of the jeweler's building and watched as Stanley sent him more signs, then moved his eyes heavy to the right. Marleski followed his hand signals, then his eyes as they rested on two big, burly white gentile males, standing at the corner.

Marleski's back was up against the building and he was not visible to the two men. He made similar baseball signs back to the reporter, pointing to his head and indicating a large brimmed hat.

Stanley looked left and right, touched the brim of his baseball cap and nodded yes, then put up two fingers.

"Two gooney birds," Marleski mumbled to himself. "Okay, then who is this reporter?"

Father Marleski checked his disguise, making sure his sunglasses were on straight, put his head down and turned to the right, shoved his hands into his pockets and started walking away from the building, in the opposite direction of the gooney birds. He didn't want to take a chance that one of them was Eldron Burt.

He walked half a block and Stanley pulled up and tapped the car horn. Marleski shrugged him off with a quick hand gesture, but Stanley just idled the car in first gear, and followed the priest. At the next intersection Stanley pulled up to the curb and hollered out, "It's not what you think. C'mon get in."

"I don't like to be conned," Marleski said, staring straight ahead. "You're a cop just like they are."

"Get in, I'll explain," Stanley insisted.

Father Marleski surveyed the scene. He wanted to make sure that Stanley wasn't setting him up for some sort of ambush.

"Okay, it better be good, what gives?"

"I use it all the time when I want to double-park. It's a fake sign that let's me get close to the action."

"You're dangerous," the priest said. "And what about the baseball cap, NYPD. What if you get stopped by a real cop?"

"I'll just tell them it means New York Post Dispatch."

Marleski shook his head at the guts of this reporter and decided to take the offer of the ride. He got back into the Dodge, leaned back on the seat and

41

laughed hard. He was impressed with the ingenuity of his new sidekick.

"Maybe you'll open up and tell me what this is all about," Stanley said.

"Not today," Marleski said. "It's too dangerous. Hey, drop me off at St. Patrick's Cathedral. I'd like to make a small visit. I need all the inspiration I can get right now."

The reporter agreed and headed back to Fifth Avenue granting the priest his wish. Father Marleski smiled as the big sedan pulled up to the curb. He waited for a moment to try to put everything together, but thought the better of it. He waved good-bye to his new friend and went inside the large Gothic masterpiece.

As he entered, he felt a rush of nostalgia about the large cathedrals in Europe he had visited. The massive structure was cold inside and echoed easily, but extended an awkward welcome from the corrupt world several blocks away. Father Marleski pushed his sunglasses up on his head, surveyed the empty church and selected a pew near the back. He edged into the old wooden oak pew, knelt down and prayed. The serenity of the dark church was comforting and allowed him some rest. He was hoping for a major inspiration to his problems as he focused on the sharp beam from the spotlight as it covered the marble altar.

He mumbled quietly, inaudible at first, but his words became more distinct as he closed his eyes, and bowed his head.

"Give me a sign," he whispered in a pious way. "Tell me what's going on, and where I need to go from here?"

"Listen to me," a mysterious voice whispered from about three pews behind him. "No matter how hard you pray, Duquesne will still have a tough time against Fordham."

Father Marleski lifted his head, swung around in the pew and looked squarely at his old friend.

"Art, when did you get in?"

"About an hour ago," he whispered back. "Greyhound bus."

Father Art got out of his pew and went over to Father Marleski.

"You weren't at the college, so I thought I would come down here for a quick visit. Good Lord Almighty, Dennis what happened to you?" Father Art asked as he focused on Marleski's face.

"Ran into a group of cops who don't like priests."

Father Art strained his eyes for a better look at his friend's wounds. "Man, that looks bad."

"Art it feels worse than it looks."

"Dennis, I ran that test on the handkerchief you sent me. It's real blood alright," Art said. "No tricks, no chemicals, no gimmicks, just plain blood. I'm anxious to hear more about this guy, and how or why he has the stigmata. If he really has it. As a Ph.D. scientist I am skeptical. As a religious person, well anything is possible."

"Let's get back to the college and we can talk, Art. We have a lot of things to go over. I can really use your help."

The two priests blessed themselves, genuflected and went toward the back of the church. Father Marleski stopped by the poor box, and reached in his pocket for some loose change. He lifted the lid to drop his money in and noticed it was stuffed with a fancy woman's scarf. He realized this was unusual and pulled the scarf out of the box.

Father Art watched him with a curious eye, never really knowing what his friend would do next. The scarf was expensive silk, with fine lace on the edges. It displayed more as he pulled it out further. A gaudy, but expensive necklace was attached to it. At first the jewels appeared to be fake because the gems were so large. But as the two priests examined it closer they were convinced it was real.

"There's probably a note with it," Dennis said. "There usually is."

"Ahem." A man standing in the shadows of a marble pillar cleared his throat in an obvious attempt to get their attention. The noise this maintenance man made clearing his throat echoed throughout the back of the church.

"At St. Patrick's we don't make a habit of letting people examine the poor box," the janitor said.

"I'm a priest," Father Marleski protested in a whisper. "This is Father Art, he's from Pittsburgh."

It took a while, but Father Marleski was able to explain to the worker what was going on, but he felt terribly clumsy when it came to the part about the healer.

"It started at St. Mark's," Marleski said. "People were dropping their jewels in the basket. I'm surprised it would happen here, too."

The worker was unimpressed, scoffing at the priests as if they were commoners when they mentioned St. Mark's. He took the scarf and jewels from the priest's hands and stuffed them back into the box. He eyed the priests and waited by the box, guarding it, as they made a clumsy good-bye gesture and left the church.

Outside, the two priests talked freely as they made their way back to the college. Solomon Weinstein was healing people. There were obvious reasons why he would not want people to know about his powers. Was it possible the reporter from the *Daily News* really knew something, but didn't know enough?

When they got to the steps of Father Marleski's apartment building, they noticed the monsignor from St. Mark's sitting on a bench waiting patiently.

"Monsignor Brody, what are you doing here?"

"Father Dennis, I need to talk to you. It's really important."

Father Dennis introduced the monsignor to Father Art, and all three men went inside to find an appropriate place to sit and talk. Father Dennis found a small, empty, conference room where they could talk. They pulled up student chairs around a heavy black wooden table and waited for the monsignor to begin.

He made sure the door was locked as he reached into the center of his long black habit and pulled out an eight by ten manila folder. He undid the brass clasp and poured the contents onto the round table.

Father Art backed up as he saw more jewels and watches than he had ever seen before: necklaces, rings, bracelets, and gold cuff links.

"They all have the same kind of note," the monsignor said. "Except some of them are now in Spanish."

"Of course," Father Dennis said. "Old man Weinstein told me he had Cuban and Puerto Rican friends."

Monsignor Brody fished through the manila envelope again and produced a regular white envelope with Father Marleski's name on it.

"Whenever we receive an envelope in the collection basket with a specific priest's name on it, we let that priest open it," the monsignor said.

Father Marleski stared at Father Brody as he analyzed the envelope. He was suspicious of it and hesitated tearing it open.

"Go ahead, Dennis" the monsignor said. "I'm sure it won't bite."

Father Marleski felt the slight weight and figured it to be a two or three page letter. He tore off one end and pulled out the contents: a one-page letter, and five new, stiff, one hundred-dollar bills.

"What the heck," Art said, in a surprising tone. "These New Yorkers sure have the money."

The monsignor was also surprised as Father Dennis unfolded the perfectly folded white stationery. He displayed the letter to the other priests showing them the official seal of the United States Treasury Department. They looked at it in stone silence as he read.

*Dear Father Marleski. This is not
a prank. We need for you and your
special friend to come to Washington.
The money is for your expenses. Of
course you must keep it quiet. Somebody
very high in government needs his
services. Call this number collect
and use the password, 'holy water'.
We will explain the rest.*

"Five hundred dollars?" Art exclaimed in disbelief.

Father Marleski stood up, folded his hands over his head and walked around the small room. He paced with a deliberate and slow gait, hoping that some great inspiration would cross his mind. He looked at Art and focused on him, begging him to come up with something.

Art fingered the bills, rubbed them against the white paper, smelled them and examined the watermark.

"They're real Dennis, they are perfectly new and have consecutive serial numbers. Not only that, but they came from the Richmond mint. They're definitely from DC."

"Father Marleski," the monsignor said. "I'll help you in any way I can. Should we call on the bishop?"

"No, Monsignor, it will only make trouble for you. I have to get Weinstein. We'll make that call and see what this is all about."

Father Dennis folded the money back into the letter and placed it in the back pocket of his jeans. The monsignor gathered up all the jewels and placed them back into the manila folder, and then put it back into the center pocket of his black habit.

All three men left the small conference room and headed for the hallway. The monsignor continued down the hallway and out the side door. The two priests walked over to the admin office and arranged for a visitor's room for Father Art. The clerk on duty was happy to oblige, and gave Father Art a room key and a clean set of linens.

"Will you be staying long, Father?" the clerk asked.

"No longer than a week," Father Art answered. "I can't take much more excitement than that."

On the way out the door, Father Marleski spotted a bottle of aspirins sitting next to a First Aid kit on a thin shelf.

"Excuse me," he said to the clerk. "Would it be alright if I took a couple of these?"

"With all due respect, Father. You can take the whole bottle."

The two priests nodded their thanks to the clerk and headed for their rooms.

"Just remember, Father," the young clerk cautioned. "Never take aspirins on an empty stomach. It'll make you very sick."

Marleski stared at the young man, fingered the bottle of aspirins and wondered why in the world he would come up with such advice.

"Thanks, I'll remember that, young man." Marleski said. "See that, Art, New Yorkers really are helpful."

Chapter Four

Both priests had a great night's sleep. Father Art was exhausted from his trip and his immediate initiation to New York. Father Dennis was still recuperating, but determined to shake off the pain and go on to class.

They each were able to say Mass in one of the small chapels on campus and met in the faculty mess hall afterwards for breakfast. Father Art was famished and ate more than normal. Father Dennis resorted to his typical two cups of black coffee and one fried egg over easy with two pieces of toast.

"Need any help with your class today?" Art asked

"No, but if you want to tag along you might learn something about Socrates."

"Greeks bore me. That's why I love science."

The two men enjoyed kidding each other often and Father Art was concerned about the unsightly bandage still on Father Dennis' head.

"When do you get the stitches out?" Art asked.

"Probably next week. Those aspirins that kid gave me last night really helped."

"You shouldn't take that stuff on an empty stomach. It'll tear a hole in the lining and double you up like a wounded crab."

"Yeah, you're right, Art, but I guess I can take a couple now."

"Should be alright, but you haven't put very much in your belly. If it starts to irritate you, pour something else in there like more toast or something."

"Thanks, Art."

Father Dennis packed up his briefcase after breakfast and both men headed off to class. The curious were glued to the hallway waiting for the priest to show since he had canceled his session yesterday. The word about what happened to the priest got around campus with the speed of a fraternity party announcement.

He walked closer to the classroom and the students ran down the marble-floored hall calling out to him.

47

"Father, what happened? Did you get mugged or something?"

"Something like that," he said. "I hope that you guys are going to make up for what we missed yesterday. I don't like to cut a program short."

The concerned students were afraid to say anymore. They simply followed him into the lecture hall.

He swung his large black briefcase up and dropped it unceremoniously on his man-sized, time-honored, scratched brown desk. He went over to the huge blackboard and erased all the math codes written in yellow, red and white chalk, left there by the professor before him.

He waited until the dust settled in the class and practically everyone had found a seat, when he started.

"Okay, where did we leave off?"

"Father, you have to tell us what happened. We'll never be able to get through the first part of today's lecture unless you do."

Father Art who had taken a seat on the side of the room looked at Father Marleski and nodded that it would be a good idea.

"Well, believe it or not, I got beat up by a cop, in the back alley of a bar, because I was defending the honor of a fervently religious Jewish man."

"Yikes, Father," a younger student in the front row shot back. "You gotta do better than that."

"Okay, you asked, and now let's get on with the class."

He poured himself into the lecture. It was as if he wanted not only make up for missing yesterday's class, but also because he was damn mad at being banged up and wanted to release the energy of his anger through his lecture. He was animated more so than usual. He waved his arms like an Italian music conductor, and paced back and forth like a German officer giving out punishments. He turned with abrupt behavior to the blackboard and wrote with forceful heavy pressure, often using the yellow chalk of the math teacher for emphasis.

When he signaled the end of the class, many of the students applauded as they clapped their hands indicating the finality of the symphony. He needed something to bring the tone down and back to a lighter note.

"Now, go in peace to love and serve the Lord."

"Thank you, Father," the response came from many of the students as they closed their spiral notebooks, let out with heavy laughing and dashed for the door.

Father Marleski waited for the room to empty and went over to where Father Art was sitting.

"Well, old boy, what's on your agenda for today?"

Father Art looked at him. "Dennis this is New York, the cultural capitol of the world. I'd love to see the Met, or one of the other millions of museums they have here."

"Great idea. We can get tickets at the admin office with a faculty discount."

Father Marleski was delighted with Art's idea, but he was preoccupied with the Weinstein problem.

"Dennis, why don't we go find that Jewish guy first. Take care of him, get him off your mind, and then we can see the museums later."

Father Marleski smiled. He knew Father Art wasn't going to let him slip out of his responsibility.

The two priests walked out of the lecture room, down the hall and into a small office for teachers. Father Art made himself comfortable in a wooden student chair, while Father Dennis slid behind the small metal desk and grabbed for the phone. He pulled the wrinkled piece of paper out of his pocket given to him by the old Jewish man at the diamond center. The paper resembled a cash register receipt. Father Dennis examined it casually and smoothed out the wrinkles to read the writing better. He dashed through the numbers and leaned back in his chair, waiting for a response.

The phone rang about ten times, and Father Dennis focused his eyes on Father Art with an empty expression to let him know nothing was happening.

The phone quit ringing, there was somebody on the other end, but no voice.

"Hello?" Father Dennis said. "Mr. Weinstein? Are you there?"

No response.

"Solomon is that you? It's…" he paused and realized that using his real name might be a problem.

"It's the padre."

Still there was no response.

"I was told to give you a call," Father Dennis said.

"Go to Morty's deli on Forty-Ninth, near Park. I'll call you there."

He hung up.

Father Marleski held the receiver in his hand and stared up at the ceiling like a wounded teenager stood up for a date. He looked at Father Art and then dropped his head toward the metal desk, stopping short of banging it.

"Art? How in the living name of the good saints do I get myself into these things?"

49

"What's up?" Art asked.

"I have to meet him at Morty's deli on Forty-Ninth."

"Good, I can't wait to eat again."

The two priests left the small office, headed straight for the medieval double doors near the end of the hall and down the short ten steps to the street. They were both in great condition for their age, and each of them enjoyed walking. Father Marleski was the taller of the two and had a longer stride and quicker gait, often pushing Father Art to the limit when he walked.

It was a quick walk for the two men as they gabbed on about many of the things that were happening for the day.

Father Art pointed to a newspaper stand as they neared the deli. The *Daily News* was plastered on the side of the wooden hut. "Bay of Pigs: Rebels feel betrayed."

"How big of a deal do you think that Bay of Pigs is, Art?" Dennis asked.

"I think it goes deeper than Washington is willing to admit."

"I noticed the other day it said the Kennedys screwed up. It used the plural."

"It's because JFK lets Bobby run the show on many issues."

"Where does that put LBJ or McNamara?"

"Under Bobby with everybody else. It's a new form of government: The Kennedys are first, any relative of the Kennedys comes second, then the vice-president maybe, and then all the rest after that."

"Dangerous," Dennis said.

The two men finished their conversation as they wheeled through the narrow glass doors to the deli. Immediately Father Marleski lit up when he recognized a couple familiar faces from Lucky's bar. Morty, the guy who owned the deli, was one of the guys who took him to the hospital after he was beat up by the crooked cop.

"Hey, Morty," Father Dennis said. "What's going on?"

Morty didn't let out with a wondrous round of applause for the priest, but just signaled hello with his eyes and motioned with a slight turn of his head for the priest to take a corner booth.

As with everything else in this New York atmosphere, Father Dennis learned quickly and words weren't always the best way to communicate. The two priests made themselves comfortable and sat in the corner and Morty brought a couple Cokes over to them.

"Want something to eat?"

Thanks, but we finished breakfast not too long ago. We're supposed to meet…." Dennis was stopped abruptly as a haggard and disheveled Solomon came out of the back room and sat down next to the two priests on the hard brown bench in the booth. Solomon was pale, slow in walking, and hunched over. He was gravely ill by his appearance and could barely keep his balance.

"Solomon," Dennis whispered. "What gives?"

"Who's this?" Solomon asked in a barely audible voice.

"My friend from Pittsburgh, Father Art."

Father Art reached out to shake hands with Solomon, but the old man preferred to use his hand to steady himself on the deli booth table.

"Does he know?" Solomon asked.

"Yes, he's here to help."

"You a doctor?" Solomon asked.

"Something like that. Big on anatomy."

"Padre, I need to get to a hospital real bad, but anywhere I go they'll have the six o'clock news there to see the religious freak, and then the gooney birds will be there to stuff a pillow over my head."

"No they won't," Dennis declared with an authoritative voice. "I'm making some arrangements now. Actually, let me get up and I'll call to get the directions."

Dennis slid out of the booth and went over to Morty's pay phone on the wall. He clunked in his change and dialed a well memorized number.

"Monsignor? Father Marleski. Any luck?" There was a pause as Father Dennis listened to the monsignor and shuffled his body weight on his feet trying to get comfortable. "Great. What's the address?" Dennis grabbed a pen from his pocket and looked for something to scribble on. "You have a phone number?"

He grabbed a napkin from a nearby table but it proved to be a lousy tablet. He settled for the wall above the phone, picking a spot higher than anybody else did and scribbled away.

"Anybody in particular we're supposed to see when we get there?"

The monsignor talked for a while.

"Thanks, Monsignor. I appreciate it."

Father Dennis hung up the phone and went over to Morty's cutting table and grabbed a lonely order pad. He went back to the phone and copied the name, phone number and address the monsignor gave him. He checked his numbers again and went over to Solomon and Father Art.

"Okay," he said, returning to the booth. "Got all the particulars. Are you ready?"

"Gotta wait for my friend, Moe," Solomon said. "He wants to make sure I'm not alone. He's going to stay with me for a few nights."

"It's okay with me," Dennis said as he passed the address to Father Art. "That's where we have to take this man," Dennis said as he pointed to Solomon with the nod of his head. "It's a small Catholic hospital on the upper West Side run by a bunch of Spanish nuns."

Father Art looked at the address and continued to study it, but for no apparent reason. It was something to do to waste time until Solomon's friend Moe showed up.

Father Marleski was growing impatient, but was still sympathetic to the needs of Solomon.

"Are you eating anything?" Fr. Dennis asked.

"Can't eat, stomach hurts too much," Solomon said as he stayed bent over in his seat.

Just as he finished saying that his friend Morty came over and delivered a small glass of buttermilk.

"Father see if you can get him to drink this. He needs something in him."

Father Art picked up the glass of milk and coaxed it toward Solomon's lips. Solomon looked at the priest and shook him off at first, but he responded to the well intentioned look on the priest's face and made a desperate try. His hands and lips were both shaking as the glass got nearer to him. Father Art steadied the glass and didn't allow the old man to hold it himself, but tipped it up and the milk flowed past the bushy black and grey mustache and spilled over his lips and down his scrawny cheeks.

He tried to sip the milk more and succeeded in getting some of it in his mouth. It helped pick up his spirits at his success and he nodded to Father Art to try again. They repeated the process until half of the glass was finished and Solomon nodded that he was satisfied.

"No more aspirins," Father Dennis said in a demanding way. "You have to get some food in you."

"The pain is terrific, Padre. Not only the pain in my hands from Christ's wounds, but also the pain in my belly. You wanna trade? You can walk around and heal people and I'll go back and cut my diamonds."

Father Marleski reached over and gave Solomon a sympathetic hug with his long arm. Solomon was not in a jovial mood and did not respond to the affection, but looked at Father Art and signaled with his eyes to try the buttermilk again. Father Art complied and picked up the glass again to repeat the routine.

"I guess this is Moe?" Father Dennis said, as he spotted a Hassidic Jewish man coming through the glass doors. It was the same man who gave him the note on the sixth floor of the jewelers' building about Solomon.

"That's Moe," Solomon said breaking into a smile at seeing his friend. "Hey, Father," he whispered to Father Dennis. "Tell him we look alike. He likes to hear people say that." It was the first sign of real life out of Solomon.

Father Marleski stood up and caught Moe's attention by waving a white paper napkin. The place was small enough that Dennis could have called out, but he didn't. He preferred the quieter approach.

Moe came over and introduced himself to the two priests.

"My name's Moe Kessler. I'm Solomon's friend."

"You two relatives?" Father Art asked.

"Everybody thinks we look alike," Moe said with a big smile as he pointed his hand toward the sitting man. "But right now I think he's not looking so healthy. I wish I could get some good hot chicken soup in him."

"Well, we're going to get this straightened out soon," Dennis said. There's a group of doctors over at Saint Gabriel's hospital who are going to take care of him.

"Where?" Moe asked with a concerned and nervous demeanor.

Father Art showed him the small order pad slip with the address scribbled in.

"That's a pretty crummy neighborhood," Moe said.

"It's okay," Father Dennis said. "He won't be outside on the streets, he's going to be in a hospital bed with a security guard at the front door."

"Do they take Blue Cross?" Solomon whispered.

"Yes they do the priest said. Blue Cross, Red Cross, whatever Cross you have. The monsignor told me to tell you not to worry about the bill."

"I'm ready," Solomon said as he nodded to Father Art to try one more time with the buttermilk.

Father Dennis and Moe watched as Solomon slurped with a valiant try, then started coughing and choking.

Father Dennis grabbed the old man and slapped his back to get the milk to go down the right pipe. Solomon waved him off and pointed toward the door. Dennis didn't get the idea immediately and had to have Solomon wave again.

There he was. The jerk of all jerks, Dennis thought; Eldron Burt, the head of the gooney bird cops.

The cop caught the eye of Father Dennis immediately and started his arrogant head-sheriff of the west walk toward the booth full of holy men.

"Well, well, well. As I live and breathe, the tough guy, ohhhhh, and he has another priesty friend with him and two of the crookedest Jews around. Where have you been old man?" he asked as he walked over to the booth and leaned his two massive fists on the table for effect.

"I've been looking all over for you," Burt said as his face got closer to the sick old man.

The people in the booth next to the foursome scurried out of their booth, sandwiches and Cokes in hand, hustling toward the counter and then out the door.

Morty didn't see the burly cop come in, but when the customers jumped out of the booth and several others left the deli he immediately knew something was drastically wrong. He reached under the counter to make sure his wooden two-foot nightstick was handy. If Eldron Burt started something, Morty wasn't about to let it end there. He would protect his friend Solomon by any means. If Solomon were arrested then he would surely die in jail.

"Hey, old man," Eldron started again with his dry, sarcastic, acid tongue. "I'm talking to you." He leaned closer to Solomon and found Father Dennis' hand stopping him from getting his face any closer. "You got these tough priests backing you up now? You owe me a lot of money, Jew boy. When are you going to pay up?"

"You're going to get yours, Mister tough guy. Crooked cops don't last long." Solomon said.

"Ohhh, listen to the tough Jew bagel. Okay let's go. You two Jew guys are under arrest."

"What for?" Father Dennis and Father Art both said in a protesting manner.

"Oh, you tough guys gotta have a reason? Okay, how's this one," he said as he leaned closer and the biting words had small spit coming out of his mouth. "It's illegal to wear black leather gloves in a Jewish deli on a Tuesday afternoon in May. Good Enough? C'mon let's go," he said and pulled a couple sets of handcuffs out of his crumpled suit jacket.

Father Art and Father Dennis both jumped out of the booth and pushed themselves against Eldron blocking him from arresting the two Jewish guys.

"Get outta my way or I'll arrest you guys, too."

"Go ahead, tough guy," Dennis said. "We happen to be close friends of Bobby Kennedy. We're real tight with the Kennedy family and if you bust these two guys we'll have the justice department down on your ass in a minute."

Eldron Burt got furious and he started to holler as he pushed Father Dennis out of the way and reached around for Solomon.

"Are you threatening me? I'll take you outside and kick your ass."

"You and what army," Father Art said jumping in. "He fought golden gloves when he was younger." He was pointing to Father Dennis. "We call him the Joe Louis of the priests."

Eldron stared straight at Father Dennis while he answered Father Art. "The only thing your Joe Louis priest can do is kick a guy in the balls and fall down. Who do you think gave him those two black eyes and that big bump on his head?"

Father Art shut up. He realized he painted Dennis into a corner.

"Let's go outside and finish this like a couple of men," Father Dennis said.

"Oh, we're going outside alright," Eldron said, as he pulled the two old Jewish men out of the booth and started parading them to the front door. He locked the handcuffs on them with their hands behind their back.

Morty grabbed his nightstick and went over and smacked Eldron in the back of the head, knocking his hat flying toward the door, but another crooked plainclothes cop was waiting just outside the glass doors, ran in and grabbed Morty before he could do it again. It was the same cop who smashed Fr. Dennis in the head with the gun.

Father Art made a desperate attempt to be a human blockade as he spread his arms out and made it tougher for the two cops to pass with their prisoners.

"He's a sick man," Dennis insisted as he continued to grapple with Eldron. "Leave him alone. We gotta get him to a hospital or he'll die. He has a terrible stomach condition."

Eldron used his massive frame to force the three men out the door and pushed the two old men toward the cop car.

He pushed his prisoners toward the open back door, forcing Solomon in first and leaving him little trouble pushing Moe right behind him. The engine was running and squawking sounds were coming out of the cop radio.

Father Dennis grabbed Eldron's arm and pulled it back behind him in a hammerlock, while Morty swung his bat-like nightstick at the other cop.

"Look at him, priest," the tough cop screamed. "You know why he's sick? Because he keeps putting acid on his fingers to change his fingerprints. He thinks covering them with those black leather gloves is going to help hide what he's doing. It's the acid that's killing him, not any damned stomach condition."

Father Dennis and Eldron were in an awkward bear hug as they pushed

55

each other from the deli to the side of the car, then back again to the glass wall of the deli. Each man tried to get the better of the other, grabbing punching, holding or doing anything he could.

The other cop had the better of Morty and pinned him to the concrete as the customers fled the store. None of them wanted to be around when the black and white squad car showed up. The fight continued and Father Dennis looked at Father Art, with his eyes aimed at the cop car. Father Dennis pushed Eldron back toward the entrance of the deli and tripped him over the other bad cop who had Morty pinned down. Father Dennis remembered some of the marine corps training he had and started screaming in Eldron's face to disorient him. He now had the upper hand as Father Art ran over to the driver's door of Eldron's plainclothes cop car, jumped behind the wheel and jammed the automatic transmission of the big black Buick into low gear.

The tires screamed on the hot New York asphalt as Father Art gave it too much gas and slammed into the parked car in front of him. He slammed the car in reverse and did the same thing. Again, the excessive gas shot the car backward and smashed the front end of the parked car behind them, pushing the shiny chrome Buick bumper through the radiator of a proud Caddy. The crash sent him, and his Jewish passengers in the back seat, to a mighty jolt, plastering them to the back seat like wet pancake batter.

Moe and Solomon smashed against the front seat on the first wreck and now they were smashed against the back seat on the second wreck. Father Dennis startled by Art's driving was determined to keep Eldron pinned to the sidewalk until Art learned how to drive the car. Father Dennis continued to scream into Eldron's face while he pulled his hands free and pummeled the other cop on the side of the head with repeated punches. Priest or no priest, sacred hands or not, it was now survival for himself as well as the old Jewish guy.

Father Art was sweating as he tried desperately to get the car to go forward again. He pulled the steering wheel hard to the left, and gunned it again. This time he smashed the left rear fender of an old Ford in front of him and pushed the car about two feet out of the way as the Eldron's Buick shot out of the parked space like a rocket.

Moe and Solomon were still in the back seat, but now in shock as they tried to maneuver themselves, but having their hands cuffed behind them this was a terrible feat. Father Art bounced the Buick off two or three more cars as he disappeared at the end of the block, screeching rubber all the way.

"Hello, police?" an old woman said as she called in the riot. "You got some plainclothes cops beating up on some priests and rabbis at Morty's deli on 49th near Park. You better get somebody over there soon."

The dispatcher tried to remain serious as he tried to get more information from the old lady.

"Do we have anybody in the vicinity of 49th and Park?" the dispatcher called out on the radio. "A couple priests and rabbis are getting beat up by a couple plainclothes cops. Does anybody copy this message?"

"Hey dispatch, this is DeNardo in car 24. Lou and I will get it, but we ain't had our break yet." The laughing from the cops and the dispatcher was so loud that it broke the squelch-meter on the radio causing heavy static.

"Okay, 24, but get there when you can. I have a funny feeling it's Burt and his guys breaking a couple Jewish heads again."

"Yeah, you got that right, Sarge."

"Go right," Moe hollered from the back seat. "Go right."

Father Art hadn't driven a car in at least ten years, and this was the first one he ever drove with an automatic transmission. He kept reaching for the clutch, but kept hitting the left side of the large Buick brake pedal instead. The double crash broke the driver's seat and pushed it back about a foot making it difficult for Father Art to reach the pedals and see over the steering wheel and steer the car.

"Go right," Moe screamed again and Father Art pulled a wide turn onto Park. He missed the correct lane turning right, made a long slow wide right turn and ended up in the oncoming traffic lane.

"Get down," Moe said to Solomon, as they both hit the floor. "He's gonna kill us all."

Father Art hunched forward and with both feet, slammed on the brake and slid the plainclothes cop car into two parked cars. He grabbed the gearshift lever and forced it into reverse and gave it his patented floorboard gas treatment, swerving the car and forcing all traffic to stop while he completed his daredevil routine.

He straightened the car out and the sideways crash with the parked cars jolted the seat upward and forward almost to its rightful position, but left the passenger door wide open. Somehow he came up with a new driving technique, pushing on the gas and the brake at the same time smoothing out the jerking motion.

The car moved along about twenty miles an hour and Father Art let out with a large gusto of "yes, yes, yes..." as he drove Northward on Park.

"Hey Moe, where am I going? " Fr. Art asked.

"How the hell do I know," Moe said, as he and Solomon kept their faces and bodies hidden from anymore serious accidents or flying objects.

The car was a sight: smashed-in front grille, passenger door open, and the beautiful shiny chrome bumper trailing on the right rear, making a horrible metal screeching sound as it shot sparks off the concrete.

"I wonder how Father Dennis is doing?" Art said.

"Pull over somewhere so we can get these handcuffs off and check on Solomon. He's back here groaning. But put the brake on easy."

Father Art looked down at the pedals and let off the gas. The car started to slow down in a wonderful gradual pace. He got closer to 60th street and prepared for the traffic light that was yellow.

"Easy," Moe said, as he leaned over the front seat and coached Father Art. "Easy. Easy. Easy," he kept saying anticipating a sudden teeth-rattling stop.

Father Art did it with the precision of an experienced truck driver until the last second when he panicked and pushed a little too hard pushing Moe over the top of the vinyl seat and head first toward the floorboard of the front seat. Father Art reached over and grabbed him before he smacked his head, and at the same time smashed the brake pedal to the floor causing the car to come to a screeching, death-rattling halt.

He had to think fast. He rolled down his window, pulled the portable red light off the dashboard, and slammed it on the roof, reaching for the button on the dash and turning it on.

The heavy walking traffic nearby came to an abrupt halt as the pedestrians stared in shock at the Buick and its riders. Father Art managed to figure out how to get the car into park and helped his two Jewish friends into a comfortable position despite their cuffs. He had no idea where a handcuff key would be in the car.

An old lady standing in front of the black Buick with the smashed front end and a bumper hanging rear end stared jabbering at Father Art as he tried to force the wedged passenger door closed.

"You know, you cops need to wear uniforms. I think it's disgraceful trying to look like priests. What if the priests dressed up like you guys? You'd be madder than hell. Right?"

"God Bless you, ma'am," Father Art said as he slid back behind the wheel one more time.

Father Dennis hated the idea that he actually struck the cop and wished that he hadn't done it. He kept telling the cop on the bottom of the pile he was sorry but he had to keep up the barrage as Eldron Burt tried strangling him.

"I'll kill you," Eldron kept saying to Father Dennis.

Father Dennis retaliated by yelling back into Eldron's face with a kamikaze-type scream. Finally, he grabbed Eldron's massive arm and twisted it, causing the cop to scream out and curse the priest.

Reporter Tom Stanley was sitting in a typical reporter's type small beer garden at 42nd and First Avenue.

He sat brooding over a boring and dull day with nothing to write about when he heard the call from the police radio of a couple plainclothes cops beating up on some Jews at 49th.

"The gooney birds," he hollered out as he jumped up from his well-preserved spot at the bar leaving a two-hour stale beer behind in his wake. He bolted for the front door and first thought about running up to 49th, but later thought the best of it and ran for his car. He was panicky. He worried that he would get there too late and report on nothing but broken windows, broken barstools, and broken hearts. He fished for the keys to his brown Dodge as he ran back over First Avenue toward his parking place.

It didn't take him long to start his car slam it into gear, lean on the horn and scream away north up First. He went through every red light in his way and when he got to 49th, with his horn still blowing and his high beams flashing, pulled a hard left turn, and pushed the Dodge toward Park Avenue. He found the raucous lot easily enough. There was a big crowd of people and stopped traffic.

He pulled his car over and onto the curb and with his horn blowing and his lights still flashing drove recklessly up the sidewalk until he got closer to the deli.

He couldn't go any further when he reached a bunch of tables at a sidewalk café. He stopped the car, reached in the back seat for his baseball cap with NYPD on it, put it on his head and ran the rest of the way.

Father Dennis was grappling with Eldron still and the fight was intense. Blood was now pouring from Eldron's nose and the bandage on Father Dennis' head was torn off. The other bad cop got off Morty and had Father Dennis around the neck with a chokehold while Eldron poured the punches to the priest's belly.

"Take that," Eldron said as he delivered a fierce blow. "Let your friend

Bobby Kennedy save you from this."

Wham, another blow to the priest's belly. Father Dennis took two mighty blows and wasn't about to take another. He pulled himself up in a chinup type position and folded both his knees tight to his chest, like a rattlesnake, and delivered a tremendous wrestler-type kick to the chest of Eldron shooting him back into the six-foot high deli glass window and right through it.

Tom Stanley arrived just in time to give a flying block to the other cop who had Father Dennis with a neck hold and bounced him to the ground like a Green Bay Packer tight end. The priest, the reporter, and the bad cop all went crashing to the ground with the bad cop striking his head, getting knocked out.

Father Dennis was freed from the grip and the crowd standing around shoved him clear of the two cops so he could run away. Father Dennis did run. Up 49th to Park and then he stopped. He tried to grab his breath and looked back to see who was following him. He didn't escape clean. His clothes were a horrible mess and his face was bloody and scraped.

The black Buick and the erratic driver were attracting too much attention, even for New York. Moe Kessler tried hard to coach Father Art on the dexterity of driving the car, but had little success.

"Get these cuffs off me, Art and I'll show you how to drive."

Father Art reached over and opened the glove compartment and rifled through the contents. He found some official looking papers but no key. One of the papers was a warrant with the official looking seal of the city of New York. He clutched them in his teeth and tried to think hard what to do with them.

He saw a beat cop standing on the corner near 58th and pulled the car over.

"Hey you," Father Art called out of the wrecked Buick to the cop. "Hey, you," he called again. "Get over here?"

The beat cop was madder than hell at being called 'hey you,' but seeing the flashing light on the top of the wrecked car he had to at least figure it was some kind of plainclothes cop and most probably somebody with a higher rank than he was. He walked closer to the car with his hands behind him grasping his nightstick. He wasn't about to take any chances with this weird situation.

"You got a handcuff key on you?" Father Art called out.

The cop got closer but was still silent.

Father Art realized that tough cops talked tough and there wasn't any such thing as a nice cop who spoke the King's English and exhibited the highest level of decorum.

"Hey, you wanna get the lead out of your ass and help me?" Father Art boomed. His face was red and his voice was raspy and deep. He jumped out of the car and slammed his door, going straight for the cop.

The cop was still analyzing the situation, and slow to react.

"Name's Walker, special federal detail from Washington." Father Art said as he flashed the fancy looking summons at the cop. "Help me get these guys' handcuffs off."

The beat cop worked as slow as a monkey full of bananas. He reached in his pocket and grabbed a key and went for Moe Kessler first.

"Where's your key, Walker?" the cop asked.

"Where's your key, Walker?" the priest said as he mimicked back with a grade school girl sarcastic pitch. "I lost it in a fight. Now come on. We're in a hurry."

"Hey, a priest outfit for undercover. You think you could get me in on it?" the beat cop asked.

"Sure what's your name?"

"Flaherty, Jimmy Flaherty, best beat cop right here in this section of midtown."

"Great, I can use a good smart Irish cop like you. I'll call your commander later, but we gotta go. Thanks for your help."

With the red light still flashing, and the rear bumper still dragging and the front end smashed in and now starting to steam from the smashed in radiator, the priest and the two Hassidic Jews pressed on. Moe Kessler jumped behind the wheel and Father Art wrestled with the crumpled passenger door as he slammed it shut and called back again as they pulled away.

"I'll call you, Flaherty. Keep up the good work."

Father Dennis knew he had to go north on Park, and did that, but seemed to wander aimlessly and stumbled for about a block and slowed as his breathing became labored. He was about to pass out when the brown Dodge of the newsman came speeding up toward him, blowing the horn for half a block.

"Get in," Stanley hollered out.

The priest didn't hesitate, and made his way to the opened passenger door by sneaking between two parked cars.

"Where we going?" the reporter asked.

"Near Columbia University. There's a small Catholic hospital called Saint Gabriel's."

"Never heard of it. Do they have an emergency room?" Stanley asked.

"Don't know. We aren't going for me. It's somebody else I have to see."

"You going to tell me what this is all about, right?" the reporter asked the priest.

"Someday, Stanley," the priest said, as he grabbed for his ribs again, and doubled over to ease the pain. "Go a little slower. The bumps kill."

Tom Stanley did just that. He put his foot on the brake and slowed the car to a respectable fifteen miles an hour.

Father Dennis couldn't remember the exact address, but he remembered the monsignor saying it was north of Columbia University, run by a group of Spanish speaking nuns. They stopped near a small Puerto Rican grocery store long enough for the two men to go in and call back to Morty's deli. The priest instructed the worker to go to the payphone and look for the highest writing on the wall. The young deli worker complied and when he returned to the phone, the priest handed the receiver to the reporter.

"Got it," Stanley said, as he wrote all the information down. "I had no idea there was a hospital there. It's in the most unlikely neighborhood."

The priest and the reporter made it to the destination on the West Side and it was as the reporter had anticipated; in a badly rundown neighborhood, with boarded up buildings, abandoned cars, and rubbish and dumpsters everywhere.

"There it is," Father Dennis said, pointing off Stanley's left side. "The building with the Archangel Gabriel in front."

Tom Stanley gulped in disbelief. "Here? This is it?"

"It affords priests and nuns a lot of privacy when they have to be hospitalized," Father Dennis said. "Hey, there's Burt's car, the crooked cop. Looks like Father Art made it."

Stanley pulled his Dodge up to the side drive next to the wrecked Buick. Father Dennis got out of the car and headed for the side steps and up into the entrance of the hidden hospital. He smiled at the irony of the concrete St. Gabriel statue. Nicely painted milky white, but with a large chunk cracked off its right wing. He paused and waited for Tom Stanley, but was interrupted by a man sitting in the shadows near the entrance.

"Hey, man, can you spare me some money for food? I ain't had nothin' to eat in about two days."

Father Dennis focused on the man and couldn't refuse. Back in Pittsburgh,

Father Dennis was one of the main volunteers at the St. Anthony's soup kitchen.

"Sure, I can help," Father Dennis said as he reached in his pocket and pulled out a couple bucks and some loose change. "But you have to do me a small favor."

"What's that man?" the derelict said, in a disappointed manner.

"See that black car there?"

"Yeah."

"Drive it away from here. Anywhere. Take it to your buddies and have them take the hubcaps and tires and engine and all that stuff."

"Why?"

"My brother is a terrible driver and I don't want him behind the wheel anymore. He could kill somebody."

"Can I keep the car?" The bum said. His eyes got as big as saucers.

"Anything you want," the priest said. "Just get it as far from here as you can."

"Lord have mercy!" the man cried as he got up from the cold concrete steps and went for the car. He waddled down the steps and straight for the driver's door.

"Oooooohhhweee, Black Buicks are my favorite cars. Thank you, Jesus. Wait til my buddies up in Harlem see this."

The bum jumped behind the wheel before the priest could change his mind, started the car and squealed the wheels as he shot away from the hospital. As he got closer to the end of the block he blew the horn for a long time as a final farewell to poverty row.

Tom Stanley witnessed the great gift giving of the priest and jumped up the steps to go into the hospital with him.

"You can't come in, Tom. This place really is supposed to be secret."

"Man, you give a bum a couple bucks and a new Buick, and he didn't do anything for you. I save your life from the gooney squad and you tell me good-bye, out here in the middle of a war zone."

"Okay, but you don't write a word until I tell you it's safe for the old man. Got it? One slip and he's dead."

"Got it," Stanley said, as they entered the sixty-year old, brick building.

63

Chapter Five

The customers and friends of Morty helped with the cleanup of the nasty mess. There were overturned tables, broken chairs, glasses, sandwich plates, and a smashed glass front window caused by the bulging linebacker Eldron Burt going through it.

Morty expected that he would be arrested, taken away and never seen or heard from again. He was surprised when Eldron Burt told the two uniformed cops, when they arrived, that they should help Morty get the place cleaned up.

"Hey, Detective. We're cops. We aren't cleanup guys."

"Yeah, I know, but you got a lot of people hanging around here. They like this guy. Arresting him would be stupid. Just make it look good, go through the motions. Wait till the people leave and you can go. I gotta get my partner to a hospital. He took a nasty smash on the sidewalk and his head is about the size of a basketball."

Eldron stepped off the high curb and onto the street directly into the oncoming traffic. He lunged out in front of a cab with his arm outstretched straight forward, and his hand upturned like a human stop sign. His arrogance was overwhelming. He didn't suggest that the cabbie could stop the car in time without killing him. He demanded it. The cabbie slammed on the brakes with both feet, causing the cab to slide sideways, banging against a parked car with the tail end.

"Hey, stupid, what the hell you doing. I can't stop that fast."

"Take us to the hospital," Eldron demanded, as the two uniformed cops carried the injured assistant to the back door of the cab.

"I gotta fare, or are you blind?"

"I'm a cop," Eldron shouted at the driver.

"So what the hell do you want me to do with the lady in the back seat?"

"Get out," Eldron demanded. "I gotta have this cab."

The ruthless cop opened the back door of the cab and dragged the grey haired woman by the arm, pulling her out.

"C'mon, c'mon, lady. I ain't got all day."

64

"You can't do that, you meat hook," the cabbie screamed as he got out and ran around the cab to defend his rider.

The uniformed cops continued to carry the unconscious plainclothes cop and had a horrible time getting him into the backseat. He was dead weight.

Eldron ran around the driver's side of the cab, opened the back door and helped pull his buddy in. The cabbie was still protesting and the woman was screaming along with many other pedestrians.

"Get outta my way, you punk," Eldron said as he pushed a well-meaning passerby who tried to get involved.

"This is police business. This cop is hurt bad."

Eldron pushed the protesting cabbie aside and as both back doors were closed he jumped into the driver's seat and threw the cab in gear. The tires screamed and smoked and the cab swerved like a scared snake as it pulled away from the deli scene.

"Come back here with my cab, you lousy bastard," the cabbie screamed as he ran almost half a block. His efforts were useless. He gave up running, stopping awkwardly, bending over with his hands on his knees, and grabbing for a precious bag of New York City polluted air to fill his lungs.

He turned around and headed back toward the deli, still puffing his flabby cheeks to force more air into his body. His face was red from fright and anger. He tried to focus on the old lady's problems, but his concern for his cab was much more important to him.

The crowd at the deli was hollering and screaming at the uniformed cops, who were getting into their black and white and wasted no time getting out of there. As they pulled away from their double-parked position, a long black Cadillac limo pulled up behind them and parked. The passengers in the limo waited until the cop car left and then they got out and surveyed the damage.

There were several men in black suits who got out of the limo, and went straight for Morty. They talked to him for a few minutes, asked a lot of questions, looked around at the partisan crowd, and went back to the limo. The window in the back door came down with the flick of a button, but no face was seen, only the hefty wave of whitish-grey cigar smoke. The men in suits leaned on the limo toward the opened window and talked for a while. They waited for several minutes and then the back door opened.

Out stepped a middle-aged, and impeccably dressed, businessman in a shiny black suit, white shirt with large gold cuff links, brilliant red silk tie, and beautifully polished black pointy shoes. He looked Latin, maybe Italian or Puerto Rican. He was average in height and build, but as he walked toward the deli he looked strong and invincible. He watched every step that he took as he walked closer to Morty who was sweeping up the last bit of broken glass. He made sure the glass didn't scratch his magnificent shoes. He stared straight at Morty and paused for a profound effect, before speaking, to allow his presence to be captured in the memory of all those standing around.

He reached his one hand out and placed it on Morty's shoulder.

"Your troubles are only going to be temporary," the man said. "I'll take care of this jerk Eldron Burt and his cronies."

"I don't want your help," Morty said. "I just wanna be left alone."

"Don't worry, nobody's gonna bother you again."

The man surveyed the crowd, dropped his hand from Morty's shoulder and walked back to the limo with an exaggerated pompous strut.

"I'm going to take care of the goons. Just give me a little time." With that he dismissed himself, entered the back of his limo, with his bodyguards in tow, and nodded to his driver to pull away. He kept his window down to make sure the crowd got a long cold look at him. He gave them a slight wondering stare and plastic smile to emphasize his confidence in dealing with the corrupt cops, and tipped a half-hearted salute to them as the limo pulled away.

The scene inside St. Gabriel's hospital was quite different from the look outside. It was bright, clean, friendly, and busy with people scurrying around. Their white smocks and white shirts, but no ties easily distinguished two doctors writing at the front desk. The nurses, who were nuns, wore white loose pleated skirts that went past their knees, and heavy cotton blouses that were similar to a man's dress shirt. They wore a simple kitchen-type apron over their blouses with a small green cross, crocheted on the upper left. Their nurses' caps were larger than normal, with pointed edges on the side, and a small green cross in the middle.

The nurses who were not nuns, wore the more typical straight white skirt outfit, regular nurse blouses and caps. The volunteer women and nursing students wore candy striper outfits, the same as every other hospital.

There were people in the long hallway, sitting on wooden pews salvaged from a church somewhere. Some were patients waiting to be seen, others were accompanying patients that they brought in. All of the people who were waiting looked poor and pathetic. Their sad eyes told stories of depression, frustration and despair. They were in physical and emotional hell.

"Can I help you?" one of the nuns asked, with a Spanish accent.

"Yes," Father Marleski said, holding his ribs and waiting for a lungful of air. "We're here to see...."

He didn't make much sense, so Tom Stanley chimed in.

"There was a priest who just came in here with two Jewish men. Which way did they go?"

"Second floor, but you can't go up," she said, she staring directly at Tom Stanley.

Father Marleski asked with his eyes, "Why not?"

"Because we don't allow no policemen in this hospital without a really good reason."

"I'm not a policemen," Stanley protested.

The nun pointed to his hat.

"Oh, that. I just wear that to keep myself from getting mugged, but I'm not really a cop." He took the cap off and fumbled with it.

"Well then, you must not have it in here," the nun said with a military stare.

Stanley obliged and stuck the bill of his baseball cap with the NYPD logo in the back part of his belt.

She eyed him one more time, and Father Marleski, still holding his ribs, nodded repeatedly that he was telling the truth.

"Father, you better sit down and have a doctor look at you. Why are you holding your ribs like that?" the nun asked. "What happened to your face?"

"I'll be okay, where's the elevator?"

She leaned over her desk, stretching, and pointed to the stairs first and the elevator second. Father Dennis and Tom Stanley ended up using the stairs after they waited a long time for the elevator. The climb seemed like an unjust punishment for Father Marleski because he had to stop every three or four steps for more air.

The stairway was a killer. The place was an old factory built around the turn of the century. It had fourteen-foot high ceilings and twenty steps in between each floor. The factory refurbished in the fifties as a mercy hospital, was originally heavy industrial with exposed wooden beams and rough-hewn joists.

The new place now, the hospital, was run by an order of Spanish nuns to take care of their indigent countrymen.

In the early days of the hospital they exhibited a high profile, but ran afoul of the city politics. Now the hospital was run as a quiet place, and helped mostly elderly priests, and nuns who wanted privacy. However, the compassion of the doctors and nurses was still extended to the poorest of the

67

Spanish speaking community. Only those persons who were troublemakers were turned away. The staff at St. Gabriels' hated publicity, whether it was good or bad.

"Father, are you going to make it?" Tom Stanley asked.

Father Dennis kept pushing along. Stubbornness was his greatest virtue. When they finally reached the second floor, a beautiful woman met them with an infectious smile. She looked more like a princess than a nun.

"My name is Sister Mary Beth Acree," she said. "I'm the nurse in charge of the second floor."

She had the perfect complexion, and smile of the prettiest Latin woman either man had ever seen. Her eyes were dark with perfectly arched eyebrows, high cheekbones, thick eyelashes, (of course no makeup) and her hair was made out of black silk from the Far East.

"Acree that's not Spanish," Father Dennis said, trying to grab his breath.

"My father had to change our name when we left Cuba several years ago. How can I help you?"

"We're looking for Father Art and the two Jewish men."

"Follow me," she said.

Sister Mary Beth had a certain way of making everybody feel comfortable and loved. As she walked down the hall, she touched the faces of the older people who were waiting for one of the doctors to give them some attention. She consoled them in small shots of Spanish that were assuring but not patronizing. She touched their faces with her perfectly clean hand and gave them the loving support they needed.

"Down this way, Father. He's in a semi-private room. What happened to you, Father?" she asked in the same quick breath of a sentence.

"Oh, had a fight in a deli. Didn't like the pastrami."

Sister Mary Beth turned around as she walked, giving the priest his credit for the quick joke, but never losing her stride. She displayed the huge smile from her beautiful full lips, showing perfectly white teeth that her father must have paid thousands for, and wheeled around forward again toward the room.

The three walked the length of the hallway, leaving the busiest sounds back at the center desk by the stairway. It got quieter as they walked into the room, somewhat darkened by the drawn blinds, and packed with beds, but very little noise.

"He's back here," she said.

Father Marleski and Tom Stanley walked to the end of the room near a large metal casement window covered with light green Venetian blinds.

There was a small crowd gathered in the corner around Solomon's bed. The semi-private room the nun talked about was really a small ward of about six other beds, but they liked to call it semi-private, because the wards had twenty beds.

As they got closer to their group of friends, they were able to hear the doctor carry on a quiet and clinical conversation with the nuns.

Solomon had been stripped of his Jewish clothes, given a wonderful sponge bath and placed in the most comfortable looking army hospital bed in all of New York. He looked angelic with his hair wet but combed back and his raggedy beard cleaned up and presentable. He seemed comfortable lying in the bed, wearing his white hospital gown. Solomon looked peaceful and confident as the doctor started his exam. He was lying on his back staring straight up at the doctor. His black wired glasses made him look more like a professor than a Hassidic Jew.

Doctor Salvatore Perez was attending to Solomon and called out important clinical information to the two nurses who were standing at Solomon's side as they were writing.

"Let's get him started on an IV immediately," the doctor said.

The directions went on for quite a while and the nurses followed everything he said. They whipped into action pulling a chrome IV stand over, hooking up a bag and getting the needle into Solomon's arm with incredible speed and accuracy. With the knowledge from Father Art that Solomon was living on aspirin and not much more, Doctor Perez ordered the nurses to inject the old man with certain medications to counteract the destruction the aspirins did to his stomach.

Doctor Perez surveyed Solomon's face with his hands, touching his jaw, then pulling down his eyelids, shining a small light into Solomon's eyes, dilating his pupils. He continued to check his glands, lymph nodes, chest, breathing, and even checked his breath. He poked some probing but tender fingers into Solomon's abdomen, and watched the old man's face for a reaction. He moved his exam lower and got to Solomon's bandaged hands. He took a safety scissors from Sister Mary Beth and cut away the gauze, much like a trainer cuts the wrapping off a fighter.

"What's this?" Perez said, holding the patient's hands up for a closer exam.

Father Art moved closer to the doctor to get a view for himself.

"I've never seen this before," Perez said.

"Stigmata?" Stanley said quietly.

Everyone froze. The two nuns made the sign of the cross and kissed their fingers.

Father Marleski looked at the doctor, then Sister Mary Beth with a puzzled gaze. He was sure that the monsignor had briefed them about the Jewish man, but apparently, the monsignor didn't get the whole story out.

"How did you do this?" Doctor Perez asked with the kindest voice.

"I stood near a crucifix when a lightning bolt hit," Solomon answered, as he broke his mustache into the cutest smile.

"It looks pretty real," Sister Mary Beth said.

"It is real," Moe Kessler said in a definitive whisper.

There was a church-like, almost funereal silence. The doctor stared at the hands closer and touched the tender wounds. Blood trickled slightly as he pressed his index finger on Solomon's palm. The wounds looked fresh, exactly what iron spikes would cause if driven through a man's hands.

"Does that hurt?" he asked, as he pushed an index finger again.

"Yes, it's very painful. That's why I lived on aspirins."

Doctor Perez gently laid Solomon's hand back to the bed and put his professional fingers on his wrist to check a pulse.

"He must have lost a lot of blood and his body can't rebuild it. Let's get some blood in him, Sister. I think that would be a good start. Then let's try some xylocaine salve on his wounds to make him more comfortable. Then after that, well...."

Doctor Perez looked at everyone around the bed and smiled with perfect confidence that he would come up with something to help this man. He shifted his weight a couple times hoping to make himself more comfortable. He wrote some important details in Solomon's chart, stuck the chart on the footboard of the army hospital bed and slowly walked backwards out of the room, holding both hands up slightly in a polite gesture of good-bye.

Once the doctor left, the group of people surrounding Solomon felt out of place standing there waiting for the old man to get better. Each of them felt they must do something to remove the awkward feeling.

"Sister, is there anything we can do to help?" Father Marleski asked.

She looked at the priest with his ripped suit jacket, black eyes, badly tattered forehead with stitches, and holding his ribs.

"Yes, Father. Go stand outside, wave to everybody who goes by and tell them you are a billboard for this hospital."

Father Marleski was shocked at her direct approach.

"I want you to go down the hall, strip all your clothes off, get an x-ray, and then get into a bed. We need to fix you up as much as we have to fix up this man," she said pointing to Solomon.

Father Marleski protested, but a short, strong, Spanish nurse led him away by the arm and brought him down the hall. Father Art went with the nurse to be of some help, while Tom Stanley and Moe Kessler stayed with the old man. The two Jewish men talked to each other in Yiddish for privacy, as they eyed Stanley hoping he would walk away.

Stanley took the cue and backed up to the next bed about ten feet away, and watched as Solomon started to nod off to sleep. He backed into another patient's bed and jostled the man.

"Pssst. Hey, buddy," his raspy voice called out. "What's that guy in here for?"

Stanley thought for a moment, excused himself for bumping into the guy's bed, but knew that the truth would be ridiculed.

"Oh, he's just a sick man. Stomach problems."

"What about the hands? Why did the nuns bless themselves?"

Stanley had to think fast. "I guess it's a hopeless case."

"No worse than mine," the guy said.

"What are you in for?" Stanley asked.

"Emphysema. Too many years of smokes, only God can save me now. I pray every day. My faith is all I've got. Good thing I'm a priest."

Stanley showed surprise on his face. Somehow he couldn't put this all together.

"Can I get you anything?" he asked the old priest.

"No," the priest said. "Just a compassionate moment is all I ask."

Stanley reached over shook the priest's hand and went out of the room to the hallway. Moe was the only one left with Solomon, and he too nodded off to sleep, sitting in a hard wooden early American armchair by his friend's bed.

The room with its high ceilings, and brick walls, became an echo chamber. The oak plank floors of the converted factory acted like a soundboard in a grand piano amplifying every slight movement of a patient in his bed, wrestling with his sheets, or shifting his weight. The noises were growing more silent as the hours wore on and most of the patients began falling off to sleep.

About five minutes after Stanley left the room there was a slight movement: a sagging spring and a creaking metal bed frame. The tussle of fresh sheets coming off a bed, and a slight jarring of the skinny legs of a night table being pushed along the floor. Then a spooky thump as a heavy weight dropped down to the floor. A dragging sound followed, with the squeaking of flesh catching on the waxed wooden planks. The dragging sound was going in the direction of Solomon, who was in a deep sleep now. There weren't any footsteps, but raspy breathing, mixed with body dragging sounds. The person had the cunning of a hunter. Like that of a Cherokee Indian in the brambles sneaking up on a deer; cautious and stealth-like, coming after the defenseless old Jewish man.

The predator got closer to Solomon. He reached up to Solomon's bed and held on to the corner sheets with one hand and the metal box frame with the other. He tried to remain quiet but his breathing was labored, like the leather bellows that aids the fire in the winter hearth. He was kneeling now, resting for air, next to the snoring Moe Kessler who was stretched out in the wooden chair. The man reached up further and touched Solomon, worried at first that he might wake him, but anxious all the same.

Solomon didn't budge. The thief tested Solomon's reflexes again, touching his hand with a few gentle fingers, but keeping an eye on the bodyguard Moe. He looked at the Jewish man's wounded hand but couldn't make out what the fuss was all about. He turned Solomon's hand toward the window catching the slight stream of light coming through the Venetian blinds. He saw, but he wasn't sure. He squinted his eyes for a better look. He reached out with an index finger and pushed on Solomon's palm, causing drops of blood to flow and scaring himself with what seemed like a jolt of electricity.

He lost his balance and fell to the floor, with Solomon's hand dropping on top of him. He felt the bony presence of the Jewish man's hand on his head and gasped for air.

"Sweet Jesus, let it be real," the priest said with his raspy voice. "Let me breathe again."

Neither Moe nor Solomon woke up, but the priest moved into position to place Solomon's lifeless hand more securely on his head. He paused for a moment and whispered a prayer. At first he was ashamed for being selfish in his thoughts, but stayed in this position for a few more moments, swallowing hard to fight back the emotion, and trying to remain calm enough to not wake Moe. His feeling of unworthiness was mixed with his human desire to be healed. He accepted whatever fate there would be, let loose with Solomon's hand in a soft and gentle way, and crawled back to his bed.

The long trek back to his bed was exhausting. He was too sick to pull himself up, but lay there knowing somebody eventually would come into the room. He let out with a goofy light laugh, realizing the irony of the situation. "I do believe, Jesus. I do believe," he said, with the faintest whisper from his worn out lungs. "Thy will be done."

The priest gave up trying to pull himself up onto his bed. He smiled at the futility of his strength, rolled over on his back and fell asleep on the floor.

The rustling of sheets, and tiny bedspring squeaks had ended. The semi-private wardroom was quiet with the silence of a still night in May. Only the shadow of a woman with a large brimmed cap slid along the floor, breaking the scene of the Rubens-like painting. Sister Mary Beth was standing motionless near the doorway now, behind a sanitized white cotton curtain, watching the entire ordeal of the old priest. She clutched her fist toward her mouth to prevent herself from crying. The scene moved her to tears as she tiptoed away from the curtain and toward the center of the hall.

Chapter Six

Several days had passed since Father Marleski, and Solomon Weinstein had been admitted to St. Gabriel's hospital. Father Art was staying at his guest quarters at Fordham and was shuttled back and forth by students or members of the hospital staff. He was concerned about the safety of Father Marleski. He knew mean old Detective Burt would find them sooner or later.

Father Art went casual, wearing jeans or khakis instead of his typical religious garb. He knew he could easily be followed dressed in priest's clothing.

Moe Kessler was different from Father Art. He would never give up his Hassidic Jewish clothing. However, Moe rarely left the hospital. He was the vigilant warrior who sat at the foot of his friend's bed. He would go to the nurses' station now and then to make a phone call to his wife and let her know how everything was going, but he steadfastly remained near Solomon's bedside. Moe ate the simple hospital food along with the patients, and a friend of his brought him clean clothes on a daily basis.

Moe would sit and talk to Solomon, wipe his forehead now and then, help him with his food and give him the general love and support of an honest friend. Solomon was improving. The nuns were fastidious in their attempts to keep him alive. His color was improving. He was taking some solid food, and forced himself to get out of bed everyday to exercise and fight to regain his strength.

The doctors maintained a rigid discipline of medication and vitamins to bolster Solomon's health. Everything was coming along well, except the wounds on his hands. They still bled, although not as much as they had. The xylocaine treatments were effective in slowing down the flow of blood and easing the pain. The Vaseline consistency of the ointment was easy for Solomon to tolerate because he was used to having gauze bandages on for long periods of time.

His spirits had lifted and he felt safe in the odd environment of the Hispanic Catholic hospital.

"Hey, Moe. Can you believe this? If I die in here make sure you tell everybody that I didn't become a Catholic. Tell them I was here because I caught some kind of Mexican or Cuban disease from the neighborhood."

Moe laughed, breaking the demeanor of worry he was living with over the past several days.

Solomon was in a good mood. He knew he was getting better and looked forward to leaving the place.

"What do you want to do when you get out of here, Sol? You know that bastard Burt will be looking for you."

"Moe I wanna go see Millie. I miss her and the boys. I'm sure once I get to Tel Aviv I can explain about my breakdown and all that. I know she still loves me and I still love her."

"What about your passport? Burt called the Feds and told them you were a fugitive. You can't get on a plane or a boat. You going to swim?"

Solomon folded his hands behind his head and pulled himself up a little to view Moe better.

"So help me, Moe. If I have to swim I'll get there. I gotta get somebody with pull to get me my papers."

"The rabbi is working on it. I'm sure something will turn up," Moe answered in an assuring voice.

Moe shifted in his hard wooden chair for a more comfortable spot and focused on the old priest with emphysema lying in the bed nearby. The priest could hear everything they were saying, but never offered any advice or words of encouragement to the two men.

Moe leaned toward his friend Solomon and whispered.

"Don't worry, Sol, any of those bastard cops come around, I got a gun." Moe lifted the lapel on his suit jacket revealing the handle of a small .25 caliber pistol stuck inside his coat.

"How you gonna stop a cop with that pea-shooter?"

"If they come close, I'll surprise them." Moe said, beaming with confidence.

The old priest just lay there in bed facing the two men, but faking to be asleep.

Over in another room, Father Marleski was sitting up, stretching his legs and arms, testing out the pain in his ribs. He also was recuperating with the loving care of the Spanish nuns. Sister Mary Beth Acree was a tireless and dedicated woman. She worked day and night at the hospital and never seemed to complain about the hours.

Father Marleski's determination for a quick recovery was an excellent example for the other patients. They were all amazed at how fast he was able to get up and move around.

"I guess you'll be leaving us soon, Father," Sister Mary Beth said.

"I love this place, Sister, but I need to get back to work."

She smiled, nodded, and moved on with a quick step to another patient.

"Oh, Sister, tell me something. The last couple nights I heard people crying and praying out loud in Spanish. It seemed to be coming from Solomon's room. What's going on? Is he alright?"

She smiled again with those beautiful perfect teeth and her gorgeous Latin lips.

"Everything is fine, Father. It's just that I had Mr. Weinstein help me with some of the older patients. I think we're going to keep him here for a long time. Great socialized medicine for old Hispanic people who really believe."

Father Marleski stared with his mouth open. Did the nun actually line up old sick people at night to visit Solomon?

He had to get out of that bed and go see him. He was anxious to witness a healing. Could it happen while he was around?

Father Dennis worked himself out of his bed, standing up straight and stretching again. He looked a sight in the uniformed white hospital gown with the ties in the back. He had the worst time dealing with the way they fastened, but tried to be a sport about wearing it and following hospital rules.

Down the hall he walked, with one hand behind his back holding the flaps shut on the gown.

"Father, can I get you something?" one of the Spanish nuns asked in her perfect accent.

"Thank you, no. I'm just going to see the old man."

He hesitated before going into Solomon's room and went down the hall looking for a service closet. He was determined to find something else to wear besides these sissy-boy clothes.

Outside at the side door of the hospital there was a commotion going on. Two detectives were sitting in their car with a derelict in the back seat. It was the same man who had taken Eldron Burt's car up to Harlem. The cops had the man in the back seat of their car and continued to threaten him unless he gave them more information.

"I ain't lying, man. A priest gave me the car. Told me to take it home. Told me it was a present to a poor man like me. I thought it belonged to the priest. It was black."

"Hey, Frank. We better call this in. We shouldn't be investigating without Burt. He'll be madder than hell if we blow this."

"What can we screw up, Harry? We go inside, show our badges, break a few heads, kick a couple asses, arrest a couple of old priests, and then we bring them over to Burt. You wanna get ahead in this special department or what?"

"Of course I do, Frank. Don't be so damn stupid. It's just that Burt's been having one lousy time with these guys and he doesn't want any more screw-ups."

"You coming in? Or are you gonna sit here and suck your thumb," Frank asked. He was upset, but burning with ambition at the same time.

Both men checked their guns. Pulled them out of the holsters, made sure they were loaded, put them back into the holsters, and got out of the car. They closed the doors quietly, and walked with a slow and measured pace toward the side steps. They walked up, opened the door and found themselves in the first floor hallway. People were everywhere; mostly Spanish people, some black, but almost all of them wearing the look of poverty and despair.

"Can I help you gentlemen?" a kind nun asked, with a distinct Spanish accent.

"Ah yeah," Frank said as he leaned closer to the desk counter. He kept his hands in his pockets and shifted his weight like a typical roughshod hoodlum.

"We're looking for a couple of priests who came in here a couple days ago."

"Lots of priests come in here," Sister Rosa said. She leaned up against the counter and pressed a small button under the counter. It rang on the second floor and startled Sister Mary Beth. It was three quick buzzes that could only be heard on the second floor.

"Today?" the nun at the desk asked.

"No. Several days ago, I said. What's the matter? You don't understands no English?"

"Are they patients?" the nun asked, doing what she could to buy some time for the workers on the second floor.

"Don't know. You tell me," Frank said. He was a mean and sarcastic character. He smiled and exposed his half-rotten teeth, balancing a toothpick in them as he talked.

"And what is your names, please?" Sister Rosa asked as if there was a special routine that visitors had to follow.

The two detectives were eager to show their badges.

"I'm detective Frank Curry and this is Detective Harry Johns." Both men displayed their badges.

Sister Rosa leaned against the counter again. There was a series of short buzzes.

Sister Mary Beth swung into action. "Quick, Sisters, Immigration."

The nuns and nurses bolted into action. They ran down the hall and grabbed four beds out of the smallest ward, pushing them the length of the hall and into a room marked with an ugly bright yellow sign: Radiology Medicine. Authorized Personnel Only.

The nurses pushed the patients' beds into the small room.

"Quickly, cover them up with those canvasses that the painter uses."

In a matter of ten seconds, the patients were secure in this small room and instructed to lie still in their beds and keep quiet, as the painting tarps were laid over them.

"We'll be back as soon as they leave," Sister Mary Beth whispered to them. "Say a prayer and be quiet."

They did as they were told. Sister Mary Beth was the last of the nurses to leave the room. She turned off the lights and placed a large padlock on the outside of the door, snapping the lock closed with an ominous metal clicking sound. She turned around again, composed herself and walked back toward her center hall counter. She noticed the cops coming toward her.

"Gentlemen, can I help you?" She was short of breath.

"Running somewhere?" one of the cops asked showing a definite suspicion on his face.

"I need to run all the time in this hospital," she said with a semi-genuine smile, acting out the role of he dutiful nurse. "Here to see somebody?"

"We're looking for a couple of priests. We believe that one of them is a patient here in the hospital. Tall guy white hair, big guy, looks like an old football player fifty-five, maybe sixty years old."

Father Marleski was just about to come out of the utility closet when he heard the two men talking about him. He leaned behind the door and looked through the crack between the door and the frame.

"Are you a friend of his?" Sister Mary Beth said, as she walked past the men and went behind her counter faking interest in her charts lying there. She leaned on the counter and pressed her panic buzzer two times. The sound buzzed downstairs only, and Sister Rosa jumped into action. She shoved her hand into her pocket grabbing her keys and went straight for the high security closet with the dangerous drugs.

Sister Rosa motioned to another nurse for help. They grabbed two large syringes with deadly looking needles at the end and nervously filled each syringe with ten cc's of a knockout drug. Sister Rosa took the two needles and ran up the back steps to the second floor. She walked slowly toward Sister Mary Beth as she continued to talk to the men.

Father Marleski was still in the small utility room, peeking out, and he saw Sister Rosa tip toeing down the hall. He found a set of official looking green garments that were used by the orderlies and threw them on. He was without shoes and found a pair of white cloth shoe covers used in the operating room. He snapped them on his feet. They looked weird, because it was obvious he was without shoes, but he had no choice. He completed his quick-change outfit with one of the thousands of paper masks sitting on the shelves. He tied the bottom strings of the mask behind his neck and left the top strings hanging loose. He found a green paper hat and pulled it down over his head covering up most of his grey hair. He looked just like a doctor who had come out of surgery, except for his feet, and his still badly bruised face. He walked out of the closet and surprised Sister Rosa.

"Ahh there you are, Sister."

She was startled and froze in her shoes putting the two syringes behind her back. She didn't talk. The panic in her face was obvious as she tried to figure out what Father Marleski was doing.

Father Marleski shifted his eyes pointing them toward the center nurse's counter. He winked at Sister Rosa indicating to her that he knew the cops were there. He walked with her toward Sister Mary Beth.

"Oh there you are, Doctor," Sister Mary Beth said, as he got closer to the counter. "These men are looking for a priest."

"I'm sure the churches are full of them," he said with a pleasant smile hiding any fear.

"Yeah, Doctor, we're looking for a special priest, big guy, grey hair built like a football player, about your height and build."

"Hey, Doctor," Harry said, as he reached into his jacket and put his hand on his gun. "You always operate without shoes and a banged up face?"

"Always. It's kind of a rule here. No static electricity."

"Yeah, you're gonna get static electricity," Harry said. "We're taking you in." He pulled his gun out and shoved it into Father Marleski's sore ribs.

Marleski with a quick and agile elbow knocked the gun out of he cop's

79

hand, bounced him off a wall and made a hard right turn and ran down the end of the hall. The loose shoe covers betrayed him as he fell on the slippery floor and slid about five feet and right into Solomon's bed.

The cops and the nuns came after him. Sister Mary Beth jumped on Harry's back and the gun went off shooting out plaster in the ceiling and splattering white dust everywhere. The scuffle and the gunshot had patients scrambling. Nobody knew exactly where it was safe to run. Everybody who could scatter, did scatter.

Harry was fighting off Sister Mary Beth as Moe was trying to help Father Marleski to his feet. He slid into the metal rail of Solomon's bed, banging his shin. He tried to get up but the loose shoe covers made him keep slipping. Moe reached down and pulled the covers of the priest's feet, giving him the traction he needed.

"Hold it," the other detective screamed as he closed in on the sprawling Marleski. Move and I'll shoot you."

"Leave my friend alone," Moe screamed as he grabbed for the gun out of the cop's hand.

"Get away, old man," he hollered back pushing Moe all the way to the next bed. Moe grabbed the cop's hand

Crack, crack, crack... the gun fired just missing old man Solomon in bed and shattering the window behind him.

Glass splattered and the gun came flying out of the cop's hand. Sister Mary Beth and Harry came running into the room hoping no one was shot. Moe was pushed into the emphysema patient, falling on his bed. The old priest acted quickly and reached for Moe Kessler's 25-caliber pistol.

"Hold it, cop," the priest screamed with what little wind he had in his lungs. "This is a real gun," he said, but his hand was shaking. "Freeze."

"Old man," Frank said as he got closer to the priest.

"You wouldn't shoot me. I'm a cop. You know how long you would be put in jail?"

"Hey, cop," the priest said as Moe moved away from him.

"Do you have any idea how long I have to live anyway. Don't come any closer."

The cop defied him. Snickered at him. "I'm gonna kick your ass, old man."

"One step closer and I shoot."

Sister Rosa nudged against Sister Mary Beth, moving their hands together, handing Sister Mary Beth a syringe full of pentathol. She then edged her way toward the cop who was closing in on the old priest.

"Go ahead old man, pull the trigger. Let's see what you're made of."

"No," Father Marleski hollered out. "It's me you want. Leave that old priest alone."

Frank Curry never flinched but kept up his snail's pace toward the old man. "Oh, so you're a priest too?"

"One more step and I fire the gun, cop."

The cop took one more step. The priest closed his eyes.

"Jesus, forgive me," he said, and pulled the trigger.

Click, click, click. Nothing happened.

"That's not a gun, that's a play toy," the cop said and reached down and grabbed the old priest by the throat.

"Now," Sister Mary Beth screamed as she slammed the pointed needle into detective Harry Johns' back.

The screaming never bothered the other cop who was strangling the old priest. Father Marleski jumped up, grabbed the cop, and wrestled him to the floor with a heavy thud. Sister Rosa took her syringe and shoved the needle deep into the cops' backside.

Seconds later both cops were passed out on the floor.

"Are they dead?" the old priest asked from his bed.

"No they're just knocked out for a couple hours."

"Hey," the old priest said. "Did you hear me holler at them? I haven't had that much air in a long time. It's because of the old man over there, the one with the stigmata. He put his hand on my head. I can breathe a lot better." The old priest was dizzy with delight at having some air and at his heroic effort.

Marleski pulled himself up from the floor, dropping the cop into a crumpled heap. He looked at the old priest, admiring him for his faith.

"If you want to live longer, Father, make sure you stay away from cheap guns."

Father Marleski picked the gun up, spun the chamber around emptying all the bullets. The firing pin in the gun was broken. He threw the empty gun to Moe. "Get rid of this thing," he said. "The only thing it will do will be to end up killing you instead of somebody else."

Moe was embarrassed. He held the gun in his hand for a while until one of the nuns took it away from him.

"We'll take care of it," the nun said.

"Hey," Marleski said. "We better get out of here. Can you nuns get Solomon dressed? Where are my clothes? We better get out of here before more cops show up. I'm sure they called in and let somebody know they were

81

coming in here."

"Right, Father," Sister Mary Beth said, as she and the rest of the hospital staff sprung into action. There was a flurry of activity. They had Solomon dressed and on his feet in a matter of minutes. One of the doctors offered Father Marleski a clean set of clothes from the lockers. They didn't fit very well, but they did the job of getting him out of there.

Sister Mary Beth unlocked the Radiation Medicine Room and had the illegal aliens put back into their old ward.

She was like an alley cat scattering after a bunch of mice doing several chores in seconds. She belted out directions to the staff, and at the same time reached for the telephone, running her fingers over the phone number she penciled on the top of her calendar.

"Hello, Signor Martello? This is Sister Mary Beth Acree at St. Gabriel's."

There was a quick conversation from the other end.

"I'm fine, Signor, but I hate to ask this. I need your help."

Very little was said on the other end and Sister Mary Beth thanked him and hung up.

She wasted little time, grabbing for her small red telephone book on her desk. "Mother of Mercy, Mother of Mercy," she muttered as she looked and scrambled through the book. She found the number, holding the page down with one hand and dialing with the other. She dialed the number so quickly that she made several mistakes. She begged herself to slow down and concentrate on dialing slowly.

The phone rang several times and Sister Mary Beth was becoming impatient. Finally there was an answer.

"Philadelphia? Mother of Mercy Hospital? Let me please speak to Doctor Eduardo Ramos, please." There was a pause.

"I am not a patient. I'm his cousin in New York City, Sister Mary Beth Acree from St. Gabriel's Hospital. It's extremely important. Please hurry."

Father Marleski was slipping on a clean shirt and a pair of too small trousers. He gathered up his priest clothes and searched the detective's pockets for car keys.

He searched more and pulled out a small notebook from Curry's pocket and some of his business cards. Marleski shoved all of the items into his own pockets.

He and Moe helped Solomon by holding him on each side. It was a pitiful sight. Moe and Solomon were exactly the same size, about five-four. Marleski was a towering six-two next to them. Solomon had one arm around

82

Moe's shoulder and another around Marleski's waist as they walked in awkward cadence down the hardwood floor hallway.

"Thank you, my cousin," Sister Mary Beth said in Spanish. "God Bless you. They'll be there by tonight."

"Sister, do you want us to take the two cops with us?" Father Marleski asked. "We could drive them down to the Bowery. Or we could drop them off in Brooklyn or something."

"No, Father. If you did that then they would just come back in a hurry. I have a better plan. I called a good friend of ours. He'll get rid of them."

Marleski stopped in his tracks. "Get rid of them?" he asked in a high-pitched, shocked voice.

"Please hurry now, Father. It's our business, not yours. God Bless you," she said as she completed a polite half genuflection.

Father Marleski moved by the tears in her eyes and tremor in her voice, leaned over and gave her a hug, kissing her on the head. He paused for another quick moment and gave his blessing. She stayed on one knee looking down, still sobbing, as he and his two Jewish friends went for the ancient elevator.

It was only a matter of five anxious moments before the three men were by the side door of the hospital. Marleski safely settled the two Jewish men in a small alcove in the hallway while he went outside and surveyed the scene. He placed his black suit on the floor and walked out the door.

He tried to appear casual as he balanced himself on the top step and whistled a slow tune. All he observed was a couple of derelicts picking through dumpsters and garbage cans. He also saw a black Buick, almost identical to the one that Eldron Burt drove. But this one was in perfect shape. No banged in bumpers, no smashed headlights or fenders and no messed up passenger door. This Buick was almost new and ready to go.

"That's it," he said. "Cop cars are so easy to spot."

He looked back inside the door and whispered for Moe and Solomon to come along. He helped Solomon negotiate the steps practically carrying him the rest of the way. When they got to the car they were shocked to see the derelict they met from several days ago.

"Oh no," the bum said. "Not you guys again."

"Oh no problem, sir," Marleski said. "Those cops got sick and decided to stay. Move over, you got company."

The three musketeers were getting into the cop car when Father Art pulled up in a cab.

"Hey, what gives?" he said.

"We gotta get out of here," Marleski shot back. "Things are too hot. We gotta get out of town."

"It's a good thing for you that I got worried," Father Art said. He reached into the back of the cab and pulled out two suitcases.

"I packed our clothes and called the dean of your department. Told him you had an emergency. He understands. Everything is okay. Told the monsignor, too. He said he understands."

Father Art paid the cabbie, who wasted no time leaving the neighborhood. The four men jumped into the cop's black Buick with Father Marleski in the driver's seat. He pulled the keys out of his pocket and stared straight ahead.

"Okay, which one of you can drive?" he asked.

Moe offered and switched places with the priest. He changed his mind once he was behind the wheel when he couldn't reach the pedals or see over the steering wheel. The cop who drove the car was wide and tall and had the seat pushed back and broken in that position.

"I'll drive," Father Art demanded.

"No, don't let him drive," Solomon hollered out. "He almost killed us getting here. I'll drive."

"Whadd'ya mean you'll drive," Moe said to his friend. "If I can't reach the pedals how can you? I'm taller than you are."

"No, you're not."

"Yes I am," Moe said with a raised voice.

"Well, I don't know how to drive," Marleski said. "These things are too complicated."

Everyone turned and looked at the derelict who was sandwiched in the back seat.

"What's your name?" Marleski asked.

"Rufus."

"Well, Rufus, you are the proud owner of a brand new, beautiful shiny black, Buick. Now get behind this wheel and show us how fast we can get the hell out of here."

Rufus hesitated only for a silent moment, but realized the desperation of the four men. He obeyed the big priest and scrambled for the front seat. He kicked the ignition of the big Buick, revving it up like a racecar. Father Art threw the suitcases in the trunk and the religious fugitives took off; heading for parts unknown.

Chapter Seven

Rufus loved driving those big cars. He never had a car of his own. The only cars he ever drove were borrowed or stolen.

"Where we goin'?" he asked Father Marleski.

"Let's go to Lucky's bar and get a German beer," Solomon answered for him. There was a big grin on his face.

"No," Marleski shot back with a tone of laughter in his voice. "No beer for you, Solomon. Not for a long time."

The priest reached over and turned on the radio. He fished for talk shows on the AM stations wanting to know if there was any news about them. He seemed paranoid about it. Father Art tried to assure him it was too soon to get word out about the two missing cops.

"I guess you're right, Art. I'm just antsy."

He fumbled some more and settled for a preachy kind of talk show host who kept jabbering about the Bay of Pigs. He became annoyed and was about to change the station.

"No," Solomon said. "Leave it. I want to hear what he has to say."

It wasn't long until Solomon was annoyed.

"Kennedy's a good man. Why is this guy tearing him apart? I don't believe he screwed up in Cuba. He's for the Cuban Liberation."

"Easy, Sol," Moe said. "Don't get yourself worked up."

"I love that man Kennedy. He's good for the Cubans. He's good for the Jews."

The ride went a while longer until Rufus had to have some direction.

"You guys gotta tell me where you wanna go. We can't just keep driving around."

"Let's go home to Brooklyn," Moe said. I gotta see my wife and get some money. If we're gonna be on the run we need money."

Rufus headed the big black Buick down through midtown and over to Brooklyn. He stopped the car near a phone booth long enough for Father Marleski to get out and make a couple calls.

85

"Hello?"

"Stanley, I need your help."

"Who is this?"

"Your friend the priest, Father Marleski."

"You ain't dead yet?" Stanley was surprised to hear his voice.

"Not yet. Listen. Meet me near that butcher shop in Brooklyn. You know the one we went to and asked abut Solomon? Meet me in about an hour. We need your help."

"There are a hundred butcher shops in Brooklyn."

"The one where we went into and asked the guys for directions about where to find Solomon."

"Oh that one. I'll be there," Stanley said. "I don't know why, but I'll be there."

Father Marleski clicked the phone long enough for it to hang up and then he called the Washington DC phone number he had scrunched up in his pocket. He realized he didn't have enough money to call direct.

"Let me place a collect call, please."

The operator obliged, but scolded him for using a code name. "This is not a good idea," she said.

"Ma'am, I was told to do it."

She obeyed and called the number.

"Justice Department, Mr. Canterbury."

"Collect call from somebody called Holy Water."

"What?" the voice said.

"See, Mister I told you, don't use stupid prank names."

"Don't hang up," Marleski hollered at the disrespectful woman. "I was told to use that name."

"Who is this?" the voice in DC said.

"One moment, sir," the operator interrupted.

"Do you have a real name?"

Marleski paused and shuffled his feet on the ground.

"Tell him it's The Healer."

"Hold on a minute, operator. Maybe somebody else knows what's going on. I'm not the regular guy on this desk."

The wait seemed agonizing. Father Marleski kept looking to his friends in the car and panicked each time a black and white squad car came down the street.

"Please hurry, Mister. Please hurry."

The wait continued. Marleski could hear people walking around the telephone, repeating the name 'Holy Water' and discussing with themselves what it could mean. He felt a fever start to grow inside him. He knew the government was bulky and awkward, but this was too wrenching to his patience.

"C'mon, damnit, c'mon," he said as he slammed his hand against the side of the phone booth several times.

"Maybe you should call back another time," the operator said with an exasperated tone in her voice.

"Lady, just hold on," Marleski said, pleading to her with the tone of his voice.

"Barnes here."

"Mister Barnes," the operator said. "I have a call for you from a prankster called Holy Water or something like that. Will you accept the call?"

"Yes, operator."

She got off the line.

"Mister Barnes. This is Holy Water."

"Why did you call collect? Did you spend the five hundred already?"

"No, we're on the run. Crooked cops are after us. Why do you want me?" Marleski asked.

"Actually, it's the old man we want. He's been trying to leave the country. We want to see him before he goes."

Marleski was in shock. Everybody wants this guy. What the hell did he do? The crooked cops were after him for protection money he didn't want to pay, and now the Feds.

"What did he do to you, Mr. Barnes?" Marleski asked intentionally showing his disgust for chasing this man.

"Oh, he didn't do anything to me. Some big shot here in DC wants to see him."

"What for?" Marleski demanded as he continued to scour the street for cops.

"Don't play games, Marleski. You know what the old man does. He heals people. Now when can you get him here?"

"Who's the big shot?"

"Can't tell you that till you get here."

"How do I know this isn't some trap to get the old man in custody."

"Don't be stupid. If we wanted to arrest him we would have done that a long time ago."

87

"Hold on a minute, I'll be right back."

Father Marleski let the receiver hang by its coiled wire while he went over to the Buick.

"Solomon, you gotta level with me. Are you trying to leave the country? Did you do something that I need to know about?"

"How did you know that?" Solomon asked.

"I'm talking to some guy in DC who seems to know a lot about you. He wants you to go to DC to heal somebody."

"What?" Solomon asked. "Who?"

"I'll find out."

Marleski went back to the phone. The conversation went on for a long time. Longer than Marleski wanted to talk. He came back to the Buick and sat in the front seat.

"Okay, Rufus, let's go." Marleski motioned for Rufus to pull ahead.

"What gives, Padre?" Solomon asked. "Who was on the phone?"

"That, my dear friend, was Mr. Barnes from the Justice Department. He knows more about you than you do. Why are you trying to leave the country?"

"I wanna go see my wife and my boys."

"Is that all?" Father Marleski demanded. He had anger in his voice.

"Yes."

"What about this illegal diamond trade you're involved in."

Solomon blew up at Marleski. "How stupid can you be?" he demanded. "Detective Burt gave that info to the Feds to stop me from leaving. I'm the president of the Jewish Diamond Council. I'm the only one who can approve protection money. Burt has to have me jailed or killed to get a new president. Maybe somebody else will approve his racket money, but I won't. That's his blackmail scheme."

Moe chimed in and finished. "We tried to get the state cops to listen to us about Burt and his cronies, but they just shrugged their shoulders. The crooked cops are too powerful."

"What about the Feds?" Marleski asked with a strict tone. "Why didn't you go to them?"

"Our last president did that. He's dead now."

"This guy Burt is pretty damn powerful," Rufus said. "We know about him all the way up to 145th street."

Marleski pushed himself against the back of the seat in a heavy resignation.

"How in the name of all the saints do I get into these things."

"Wait a minute," Father Art said. "Call the guy in DC back. I have a great idea."

All of the men in the car sat straight up. Rufus slowed down to hear what Art was going to say.

"Make them an offer they can't refuse. You heal the guy they want healed, Solomon. In return you get a clean passport and the Feds make sure Burt is taken off the street. They do their part, Solomon can do his part."

"I can only heal people who really believe," Solomon said. "It isn't a sideshow. If the person believes, whether he's Jewish or Catholic or Hindu it doesn't matter."

Rufus pulled the car to a stop on Flatbush Avenue. He turned around and looked at Solomon.

"You heal people? Like miracle healing? You mean like Jesus? Or maybe like that guy on television who makes people fall down when he touches them? Can you heal my arthritis? I got it real bad in my back. Can't work or nothin."

The car became as quiet as a cemetery on Halloween night.

"Just remember," Rufus said. "Jesus did a lot of good things for a lot of people and they crucified him. I think you should make the deal."

Father Marleski leaned forward and focused on Rufus. For a derelict, he had a brilliant sense of perception.

"Make the call," Solomon said. "I'll heal him, but the Feds have to take care of Burt."

Moe waited until several Hassidic Jewish men came near the car. He opened the door and mingled with them. He kept his head down and his hat pulled close to his eyes. He was wary as to any cops being around. He took the extra precaution of going into the apartment building next to his, rather than go into his own building. He went up two flights and knocked on the door of apartment 2C. He waited. He knocked again.

"Who's there?" a man asked, with a heavy Jewish accent.

Moe answered back in Yiddish, giving him a strange riddle. The man knew it was Moe, but the tone of his voice told him something was wrong. The door opened with a slow creaking sound and the man inside backed away. Moe walked in. The lights on the sides of the narrow stucco hallway were dim. He continued to talk in Yiddish, but he did it with a whisper as it bounced off the naked walls.

"Yitzhak, I need your help."

The tenant answered in Yiddish. "Hurry up, get in here."

Moe walked in and went straight to the heavy shadow in the skinny hallway of the Brooklyn apartment. There was a long explanation, and the two men headed for the kitchen and then the window leading to the fire escape.

The friend checked the scene out and felt comfortable. Moe thanked him and went onto the fire escape, crossed over the railing and swung onto the fire escape in his own apartment. He went to his kitchen and hunched down looked in the window. He couldn't be too careful. The gooney birds knew how close he was to Solomon. He knew they would be on him like a shadow.

The window was opened with a slight crack at the bottom giving his wife, Masha, a fresh breeze of the spring air. He stretched his neck to examine who could be there with her. She was sitting in the dining room reading from a prayer book. He waited, and watched for any movement in his apartment. He was about to stick his fingers under the bottom of the window and lift up when he saw a large shape move toward her. He waited again. The shape was a man, a large man, a gentile, about forty, dressed in suit pants, white shirt, tie and suspenders. He came closer to Moe's wife and then into the kitchen. He opened the refrigerator and pulled out a jug of orange juice.

The man, obviously a gooney bird, Moe thought, by the looks of the forty-five holstered on his side, poured himself a drink and went back to the dining room to talk to the woman again.

Moe grew angry. He whispered to himself as he sat by the kitchen.

"Son of a bitch. Not only does he take over my home, but he even drinks my orange juice."

Moe needed a plan. He went back to his friend's apartment and told him to make a call.

"Call my apartment. Disguise your voice. My wife will answer. Just say, 'give me the detective'. Then tell him that we caught the old man. Say, 'he's dead. Report back to Detective Burt.'"

Moe's friend obliged. He practiced several times making sure that he talked with a deep enough tone to disguise his Jewish accent. When Moe was satisfied with the rehearsal, the friend made the call.

"Hello," Moe's wife answered.

"Give me the detective."

Masha tried to figure out the voice, but elected to do as she was told.

"Meester? Eeets for you."

The cop got off the couch, looked at her with a curious twist of his head and picked the black receiver up.

"This is Lawson."

"We got him," Yitzhak said with an authoritative voice.

"You got him?" the cop said in a surprised tone.

"You deaf," Yitzhak said. "We got him. Burt said to leave the Jew guy's apartment and report back to him."

"Where?" the cop said with his continued high-pitched tone.

Moe was listening and mouthed out to him what to say.

"Harlem, twenty-fifth precinct." Yitzhak said.

"Harlem?" the guy said, raising his voice in heavy disbelief. "What the hell is Burt doing in Harlem?"

"Look, I don't make the rules, Burt does. He just said to get your ass over there as soon as you could."

"Okay," Lawson said. He hung up and went straight for the door.

Yitzhak put the phone down and began shaking. He had never pulled anything like this off before in his life and worried that the detective might catch on. He left his own apartment and went down to the street to make sure the cop really left the building.

After Yitzhak saw the cop get into his plainclothes sedan and head back to Manhattan, he let out a huge sigh of relief. He ran back, up the two flights of stairs to his apartment and notified Moe.

Moe thanked him for his help and went out to the fire escape again. He swung over the rail and onto the connecting fire escape to his own apartment. He was still cautious, even though he knew the cop left.

He went to the kitchen window and tapped three times. Masha did not respond. He tapped again. This time she poked her head from the dining room and squinted her age worn eyes into the kitchen.

"Masha, it's me," Moe called with a directed whisper.

"Oh, Moshe," she cried as she lifted the window. She ranted on in Yiddish about how much she missed him and that the cops were looking for him.

"I know," he said. "Listen, Solomon's in deep trouble. He won't pay off the gooney birds and they are really leaning on him."

"Is he any better?"

"He's doing better, but we have to go away for awhile for his safety. I need to get some things."

Moe went to the bedroom, grabbed as many clothes as he could for Solomon and himself, forcing the clothes ruthlessly into a large suitcase. He packed a smaller overnight bag with underwear. He looked at the bedroom door for only a moment, then pushed his bed to one side of the room.

91

Fumbling and filled with anxiety, he used his skinny fingers to loosen and pull up a floorboard in the end of the room where the bed was. He reached in and pulled out a paper bag that was wrapped tightly and about the size of a house brick. He handled the bag with the same care he would one of his diamonds and placed it into the overnight bag. He replaced the floorboard, pushed the bed back into place and started toward the kitchen again to see his wife.

She was standing in the kitchen making sure nobody was looking into their apartment. She pulled the window shades down as Moe came in and went to the refrigerator freezer door. He pulled several frozen blocks of food away handing them to his wife, and lifted up the freezer pan. Underneath it was a flat black package, about six inches long, six inches wide and an inch thick. He kissed his wife as he put the box in his overnight bag.

She returned the kiss but held onto him and started crying. "Moshe, just give the crooked cops the money. At least you'll be alive."

"We can't give in, Masha. If we keep giving in to them they'll bleed us dry. It must stop sometime and Solomon is right, now is the time."

"Where are you going now?"

"Solomon has to go to DC to see some important people to get his passport cleared up. Then he's going to Israel to escape so Burt won't kill him."

"Moshe, don't be foolish. You better take your passport with you, too, just in case you need to go with him. He's your life long friend. He may need your help in escaping."

"Masha, you are the smartest wife any man could ever have."

The two of them hugged and cried and continued unintelligible sounds of Yiddish chanting. Masha patted Moe several times on his back, held his face with her hands and kept brushing his cheeks with pecking like kisses.

"Okay, the time has come I must go," Moe said, and in several swift motions reached back placed the freezer pan in place and then the frozen food on top of it. He had practiced this ritual many times in the past just in case a day like today ever happened. Speed was essential for survival.

Masha went to the small hall closet, reached above her head, stood on tiptoes and pulled down a horribly old pink hat box with a faded green ribbon tied around it. With the speed of a seamstress she tore off the top, moved the tissue away, fingered through many important Jewish papers and found two passports. She checked hers and put it back.

She examined Moe's to make sure it had not expired and rushed back to the kitchen.

92

"Here, put this in your jacket, just in case you have to leave the country or something." She didn't wait for his approval, but shoved the passport into his inside jacket pocket.

"I love you, Masha," he said to her.

"Call me and let me know when you get there," she said. "I don't want to worry forever."

"I can't call here. They might tap the phone. I'll call Yitzhak everyday. 'The sun is shining' means everything is okay."

She was choking back tears and couldn't talk. Her hands were shaking as she threw him a kiss. Moe went back out onto the fire escape, stopped frozen, like a storefront Indian for a second to survey the scene for his safety, and then back to Yitzhak's apartment. Moe thanked him for his help, checked the hallway, and ran down the generations old steps to the black Buick waiting outside.

He was out of breath as he jumped into the backseat.

"You get it?" Solomon asked.

Moe patted his bag and told him in Yiddish.

"Everything you need, Solly; including clean underwear."

Solomon smiled. He was happy that at last maybe his dream could be coming true. He would get to see Millie and the boys soon. The two Jewish guys were laughing like young schoolboys.

Father Marleski, Father Art, and Rufus just stared at them. They were happy there were smiles and laughter, but felt odd that they were kept out of the inside joke.

"Where are we going, now?" Rufus said.

"Washington, DC," Father Marleski replied.

"In this car? A cop car? A stolen cop car?" The pitch of the black man's voice kept getting higher as he nervously evaluated the situation.

"All of a sudden you have a conscience?" Father Art asked.

"Well, you guys are gonna have to buy me something to eat," Rufus said. "I ain't had nothin' for a long time and I can't go that far."

"There's a nice little deli over there next to the butcher shop where we are going to meet Stanley," the priest said. "I'll make sure they pack us some sandwiches."

Rufus smiled and seemed pleased that he was considered as one of the gang.

The crew waited until Tom Stanley showed up. Father Marleski took the time to write down all the details necessary for Stanley to blow the whistle on

93

Burt. He had taken down the names of the two detectives who came to the hospital and had some of their papers. He had proof of the shakedown from Burt, along with a lot of other dirt the reporter would love to have.

Rufus was inside the deli coaching the counter man on how he wanted the sandwiches made, grabbing a handful of pastrami from their cutting table and shoving it into his mouth.

When Stanley arrived, Marleski and Father Art told him about the plan. He looked over the notes that Father Marleski had jotted down and made more notes of his own.

"If we don't make it, or get thrown into jail or something like that, you print everything you know," Marleski told the reporter.

"I'm going with you," Stanley said.

"You could get killed," Marleski objected.

"You go in that black Buick and you'll be killed. Half of New York is probably looking for you by now."

"It's a chance we have to take," Father Art said.

Marleski grew quiet, shoving his hands in his pockets as he began to walk away from his friends.

"Dennis, what's the matter?" Art asked. "Dennis, what'd I say?"

Marleski gave him no reply just stared with a determined force straight-ahead.

"Uh-oh," Art said. "He's thinking. I'm afraid it's dangerous. It's going to be something tricky. Dennis, c'mon out with it."

Dennis sauntered back to his friends and drew a wicked smile on his face. "Gentlemen, what do we have that old mean-ass Burt doesn't have?"

"Religion," Moe stated.

"Close," Marleski said. "His own stubborn nature will be his downfall. We have to get to his temper. Get that mean old temper working to our advantage. Look, I think I have an idea."

The four men went into the butcher shop, talked to the butchers, grabbed large amounts of brown wrapping paper, some brown twine and headed back for the car. Moe and Solomon went into a neighborhood clothing store that specialized in Hassidic clothes and dark suits, and came out shortly after.

They went to work on the black Buick. They took the large sheets of brown wrapping paper, crumpled them up and shoved them into T-shirts making roughly the top part of a man's body. The new black jackets they bought in the clothing store were wrapped around the fattened T-shirts, making fake heads using the heavy butcher paper, and magic marker scribbles for the hair and beards. Solomon and Moe finished the guys off with Hassidic black hats they purchased. Moe questioned whether they should keep the new hats for themselves, and put their old hats on the dummies. Solomon agreed and the men enjoyed the indulgence, tugging at the new stiff fit, trying desperately to make them feel comfortable. Solomon gave up and traded the dummy, taking back his old hat instead. Moe stuck with the new felt, brandishing a big smile as he checked himself out in the reflection of the car window.

When they were all finished, the setup looked terrific. Two paper-made old Jewish men in the back seat of a new late model black Buick four-door sedan, being driven by a black guy with a respectable looking suit and a makeshift chauffeur's cap, wearing a white shirt, and black tie. It looked perfect, and Rufus was delighted to shed his old smelly clothes for the new ones Moe and Solomon bought him.

"Okay, Rufus," Father Marleski said, as he reached into his back pocket and pulled out the envelope the government guy sent him. "Here's a hundred. Tomorrow morning, drive north, go through Manhattan and up toward New Rochelle. Drive real slow. You want people to see you. If you get stopped you know what to say."

"Right. Detective Frank Curry ordered me to do this. And that's the guy who owns this car."

"Perfect. Here's one of Curry's cards just to make sure, and some of his papers I took from him."

"What if nobody stops me?" Rufus asked with a puzzled look.

"Then you be the proud owner of a brand new, four door, jet black, 1961, Buick, deuce and a quarter with a government issued flashing red light that you can stick on the roof of your car and drive by all your honey girls in Harlem. Now that ain't no bad deal at all, is it?" Marleski said with a heavy laugh and a hearty handshake to the old black man.

"Oooooweeee," Rufus said. "Thanks for the car, thanks for the sandwiches, and thanks for the hundred, Father. I wish you guys luck. Hey, come and see me when you get back. I'll hook you up with some of my friends."

"Hook you up?" Solomon asked. "What does that mean?"

"Never mind Solly," Moe said. "I think it's a gentile thing."

Rufus loved his new distinction of being useful to somebody. He looked back at his butcher-papered passengers, tied in their seats with brown twine, and tipped his cap to them.

95

"You rabbis ready?" he said with a toothy grin. His face was flushed with the happiness of a little boy getting a pony on Christmas Day. "Then we goin' for a ride. Oh we gonna go by the synagogue first, just to be sure, kind of like insurance. But then we gonna go see some real queens you gonna like up in my district. Harlem, baby. Yessir, you gonna love it."

Rufus pulled the black Buick away from the curb with the skill of a diamond cutter handling a priceless gem.

The two priests, the two real Jewish guys, and all the suitcases went with Tom Stanley in his brown Dodge headed south.

"I don't think we can make it all the way to DC, tonight," Marleski said. "We better hide out for the night, maybe check into a hotel somewhere in New Jersey or Pennsylvania. We can go on to DC in the a.m."

"I have a relative in New Jersey," Moe said. "I don't like motels, or hotels, and neither does Solly. They always look at us and say, 'sorry, we don't have any vacancies'. Let's stay with my relative instead."

Solomon agreed and the other three men just raised and dropped their eyebrows.

"That's probably a good idea," Marleski said. "Some nosey motel clerk could call in a report of suspicious characters and whammo we'll all be hounded by the local police. Besides, if they search you and find out what you're carrying in that bag, we could all be in trouble. What's in there anyway?"

"I can't tell you," Moe said. "Let's just say it's Solly's freedom."

"Don't let it out of your sight, Moe," Solomon said. "Don't let it out of your sight." Solomon's words drifted off as the excitement of the day was too much for him. His head fell to the side of Moe's shoulder and he fell off to sleep.

Marleski watched as Solomon's head drooped toward Moe. He turned around and looked ahead at the road. "Okay, Tom, let's get to New Jersey. Then tomorrow we'll head south to DC, and pray to God that old Solly can do his stuff and heal that big shot, whoever he is.

Chapter Eight

Moe's call to his cousin in East Brunswick was a great idea. It allowed the fugitives to get away from the pressure of the New York cops. Moe's cousin Samuel was gracious, but surprised, because Moe didn't say anything about the two priests. It made for a few uncomfortable moments, but once Moe explained they were all in the same boat running from the law, then Samuel was well pleased to be able to help. He used to live in New York, but he too was chased out and settled in East Brunswick, away from the gendarmes.

"Any friend of Moe's is a friend of mine," Samuel said, after Moe made his long explanation.

"Thank you, Samuel," the two priests said, not daring to use the nickname Sam.

"Fortunately, we'll be leaving early in the morning."

"After breakfast," Samuel said. "I love to cook for company."

"Great," Father Art said. "I'll be ready in the morning."

Samuel realized the men were tired and Solomon was drained. Samuel put Moe and Solomon in the big guest bedroom, Father Marleski in a small bedroom, Father Art got the big couch in the den, and Tom Stanley, the youngest of the group, had to settle for the living room. It seemed like an uncomfortable jamboree at first, but within an hour, all six men were snoring.

About eight o'clock the next morning, a bright shaft of sunlight broke through the window to Samuel's house. The warm sun was a welcome sight for the travelers. They made it through the night without somebody shooting at them; one of the few nights in the last week without an event. Solomon looked a little healthier that morning, as he was the first out of bed and to the refrigerator for some orange juice.

The medicine Solomon was taking had to be effective because his appetite and strength were both improving, and the blood flow to the wounds in his hands seemed to be slowing down. The marks were still there, still quite visible, but slowing where Solomon could tolerate it.

"You're up early," Father Art said to Solomon as he joined him in the kitchen and began fussing with the coffee pot.

"I feel pretty good today, Art," Solomon said as he chomped on a piece of toast. "How about you?" Solomon extended his hands out for Father Art to examine. He was proud of the improvement and wanted Father Art to notice.

"Hmmm," Father Art said, as he held one of Solomon's hands. "Looks good. I guess that stuff the doctor gave you is working."

Solomon let out a big smile. "Thank God you guys got me to that hospital. I would have died. Hey, did you sleep well last night, Art?"

"Best night's sleep I ever had on a couch."

Soon afterward the rest of the men were up, showered, dressed in slacks and T-shirts and sitting at the kitchen table. They were ready for that advertised breakfast from Samuel. He kept to his promise: hot oatmeal, eggs, French toast, gallons of coffee and juice, and a lot of conversation.

"So what happened to the cops you guys left on the hospital floor?" Samuel asked, chomping on a piece of toast.

"The nuns said they would get rid of the bodies," Father Marleski said. "That's all I know."

Samuel choked on his eggs. "Get rid of them? Like dump them in the East River?"

"I can't imagine," Father Marleski said staring at the other men around the table. He held back a smile, but it was a weak effort. The expressions from the other men at the table reflected his thoughts.

"What time you going to make the call, Padre?" Solomon asked, trying to change the subject.

"Can't call before nine. I've never heard of a G-man getting to work before that."

The men killed a couple hours at the breakfast table with long discussions about religion, mixed in with baseball trivia, truly an unusual combination, but this was a rather unusual get-together. It was enlightening for the learned priests to hear so much history about the Jewish religion, peppered with stories about last year's World Series between the Yankees and the Pirates.

The men were finishing up their meal when Samuel went into the dining room and set up an old black Singer sewing machine. He cleared the fancy doilies and candles from the table and spread out some expensive looking black silk. Moe and Solomon excused themselves from the kitchen and followed him when they heard the whir of the old machine. The routine the three men went through next was a blur between a religious ritual and a sewing class exercise. From the precision of their actions, much without talking, it was obvious that they had performed this action before.

Marleski watched from the kitchen as Samuel cut a three feet piece of black silk with a pair of heavy-duty scissors. Then he showed the length to Moe and Solomon who sized it up, nodding their heads with approval. Next, Moe opened the small black box he was carrying and carefully took large diamonds out of the box and placed them in a cornrow on the black silk. There were about fifty diamonds, each larger than the size of a large pea. Father Marleski was amazed at the coolness with which they handled these expensive gems, but made himself realize they did this everyday for a living.

Soon, Samuel had the diamonds sewn into individual neat little pockets in the silk belt. Samuel wrapped the belt around Solomon's waist checking it for comfort and bulkiness. They tried the belt on Solomon and at the same time joked with him that if he were fatter he could be a lot richer. As it was, the belt wrapped around Solomon's waist and went partially around again. Solomon handled the new chore with ease, tying the ends of the strands of the black silk and testing its sturdiness by giving it a healthy tug.

"Fits good, Sam," Solomon said. He explained to the curious Marleski that he had done it several times before. Father Marleski shook his head and laughed.

"They'll check a Hassidic Jew's bags," Solomon said with a joking face. "But there hasn't been a customs man born yet who would ever ask a Hassidic Jew to take his clothes off. They think we have some kind of special disease."

Solomon seemed anxious about getting dressed and moving along with the mission. He kept nudging Marleski about making the call to his DC contact. Marleski took the repeated hints and went to work. He called his contact in DC, collect.

Father Marleski had to go through the same ordeal with the New Jersey operator about the code "Holy Water" when she asked for a name as he did with the last operator in New York.

"You men are all alike," she said, in a twangy nasal tone. "Always with the undercover stuff, like you're really important. Hold on."

Her attitude irritated the priest, but he begged for patience inside himself to intervene.

"Justice Department," the man in DC answered.

"Collect call for Mr. Barnes, from a Mister Holy Water."

"I'll take the call, operator."

"Barnes?" Marleski said.

"He's not here right now. He's over at the X."

"I wish you people didn't talk in riddles," Marleski said. "What's the 'X?'"

"Executive Office Building."

"Good grief. Look, we have an offer we want to make to Barnes. The old man will heal his Mister Big shot. No promises on the final outcome, you understand."

"Understood."

"In return, the old man wants a clean passport. No hooks."

"What's a hook?" the G-man said.

Marleski was surprised that he came up with jargon that the Justice guy couldn't grasp.

"No strings attached."

"So far, Holy Water, I've got you covered. I have to know where he wants to go with this passport. Cuba's off limits and so is Red China."

"He wants to go to Israel to see his family," Marleski said.

"No problem. Hold on. I'll call Barnes now."

Father Marleski waited while Barnes' assistant laid the phone down and called the boss. He could hear the G-man going through the typical governmental gyrations of explaining what was legal and what wasn't. Marleski waited for a few more moments, and then the assistant came back on the line.

"You got it, Holy Water. How soon can you get here? Our subject has a tight calendar."

"We can be there tonight," Marleski said.

"What are you driving?"

"Brown Dodge, four-door, late model."

"Give me everybody's name who is traveling with you. Spelling must be exact."

"What for?" Marleski protested.

"Trust me. I need it. I need the names to get you into a secure area."

Father Marleski hesitated. He looked into the kitchen and saw the two Jewish men, Father Art, Tom Stanley and Samuel. The lives of every one of them could be at risk if this was a trap.

"I'll give you two names: Solomon Weinstein, and Dennis Marleski."

"Anybody in your group ever been a member of a Communist party?"

"Of course not."

"Anybody in your group a Republican? Or voted Republican?"

"Two Jews, two Priests, and a guy named Stanley who is a ...an unemployed friend, a driver," Marleski almost slipped and gave away Stanley's ID as a reporter. A fatal mistake if he had. "None of them sound like Republicans or commies to me."

"Unemployed?" Stanley whispered from the kitchen.

Marleski held his finger to his mouth indicating to Stanley to keep quiet.

The G-man continued, "We just can't be too careful today. Okay, here's what I want you to do, Holy Water. We're going to put you up for several nights in a special house in Georgetown; friends of ours. They only have three extra bedrooms. Some of you will have to double up."

"We don't care," Marleski said. "We can rough it."

The G-man gave Marleski the name address and phone number of the Boyle residence. "They're old friends of ours. They know you're coming. Where are you now?"

"Jersey."

"Where in Jersey?"

Marleski was still cautious. "Not far from New York City."

"You should make it by six o'clock easy. Traffic is murder at six. Plan to be there about seven. I'll have the house man look out for you."

"Thanks, uh, what's your name?"

"Just refer to me as 'Last Pew'."

"Last Pew?"

"Yeah, you're Holy Water. I'm Last Pew, but I really am a nice guy."

"Brilliant," Marleski muttered under his breath.

"Who's the big shot who needs healing?" Stanley whispered to Marleski.

"Who's the big shot who needs healing?" Marleski asked Last Pew.

"Can't tell you, but he is Catholic and he has heard about the Jewish guy from a friend in New York who was healed."

"Okay," Marleski said to the G-Man. "We'll go to Georgetown, stay at the Boyle's and wait for instructions."

"Exactly. Have a nice trip." He hung up the phone.

Father Marleski hung up and went back to the kitchen table where everyone was sitting and staring at him. They had heard Marleski's side of the conversation and they felt comfortable with the way things were going.

The priest walked with a slow rhythm toward Solomon, who was fidgeting with his silk belt, and stared directly at him.

Marleski pulled at his slacks at the knees and crouched down by the old man. "Solomon, you have to level with me. Can your really heal people?"

"Padre, oh ye of little faith. I told you before."

"Sorry, I know the answer. They heal themselves with faith. You're just the instrument."

"Yes, it does work. But each time it does, I go through a tremendous amount of pain. I am willing, as long as the person really needs me, and believes. Whether he's Jewish or Muslim or Catholic, it really doesn't make any difference. I've healed lots of them.

"What about those who don't believe, but ask for your help."

"They only trick themselves. If they try to buy a miracle without believing, or do it just to insult me, then they always end up with worse pain. A lot worse."

Marleski wasn't satisfied. "There was a young woman on 43rd street who sells flowers. You know the one; elephant legs, but a young pretty Latin face. You could have helped her. How come you didn't?"

"Leave him alone," Moe jumped in. "It's none of your business."

Solomon stopped Moe from interfering by holding his arm up to Moe's chest. "Her father wouldn't let me touch her, so I didn't."

"What a damn, pity," Marleski said, as he pulled a chair and sat down.

"Think of all the people you healed. Why is it that somebody in D.C., somebody apparently tied to the Justice Department wants you? And somebody with a lot of money to throw around."

Solomon quit fussing with the belt, sat down, grabbed a piece of toast and began munching, smearing the grape jelly on his furry mustache. He focused on his friend Moe for help, but they both shrugged their shoulders.

"Remember," Solomon said. "I don't make deals. If somebody really needs me he finds me somehow. This is a rare situation. Maybe I can save this person's life in DC, and maybe he or she can save mine. I healed a lot of people."

Samuel and Tom Stanley sat there with their mouths opened. Stanley was dying to take notes or to have a tape recorder. Nobody would ever believe him, he thought to himself. How could he ever report this story?

"Solomon, before you go, would you go with me to visit my aunt? She has that whatchamacallit disease," Samuel said, hoping for a miracle in understanding. "She forgets everything. Doctor says there's no cure."

Solomon looked this new friend and smiled and uttered a pleasant Yiddish phrase that made Samuel smile. "I don't pick and choose," Solomon said. "But I would be happy to be able to help here. Funny isn't it?" he said. "She needs help and I need help and both of us are victims."

Samuel sat back in his chair, folded his hands on the table and relaxed his shoulders. His expression of appreciation for Solomon's compassion showed. He touched Solomon on the shoulder as he got up to get more coffee for his guests. "Thank you, my friend. Thank you."

Marleski was standing by the sink looking into a small shaving mirror examining his face and eyes and touching the wound where the cop smacked him with the gun. He stared past his own reflection and noticed Moe and Solomon whispering something to each other. He wanted to blurt out and ask what was going on as if he couldn't trust them, but couldn't bring himself to believe that these guys would ever do anything devious to him at all, or use him as a part of a mysterious ploy.

Marleski turned around and cleared his throat. "Okay, gentlemen. Let's saddle up our horses."

Samuel gave Stanley a clean T-shirt, white shirt and socks, as he was the only one who didn't have some kind of a suitcase.

"Hey, are you guys ready for the fun, now?" Marleski asked

"Yeah, you mean call that bastard Burt?" Solomon said.

"Exactly," Marleski added.

Marleski picked up the phone again and dialed Frank Curry's number on his card.

"Special Squad, Curry's desk," a bulldog of a voice answered.

Father Marleski went into his act and came up with a heavy Brooklyn accent that stunned all his compatriots still sitting at the kitchen table.

"Yooohhh, who's diss?"

"Morgan."

"Hey, Morgan. You seen dat bum Curry or dat udder bum Johns diss mornin?"

"Not in yet."

"You know why?"

"Who the hell is this?" Morgan asked.

"Give me dat udder bum named Burt. Is that big hunk of old leftover salami sitting there with his feet up on his desk."

Morgan was shocked because that's exactly what Burt was doing.

"Let me talk to the bum. Tell him it's some big news about Curry and Johns, his two best and brightest detectives."

Marleski could hear Morgan put the phone down on the desk.

"Hey, Burt. Somebody wants to talk to you, says it's important."

Burt pulled a big sloppy cigar out of his mouth, swung around on his city-issued, wooden swivel chair and grabbed the phone.

"Chief of the Special Squad, Burt here."

"Big title, big man," Marleski continued with the Brooklyn shtick. "Where's your two star detectives Curry and Johns?"

"Not in yet. Who the hell is this?"

"And dey ain't gonna be in neither. You know why? Dey got your money from the old Jewish guy and made it for Canada. I heard it was over fifty G's. Big ones. Fresh new hundred dollar bills."

"Go to hell," Burt said. He was ready to hang up the phone.

"Don't believe me, you big salami? You wanna know Curry's badge number? How about Johns? Wanna know what the Jewish guys look like?"

"What the hell's going on?" Burt demanded slamming his fist on the metal desk.

"Get some of your men to check with the New Rochelle police. Dey should be around there right about now. You want the license number? Not that I should know it or anything. Hey guess what else, Burt. He got dem Jewish guys with him to get over the border to Canada. See ya."

Father Marleski took the receiver and almost slammed it into its cradle. "I guess I got that bum."

The three Jewish guys standing nearby broke into hysterical laughter, jumping and clapping and saying all sorts of Yiddish phrases. Marleski just kept laughing and Art was patting him on the back.

"Psychology huh, Marleski? You're pretty smart for a guy who has a doctorate. You gonna let him get his own bad temper to destroy himself," Father Art was imitating Dennis' Brooklyn accent. "Wow, I wish I would have studied that stuff instead of chemistry. You never know when it's going to come in handy."

Whammmm. Burt slammed the phone and started barking out orders. "Get me a helicopter. Get me my car, quick. Get the state police. Curry and Johns are headed for the border with my money... I mean, the Jewish crooks. C'mon let's get out of here."

Burt manhandled everybody in the department. They scrambled down the two flights of steps to the alley near First Avenue, jumped in their plain black cars, sirens wailing and headed north for New Rochelle.

"Get the state police on the radio," Burt demanded. "I'm gonna kill those bastards when I catch them. Set up a roadblock."

Burt was red with rage. His face was extended like a blowfish ready to strike. He was huffing, puffing, swearing, slamming his fist on the dash and screaming at his driver to go faster.

"If I go any faster, Mr. Burt I could kill somebody."

"If you don't go faster, I'll kill you," he screamed, chomping down harder on his cigar, taking his hat off and smashing it on the dashboard of the car.

The driver took the warning and slammed on the gas, sideswiping two cabs and an old pickup truck as they headed up through Harlem.

Burt picked up the hand mike of his police radio. "State police? State police?" He was screaming now. "This is Chief of the Special Squad of New York City, Eldron Burt. I need to stop a black, 1961 Buick, government plates, headed up through New Rochelle going north."

Burt was slamming his hat harder on the dash.

"I have the governor's approval," he said. "The people in the car are escaped fugitives and criminals wanted in the city for embezzlement of city funds."

"Hold on, Burt," the dispatcher said with the patience of a Sunday school teacher. "What is it this time? Murder? Grand theft? Serial killers?"

"No these people are vicious criminals."

"Okay, Burt," the man said still uninspired by Burt's emergency tone. "What's the license number, again?"

Burt grabbed a crumpled piece of paper out of his pocket. Municipal license, City of New York, MUN456GT.

"Hold on, Burt." There was a long pause from the dispatcher.

"C'mon dammit," Burt screamed into the mike. "Do I have to talk to your supervisor?"

There was a dreadful full minute of silence before the dispatcher keyed his microphone again.

"Nooooo. Actually, you don't, Mr. Burt, super detective," he said with a rotten sarcastic tone. "Your hardened criminals have been stopped."

"They have?" he screamed back into the hand mike. "Where the hell are they? You got 'em in jail?"

There was another half-minute of dead silence before the dispatcher keyed the mike again. He paused with dead air just to aggravate Burt.

"Nooooo. They're sitting in the East Side shopping mall in New Rochelle, at the Big Kroger. They aren't going anywhere. One of our guys has them detained. I think he has a machine gun on them. Oh yes, and his partner has a bazooka trained right at their Jewish eyes. Yep, they'll never get away from us."

"Roger, thanks for your help." Burt dropped the radio hand piece. "Step on it, Eddie. I don't want those bastards to get away."

Eddie, Burt's driver and assistant, flailed the big Buick up the throughway into New Rochelle. He must have been going at least one hundred as he passed one car after another. He got off at the East Side exit, siren screaming, and sped his way into the mall parking lot.

There they were. A large contingent of state cop cars, New Rochelle cop cars, and Frank Curry's black 1961 government issued Buick. Eddie pulled his car up close and slammed on the brakes leaving acres of streaked rubber on the asphalt.

"Where are they?" Burt screamed as he jumped out of the car, and ran toward his wayward detectives. "I'll kill 'em."

The other cops standing by their cars were bent over laughing. It was a desperately funny sight to them. The big man Eldron Burt going after a poor middle-aged black man who was thrilled to be driving two butcher-papered Jewish guys around New Rochelle. Burt reached into the car and grabbed Rufus by the neck.

"Where's Curry? Where's Johns?"

"Hold it, Burt," one of the state cops said, pulling Burt off Rufus. "Better look at this. Curry gave this guy one of his cards and ordered him to drive the car around as a decoy. Told him if he didn't, he was going to put his momma in jail for prostitution. This old black man believed him and said he's been driving ever since last night. Curry even gave him a brand new one hundred dollar bill just for being a good boy and following orders."

"What? I'll kill 'em. I'll kill 'em," Burt said. His face was as red as a New England boiled lobster. "Wait til I get my hands on those two. I'll kill 'em both. I'll tear off their puny little heads and chew them up and spit them out."

The veins in Burt's neck were popped out like sewer pipes; his face was redder than a rooster's crown. He slammed his fist onto the roof of the Buick smashing his cigar into a pitiful mess.

Burt pulled his forty-five out of his holster and started shooting up the car. Rufus jumped out of the Buick with the help of a state cop and ran for his life. Burt went berserk. He shot the windows, then the tires, then he kicked the doors, till his feet were sore. He still wasn't satisfied with that. He reached into the back seat of his own car and got out his favorite weapon: a Mickey Mantle, Louisville Slugger, and smashed Curry's car until every square inch of sheet metal and glass was destroyed.

He still wasn't satisfied. He tore open the backdoor and pulled the two paper made Jewish men from their safe position.

"I hate all of you stinking Jewish bastards," he said as he bit into the paper head of one of the dummies, pulling the butcher paper out from under the black hat and into his mouth and spitting it to the ground. "Where's my money? Where's my money?" he screamed louder as he threw the dummies around and jumped on them with both feet. "I'll kill you."

He kept swinging and kicking until all of his energy was depleted. He dropped the bat and slumped to the ground dropping his arms beside him and dropping his jaw down to his chest. Spit was dropping out of his mouth, and his eyes were wide as saucers and glazed over with the frenzy of a crazed animal.

The cops around him looked at each other and made small circles around the sides of their heads with their index fingers.

"He's gone," one of the state cops said. "Which one of us is going to call in and get a paddy wagon to take him to the loony bin?"

"I've been waiting for this for a long time," another cop said as he stuck his thumbs into his black leather belt. "There aren't many Jews in the state police, but I'm one of them."

Chapter Nine

The large, black, extra wide Lincoln limousine of Signor Martello pulled up to St. Gabriel's hospital. Three oversized football players wearing expensive black suits got out of the car, went into the hospital, past the front reception nurse, and sprinted the long flight of steps to the second floor.

There was little conversation as Sister Mary Beth Acree pointed to the room down the hall where all the fighting had taken place. The three men never said a word to the nun, walked with a brisk pace to the end of the hall and stopped at the two limp bodies. They gathered up the two detectives Curry and Johns wrapped them like burritos in large brown army blankets, and carried them over their shoulders, down the noisy steel steps and back outside to the waiting limo.

The back window of the Lincoln was down and heavy white puffs of Cuban cigar smoke wafted out. The three men in suits looked like gorilla trained pallbearers as they unceremoniously dumped the two almost-lifeless bodies into the huge trunk of the car. Although they seemed tough and uncaring, the hoodlums made sure not to bang the cops' heads, being careful with placing them under soft pillows; a contrasting image of tenderness and ruthlessness. The sight of the cops lying in the trunk wrapped up was grotesque, but the action seemed natural to these three.

The hoodlums closed the trunk, jumped back into the car and took off. The limo waddled out of the area, the rear end bouncing under the strain of the extra weight, with screeching wheels and a side-to-side motion as the driver pushed for all the power he could get. He floored the gas as he went around the bend, out onto the main street and headed due south for the expressway. One could hear the East River groaning as it anticipated two more occupants for the night.

It seemed that any minute the driver would stop, all the pallbearers jump out, take the two unconscious cops and dump them. But they didn't stop. The car continued on; going through the Lincoln Tunnel and over into Jersey. Maybe *il martello* had a special dumping place for crooked cops, probably a cement plant in Newark.

The limo made it to Newark, but didn't stop. The driver continued driving the speed limit and headed further south. The limo had traveled about an hour when *il martello* ordered the driver to stop. He got out of the car, went over and opened the trunk for only one minute and closed it again. Truly it was a curious action. *Il martello* wanted to make sure that the cops weren't dead yet, giving them a new lungful of Jersey polluted air to keep them until the next stop.

Satisfied they were still alive; he slammed the trunk, puffed on his long cigar and got back into the back seat of his Lincoln.

"*Avanti,*" he called out to his driver, and on they continued, southward.

It was about two hours later, in the dead of night, when they finally came to a stop. They were in South Philadelphia, not exactly the Garden of Eden. It was an area worse than the one they left in New York at St. Gabriel's.

A slight drizzle hit the windshield of the car, making the visibility even worse in this dimly-lit area. One, not very powerful street light showed the way to a large dark grey building at the end of the street. The building had the appearance of a factory: squarish, drab, with small casement windows and very little lighting out front. As the mysterious black Lincoln pulled closer, the screeching of the windshield wipers echoed the feel of the cold rain outside. The lights of the limo shined ahead and focused on the hard, chiseled, Mother Of Mercy Hospital sign at the front door of the building. Then in smaller type at the bottom of the sign: Where Hope is Life.

As the limo pulled up to the emergency entrance of the hospital, an attendant came out to greet them. There was only a slight conversation, sending the attendant back in to use the intercom. Moments later, Doctor Eduardo Ramos came out of the swinging doors to greet his visitors in the limo. Again very little conversation in the now chilling rain, but when they finished, the long black Lincoln pulled over quietly to a side door.

Doctor Ramos looked around and then shook his head with approval. He opened the side door to the hospital and two of the tough bodyguards in black suits jumped out of the car on cue, fetched the two cops out of the trunk, and hustled them inside. No words were exchanged as they carried the two cops, still dazed, and wrapped up in their blankets into the hospital. The dexterity of the kidnapping was so smooth it looked like it had happened many times before.

Inside, the cops were unwrapped, stripped naked, tied to a gurney, had their heads shaved and wheeled off to a secure area behind bars on the third floor. Upstairs were several drone-like characters who went through a series of mechanical motions, examining, and squeezing many parts of the cops' bodies. It looked like they were checking out their eyes, but also seemed interested in listening to heartbeats as well as checking the tenderness of the patients' bellies and livers. A male nurse administered to the unconscious patients by taking a blood sample from each with a standard syringe and needle placing the blood into a lab vial for processing.

Soon after that, both cops, still naked, were placed into separate heavily padded cells, but next to each other. There were several other cells on this floor, and from the small openings in the doors of these cells, prisoners strained their necks to get into position to see what was going on. No sounds were made from the prisoners, just long stares from quick blinking eyes.

Nobody dared to call out or to ask what was going on. They knew. Detectives Frank Curry and Harry Johns were now in the complete and total custody of Mother of Mercy Hospital for the Insane, in South Philly.

It was a whole day later when the two cops finally kicked off the effects of the drugs the nuns shot into them back in New York. They were groggy, still somewhat delusional, and disoriented.

"Anybody out there?"

"Hey, Frank is that you?" Harry Johns called back

"Yeah it's me. Where the hell are we? My damned head hurts. Why am I in this padded cell? What the hell is going on? Hey, Harry you got any light in your room?"

"Probably same as yours, dark, small sink, toilet, no toilet seat, thick mattress but no bed. Small hole in the front door to the long hallway to nowhere."

"Yeah, that's the same thing I got. Where the hell are we? What happened?"

There was a deep authoritative voice from the hallway.

"No talking. You guys keep talking and you get a shock treatment." It was a man's voice that answered the cops. The voice was raspy Negro-Spiritual, and the English was American crude.

"What?" Curry screamed out. "Where the hell are we?"

"One more time," the voice called back again from the hallway. "And I go get the man."

"What man?"

"The man who take you to get the shock treatment."

"I demand to know who's in charge here," Harry yelled out. "We're cops. We're not supposed to be here. Get us the hell out of here. Who's in charge?"

Frank and Harry were calling out to the faceless voice. They could only hear the man in the hall, but couldn't see him. Frank scrunched his face sideways to look out of the small horizontal opening in his thick metal cell door.

"We demand to see the supervisor. Go get your supervisor," Frank Curry defiantly called out.

"Okay. I warned you," the voice said. "You gonna get the sting."

The man walked away, but Frank was still pleading his case.

"Hey, Mister You want money. We got lots of money. Help us get out of here."

Frank strained his eyes to see better, but caught only the back view of the man as he walked away. A tall black man with a massive frame, huge gorilla-like arms and dressed in hospital white clothing. Frank watched the orderly as he left and went toward the lone light hanging from the ceiling. As he went down the hall he stopped at a small metal desk and made a quick phone call and then hung up. The next sound was the squeaking of a heavy metal gate, then a clang. The orderly went off the floor.

It was about ten minutes later, nothing happened and Frank Curry called out again.

"Harry, they gotta feed us. Let's call out for food. When they come to feed us we can jump them."

"Great," Harry said. "I'll use my gun, you can hit them with a nightstick, we'll cuff them and get out of here. Frank, do I have to remind you we are naked? Hey, I don't even have hair on my head."

"Let's look outside the small window and see if we can find out where we are."

"The two cops struggled to get up on their toilets to see any kind of a view out of their small windows. They saw nothing but the back of another desolate looking building about thirty feet away. They both grew more confused and depressed.

"Frank, I told you we should have checked with Burt before we went into that hospital."

"Hey, wait a minute. That's where we are," Frank said. "They ganged up on us, knocked us out with some kind of drug or something, and stuck us in here. We're in their hospital."

"Yeah," Harry shot back. "All we gotta do is get somebody here to call into headquarters and straighten it all out. Maybe they forgot we're cops. We told them that didn't we? We showed them our ID. They can't drug us."

Both men mumbled a while longer, grew tired from the pentathol still in their systems and the lack of food in their bellies.

"God, I hope they bring something to eat, soon. I'm starving," Harry said. He crumpled up next to the padded door and fell on his backside in quiet resignation.

An hour had passed. The eerie squeaking and creaking sounds of the metal door at the end of the hallway started up again. It was a brazen sound of clanking, sliding metal, and hard slamming with a thunking as the heavy steel lock smacked against the iron bars of the gate.

The orderly was coming back, but he wasn't alone. The head doctor, Eduardo Ramos accompanied him and one other person pushing a kitchen-table sized food cart on wheels. When the three hospital men got to the cops' cell doors they stopped. There was another clumsy-sounding clank as a small hinged door on the bottom of their cells opened. Much like the animal food door for the lions at the zoo.

A wooden tray with food on it was slid in with a careful movement by the orderly. The door was only large enough to accommodate the food tray and anything on the tray that was no higher than eight inches.

Both Harry and Frank grabbed for the trays before they were completely into the cell. They tore into the food with ravenous pursuit: hot beef vegetable soup, a large ham sandwich on rye with mustard and tomato, a large piece of chocolate cake, several pieces of fruit, and a pint carton of white milk.

The food door closed right after the men grabbed the trays, but no conversations were started while the cops dug into their meal. The three hospital men outside the doors could hear the cops chewing and munching.

"Leave them for now," Doctor Ramos said to the two orderlies with him. "I'll stay here and see what happens."

Some time had passed and Doctor Ramos just waited outside the cells. He knew that after a good meal one of the cops would start something.

"Hey, hello. Anybody out there?" Frank asked, still chewing on a ripe apple.

"Who do you want?" Doctor Ramos answered back.

"That orderly guy, the colored guy, big guy. Is he there?"

"No. He had to go to brain surgery," Ramos answered with a huge smile, fighting back a hearty laugh.

"Brain surgery?"

"Yeah. He's one of the best brain surgeons we have."

Frank and Harry both strained their necks and then their eyes to see the new person outside their cell doors, but Doctor Ramos was standing next to the wall and couldn't be seen.

"Hey, look Mister. There has been a big mistake; you see? We're detectives. If you call our office they can straighten this all out. Somebody took our clothes and badges. If you just look for them you'll see I'm telling the truth."

Frank continued to insist the attendant call Eldron Burt repeating the phone number over and over.

"We've heard that before," Doctor Ramos said. "Every patient who's in here for life says the same thing. He's a cop or a member of the CIA. Even gives us a number to call."

"What?" they both screamed.

"In where for life?" Harry called out.

"In here. This is a special hospital for the criminally insane. Can you see out of your small holes? See all these cells to your right? All twenty of these people are here for life. Most of them claim they are cops or CIA men. Some of them even claim they are Jesus. Do you know how many Jesuses we have here? About fifteen."

"No," screamed Harry. "It was all his idea to come in here without calling in first. Please, sir, just call our supervisor Eldron Burt. He'll straighten this all out. Where's that Spanish nurse? She knows we're cops. She saw our badges."

"Sure, sure, sure," Doctor Ramos said as he pounded on the cell doors with a heavy fist. "I want you to settle down now for the night. One more word out of you and I'm coming back with the electric paddles."

"Nooooo," Harry screamed. "It was all Frank's idea. Let me go home. I need to see my girlfriend. Please call Inspector Eldron Burt of the special squad. He'll square this all away."

"You should have thought about that before you gave those nuns and Jewish people a hard time," Ramos hollered back. "Now shut up."

The screaming and pleading from the cops came to an end. No more yelling: they were shocked into submission. From Frank's cell only whimpering could be heard. From Harry's cell, crying.

Doctor Ramos sidestepped down the hallway, keeping his back to the wall. He knew the two cops could not see him through their cheat slots in their doors if he kept his body close to the wall. He had a horribly evil smile on his face and slapped a hand over his mouth to keep from breaking up. He made it to the hallway cell door, opened it quietly, making sure no squeaking sounds were heard down the hall in the cells. Opened the gate as far as he could, waited for about three painfully quiet seconds and then slammed the door with all of his might.

Whammm. The sound shot through the naked hallway and reverberated into the two cells like a billy goat kicking two empty garbage cans. The shattering sound frightened the two cops out of their quiet desolation and made them jump about two feet off the concrete cell floor. Frank jumped so high that the small carton of milk in his hand came flying out and spilled all over him, creating an even greater panic and anger.

"Get me out of here," Frank screamed over and over, pounding on the wall of his cell. "Get me out of here," he screamed with a higher pitch than before. "I'm sorry, I'm sorry, I'm sorry. I'll never pick on any Jewish or Puerto Rican people again. I promise. Help me, help me, help meeeeeee."

Harry rolled over into a fetal position, grabbed his shaven bald head and cried himself to sleep.

The next morning, Doctor Ramos and the big black orderly Kenny Washington went onto the cell floor again. They checked in with the three old-time patients who had been there for years. Kenny took each inmate out of his cell, one at a time, held him around the waist and helped the patient to exercise by walking up and down the hallway.

Each man was terribly old, over eighty and suffered from a spastic condition. All three were in special rooms just like the two cops were, but they were there for their own protection, not the protection of the citizens on the street. There were only three old men, but Doctor Ramos scared the hell out of the cops making them believe there were more. He would walk down the hallway, where the cops could see him out of their cheat door, and with a large rubber bat in his hand slammed it on empty cell doors.

"Keep it quiet in there. Oh yeah? No exercise for you today, Morgan," the doctor said to an imaginary patient. "You keep talking like that and you aren't going to get any food either. Go ahead, Morgan, push me a little harder."

He pretended to unlock an already unlocked door and entered the empty cell. He made sure the two cops could see some of his movements as he warmed up like a baseball batter in the on deck circle, and ran into the cell swinging the bat. He made all kinds of screaming noises and slammed the bat over and over against the wall, the floor, the sink and anything else that made weird funky noises. He waited for a moment for effect and then came back out of the cell, shirt ripped open, hair messed up and glasses twisted on the side of his face.

Harry saw the action and scrunched down in his cell.

"Dear God, kill me right here. Don't let me live any longer. Don't let that doctor torture me. Please, God."

"Doctor Washington," Doctor Ramos called out to the orderly. "Feed Morgan only bread and water for five days."

"Yes, Sir, Doctor Ramos," Washington said in robot like fashion.

The two cops were still scrunched down and could see out of their cheat holes. They saw Doctor Ramos coming at them and they were petrified. He inched closer to them with a deliberate and cranky mood. The look on his face was that of a maniacal dictator about to slay disloyal subjects.

"Well, how are my secret agents doing this morning?" he asked as he neared their metal doors and pounded his large black rubber baseball bat against the wall.

"Fine, Sir," they answered in perfect military courtesy as they strained their necks and covered their ears.

"You guys want to exercise today?"

"Yes, Sir. We want to exercise."

"You want Doctor Kenny Washington the brain surgeon to help you?"

"No, Sir," they insisted. "We don't need any help. We can exercise out in the hallway by ourselves."

"Oh no," Ramos declared. "Doctor Kenny Washington helps you or you don't get out."

"Okay Okay, we'll take his help."

Ramos walked back and forth and he knew they could see him.

"Well, maybe tomorrow. I'll see how I feel about this, tomorrow."

"Yes, Sir," they muttered. "Whatever you say."

The small food door to the bottom of the cell was opened and the wooden tray with a small portion of scrambled eggs, toast, and a carton of milk was pushed in: no forks, spoons or knives. Delicious food, but no utensils for eating.

Again, just as they did last night, the two cops devoured the food, caveman style, grabbing large chunks in their hands and gulping it down before somebody took it away. They grabbed the eggs by making scoops with their hands, tore into the toast and broke open the small milk cartons and quaffed the drink, spilling milk all over themselves.

"Eat well, boys," the doctor said. "You never know when your country is going to call on you to serve."

Doctor Ramos walked away and back down the hall.

The orderly Kenny Washington finished with his third patient's exercise program. Another orderly came by and went into each cell to feed the elderly patients.

Doctor Ramos left the restricted ward and went down to his office on the first floor. He reached into his top desk drawer and pulled out one of the cop's wallets. Frank Curry, Detective Special Squad, New York City Police Department. Ramos picked up the phone and called the number on the card. It rang several times, more than Doctor Ramos wanted and he began to feel edgy about his misdeeds.

"Special Squad, Curry's desk."

"Who is deees?" Ramos asked.

"Sergeant Maloney."

"Hey, do you know a Mister Eldron Burt?" Ramos asked. He was using an exaggerated Mexican accent.

"Who wants to know?" the sergeant answered back.

"I think I know where your two detectives, Curry and Johns are," Ramos answered.

"Hold on." The sergeant cupped his hand over the mouthpiece and hollered out to his boss.

"Burt!!!!! You better get your ass over here."

"Who the hell is it this time?" Burt growled back, chewing on a cheap cigar.

"Some Mexican joker says he knows where your detectives are."

"Don't be stupid, Maloney. Verify it."

Maloney shook off Burt's insult and got back on the phone to the mystery caller. "Yeah, well, he's busy. Anyway, how do I know you're for real?"

"You want me to give you their badge number? Or do you want me to give you the numbers on their drivers' license? How about blood type? Or do you want me to tell you that Curry is not circumcised?"

The man cupped his hand over the mouthpiece again and swung away from his comfortable wooden swivel chair.

"Burt!!!!!" he screamed again. "You better get your ass over here."

Eldron Burt pushed himself up from his wooden chair and swung his huge size twelve shoes off the desk. He hunched forward unwillingly and headed for Maloney.

"This better not be another stupid wild goose chase."

He grabbed the phone out of Maloney's hand and signaled for him to give up the seat.

"Yeah, this is Eldron Burt. Who the hell is this?"

"I ain't the lone ranger, but I know where your cops are."

"Yeah, Mister Mexican," Burt said sarcastically.

"They're in a special place in South Philly. They were caught with a lot of money on them and they were arrested. They are in a special crazy hospital. The head doctor can't prove who they are so they have to stay there."

"How stupid do you think I am," Burt shot back. "If they had money, then why wouldn't somebody know who they were and how do you know their badge numbers and all that other stuff? Mister Mexican smart-ass."

"Because I met them in a bar. I got them drunk and promised them Mexican women. I slipped them a mickey and stole their wallets. Then I left them on the street with their bags. I didn't know they had a lot of money in those bags, or I would have kept them."

Burt went white. He turned away from Maloney and cupped his hand over the phone, making sure that nobody else could hear him.

"Okay. Where in South Philly are they?"

"I can't tell you until you promise to give me some of the money."

"Okay, how much do you want?" Burt whispered into the phone.

"Maybe two hundred dollars. My wife is pregnant and I need the money."

"Sure," Burt whispered back. "I'll give you two hundred. Where are my guys?"

"They're in the Mother of Mercy Hospital in South Philly. You must see a Doctor Eduardo Ramos. And do not bring anybody else with you. Just you. If I see anybody else in your car when you come, then I'll call Ramos and tell him you are a liar."

"Got it," Burt whispered back. "Where does the doctor keep the money?"

"Third floor, behind a big locked door. It's a lot of money. I wish I had kept the bags for myself. The detectives told me when I got them drunk that they stole it from some Jewish guys, but I didn't know what they were talking about then. They were laughing real hard. A friend of mine who works in the hospital told me later it was a lot of money."

"Okay, hey, what's your name?" Burt said in a sickening sweet voice.

"You can call me Pablo. Leave the two hundred dollars in a paper bag and put it in the back of the church near the confessional of the church just down the street. It's called Saint Lucy's. Remember, next to the confessional. But you can pay me after you get your detectives back."

"How very kind of you, Pablo. Hey, I'm gonna give you three hundred."

Burt eased the phone back to its cradle and slammed his right fist into his left hand about three times with the force of a Bronx steam shovel.

"Yes, yes, yes," he growled.

"Hey, Burt. What's up?" Maloney asked.

"Don't know, gotta check something out."

Burt grabbed his suit jacket, flung his massive arm into the sleeve and headed for the door.

"Hey, Burt, where you going?" Maloney asked.

Burt didn't answer.

"Is it true that Curry ain't circumcised?"

Burt stopped in his tracks. "What?"

Everybody else in the office stopped what he was doing and focused solely on Maloney.

"That guy on the phone said Curry ain't circumcised. How'd he know that? He steal his shorts or something?"

Burt looked at Maloney and then at everybody else in the office frozen in a stupid pose.

"How the hell do I know? I'll be back."

"Hey, I'm going with you," Maloney said as he grabbed his jacket.

"No. Stay here in case that Mexican guy calls back. I'll call in about two o'clock. I want everybody to get busy on something. Now move."

When Burt screamed everyone jumped into action. Even those who weren't doing anything made themselves look busy immediately.

Burt ran down the two sets of concrete steps finishing off dressing with his jacket as he ran. He plowed out of the double metal doors to the street and grabbed his car keys for the new black Buick parked up on the sidewalk.

He gave his right arm a quick motion as he started up the big V8, slammed it into first and popped the clutch with chattering results to the rear wheels. Smoke and rubber flew behind him as he rudely fishtailed his way through traffic. He reached over and slammed the flashing red emergency light up onto the roof of the car. He pulled the car left and swung for the highway heading south. No sooner had he made the turn to the busy speedway than he smashed the red button on the dash for "continuous siren". The sound was deafening, but Burt loved it. It meant he had the power to shove anybody off the road anywhere. He did exactly that. He leaned his eyes to the gas gauge and quickly estimated that he had enough fuel to make it to Philadelphia with plenty to spare, even if he did eighty all the way.

Within a minute he had shifted into high gear, popped another ugly, twisted, cheap black cigar into his mouth and settled back into the protective plush seat of the Buick for a nice morning drive. The siren was blaring, the red light flashing, and with the cigar held between his teeth, he screamed out the window to almost every car he went by, "Get the hell out of my way!"

Eldron Burt was on his way to achieving justice and freeing his two unfaithful subordinates. He reached down and checked his gun, and searched his suit pocket for extra ammo. Whoever he would meet up with, he would have enough bullets to blow them away.

"Doctors or no doctors. Mother of Mercy Hospital, huh? Yeah I'll show them some mercy. Six bullets right in the head."

Chapter Ten

Burt pushed the Buick to one hundred miles an hour as he hit the Jersey turnpike. The valves in the new Buick were rapping as he slammed the gas, then the brake, passing one car after another, siren blaring constantly, red light on the roof flashing. He broke a new land speed record between Manhattan and Camden. There were state troopers who came up behind him as he drove, but he sluffed them off and didn't dare stop. He rolled down his window, and shoved his huge arm out holding his badge and wallet. One young state trooper continued to follow Burt for about twenty miles with his siren also blaring, but was called off eventually by the district supervisor when he heard it was Burt going after a criminal.

Burt got off at Cherry Hill and headed straight for Camden. It was only a short time before he attracted a convoy of County cops who wanted to know exactly what the hell he was doing. Flashing his badge wasn't enough for them.

"Pull over, you dumb bastard," one cop hollered from his car bullhorn, forcing Burt off to the side of the road.

Burt complied, pulling his car over and stopping, turning the siren off, but damn mad when he came out of the car.

"Where in the hell are you going that fast?" the Jersey cop demanded.

Burt went over to him, still in a rage, flashed his wallet and badge at the cop and then grabbed him by the neck.

"Look you wimpy ass Jersey cop. I'm going to Philly on a special mission. I have the Fed's approval to do what I need to do. You get on that mike, call your sorry ass supervisor and tell him to get out of my way. You got it?"

Spit came out of his mouth as he screamed into the cop's face.

The cop had no choice. Burt was strangling him and had him lifted off the ground and onto the hood of the car.

"Now, one more stupid problem from you people and I start breaking some heads open. You got that?"

"Got it," the cop barely uttered.

Burt pulled his meat hook hand from the cop's throat and went back to his own car. Jumped in, kicked the "continuous siren" button back on and slammed the car in gear.

Rocks and gravel went flying as he continued on his way, leaving the county cop bent over and gasping for air. The other cops who were following Burt caught up to the stopped car and rendered assistance to their comrade who was trying to get some air back into his lungs.

"Leave him alone," the cop said still choking. "He's a maniac. He'll kill you if you stop him. Leave him alone."

It didn't take Burt long to tear through that county, the Walt Whitman Bridge, and then into Philadelphia. Burt spent some time during the war at the Naval Shipyards in Philly so the city wasn't a stranger to him. He felt immortal as he captured Manhattan, then New Jersey and now Philly. Nothing was going to stop him. He knew the route he had to take and made it with relative ease. He also decided to cool it with the speed and the siren as he got into the heavily populated area of the city.

He looked around for the main street that he wanted, knowing this section of Philly was easy to follow with its perfect grid pattern and numbered cross streets.

"Here it is," he said to himself." Seventh street. Yeah, that old joint doesn't look like a hospital, does it? Why a hospital?" he asked himself. "Why did these guys get locked up in a hospital?" Burt was devilishly curious, but wanted to take no chances.

Was that guy Pablo staring at him from somewhere? He circled the block and looked for suspicious characters. He trusted nobody and enjoyed staying alive because of his paranoia and cynicism toward others.

He cruised the area, checking out the buildings and the people. He seemed satisfied that there wasn't any ambush by Pablo and planned what he would say to Doctor Ramos. He scoured the area with his suspicious eyes again and pulled the Buick over to the side of the building; purposely daring a security guard to come over and tell him to move the car from the loading zone. He waited for the security cop to get closer and then flashed his badge. He loved the power.

"I won't be long," he told the security cop. "Just gotta see a Doctor Ramos for a short visit and I'm out of here."

The security man stared at him with frozen daggers coming out of his eyes, but kept his cool. If he overstayed his welcome, a tow truck would be called, and the security cop would be the one wielding the power.

Burt checked out the sign in the front of the Hospital to make doubly sure he was in the right place. He hesitated before going in to see if anyone who looked like a Mexican was spying on him. His self-induced paranoia kept forcing him to look back. Finally he shrugged it off and went into the ancient grey building, stopping at the front desk.

He looked around and noticed the poverty of the people waiting to be seen by a doctor, and scoffed at their condition.

"Can I help you?" an older black woman who was staffing the front desk asked.

Burt pulled his badge out and tried to impress the hell out of the old woman. "Name's Eldron Burt. Head of the Special Squad, New York City. I wanna see Doctor Ramos."

"Do you have an appointment?"

Burt laughed and mocked her. "Like no, lady. I don't have an appointment. I don't need one. I'm Eldron Burt. Tell Ramos I'm here."

The old woman showed how horrified she was at Burt's behavior and called for Doctor Ramos on the intercom with a shaky voice.

It was only a half-minute before he called her back, giving instructions on what to do.

The old lady smiled at Burt. "He said to take the elevator to the third floor. He'll meet you there."

"Third floor? Yessireee, the money floor," Burt said as he spun away from the counter and quickened his pace for the elevator.

The bell to the old lift rang and opened on the first floor. Orderly Kenny Washington met Mr. Burt and opened the elevator door for him. It was a solemnly quiet short ride. The two men stared at each other with plastic smiles for the entire one-minute trip.

The door opened, third floor, and Doctor Ramos greeted Burt. The detective reached out and shook his hand and got straight to the point.

"Excuse me, Doctor, but my two detectives are supposed to be held here. Is that correct?"

"Well, if they really are detectives," Ramos answered.

"I need to see them," the detective blurted out.

" Mister Burt, we aren't sure who they are."

Burt saddled up close to the doctor and whispered. "I heard they had a lot of money on them. That money is critical evidence for a trial. If I don't get it back to New York soon, the culprits will go free. You understand that, don't you doctor?"

"Absolutely, Mister Burt. Well, the guys who claim they are detectives are in there." Ramos pointed through the bars and down the long hallway to the cell doors. From his perspective of the hallway, the cell doors appeared to be simply heavy metal doors to Burt. He had no clue that inside they were actually padded cells.

"Why the bars?" Burt asked.

"Some of the patients have to be kept in a safe area for their own good. You know, some of them actually hallucinate and stuff, thinking they are Superman and can fly out of windows," Ramos said, exhibiting the perfect psychiatrist smile.

Burt wanted to smile but wasn't sure.

"Can I see the money?" Burt asked.

"Sure. Doctor Washington here will take you to the money. We keep it in that room down there for safety. It's too much money to keep in my office. Hey, but wait a minute," Ramos said in a very patronizing voice. "How can I be sure it's the same money you are talking about?"

Burt's anger flared up. "Look, Doctor, who in the hell ever you are. I'm going in there and getting my money for the trial. Now give me the key to this gate."

"Sure, sure, take it easy. Oh, the gun, please. You must leave it here. No guns allowed on the floor."

"My gun goes where I go," Burt insisted, his face getting redder.

"Look, you want on this floor, you leave your gun here. No gun, no key, no gate, no money."

Burt was upset, but his impatience to get the money was too much. He sized up Kenny Washington, and decided that the fight might not be worth it. Washington was taller, meaner, younger, and looked quite muscular. Burt decided discretion was the better part of valor and pulled his .45 caliber from his chest holster.

"The other gun, too, Mister Burt."

"What other gun?"

Kenny Washington made a quick move like a king cobra and dropped to the floor, pulled up Burt's pantleg and pulled the small silver .25 caliber out of Burt's leg holster. Burt was stunned at Washington's speed and realized he was overmatched. He didn't object. His mind was on the money.

"Anything else, Doctor?"

"Nope, that should be it. Let him in Doctor Washington."

The orderly slipped the huge skeleton key into the lock and twisted twice, opened the gate wide for the cop and both of them entered the long hallway. Washington and Burt walked side-by-side in step with each other, in a regular military pace, as they went down the hall. Doctor Ramos waited until they were about twenty feet away from him when he quietly closed the heavy steel gate and locked it. He leaned against the bars and watched as the master went to work.

Washington and Burt walked closer to the cells where the two New York City cops were being held captive. When they came to the cell doors Washington stopped.

"You want to talk to them?" Washington asked.

"I wanna see the money first."

"Okay," Washington said and led the detective away from cells 22 and 23 and moved over to cell number 24. He shoved the large skeleton key in the lock and pulled the heavy steel door wide open. There they were, sitting on the blank and funereal bunk: two extra large suitcases, each with a Jewish symbol proudly stenciled on it in gold paint. One of the suitcases had a set of initials: S.W..

Burt stood in the doorway and just about fell to his knees as one would when adoring a shrine of the Savior.

"Yes!" he screamed. "The initials S.W. Solomon Weinstein and all of that great New York Jewish money. Thank you, thank you, thank you."

"You can examine it if you like," Washington said.

Burt rushed in and grabbed the first suitcase, pulling at the latches with a feverish pace, fumbling, bumbling, but still grabbing in anyway he could to pry it open.

"Hey, you got a key," he hollered over his back to Washington.

"A what?"

"A key, you stupid jerk. A key to open this suitcase. Didn't those guys have a key on them?"

"I'll check," Washington said, and with the speed of a karate teacher he slammed the massive door and locked the cop in the cell.

"Hey," Burt screamed as he ran to the door. "Hey, don't lock me in here. Hey…! Get back here you black bastard. Hey…!"

Kenny Washington went over to cell doors numbered 22 and 23, and stuck his face close to the horizontal slot.

"You guys wanna here a good one," he said to Detectives Curry and Johns. "There's some crazy guy in cell 24 claiming that he's your boss."

The two detectives scrambled for their horizontal peeping hole and scrunched their necks for a look.

"I can't see him," Curry called out. "Burt, are you there?"

Doctor Ramos looked with admiration at his orderly Kenny Washington and waved his hand to him with approval. He reached over to the small desk and picked up the telephone and called his cousin Sister Mary Beth Acree in New York.

"St. Gabriel's," one of the nuns said as she answered the phone.

"Sister Mary Beth, please."

"She's not here, Doctor," the voice said as she recognized his voice.

"Is this Anna?"

"Yes, Doctor."

"Tell my cousin that we have all three fish in the can."

"Yesssss, yessss, yesss!" the nun screamed out and kept him on the phone as she hollered the news all over St. Gabriel's. She even used the intercom to announce it, jumping up and down like a schoolgirl getting an "A" from a teacher. The patients, nuns, doctors, and anybody else who was around knew what it meant and jumped up and down hugging each other at the news.

Washington walked down the hall to the gate and Doctor Ramos opened it for him.

"What do you want me to do with the suitcases, Doctor?"

"Well, let him have them, Kenny. What's he going to do with two suitcases of toilet paper? Eventually over the years he'll need them."

"Yes, Doctor Ramos, and thank you for calling me Doctor when other people are around. Does that mean I am a real doctor, Doctor?"

"Well, Doctor Washington, I'll tell you what. Those three guys are your patients. You are their doctor for life. They must call you doctor and any illness that they get you will have to take care of."

"Yes, Supreme Doctor," Washington said.

The two of them made sure the gate was securely fastened, as Doctor Ramos put the two guns into a pillowcase and wrapped it under his arm. Kenny Washington opened the elevator door and they both got in and left the floor.

"You know what, Doctor Washington?"

"What's that, Supreme Doctor Ramos?"

"I'm convinced that new guy who calls himself Burt is suffering from a constricted bowel. You and a couple of your assistants should take care of it tomorrow."

"Yes, Doctor Ramos. I'll take care of it."

The cries from the third floor could be heard throughout the entire building, but they were barely a whisper.

"Hey, you bastards. Get me out of hereeeee!"

Chapter Eleven

It was about ten-thirty when the two priests, two Jewish guys and Tom Stanley left Samuel's house. They were cleaned up, well fed, well rested and ready for their new endeavor. Solomon hesitated at the front door long enough to look Samuel right in the eye.

"Where does she live?" Solomon asked, referring to Samuel's sick aunt.

Samuel lit up. "About a block from here in a small house. You wanna go see her, Sol?"

Solomon stared at Samuel and nodded his head. "It won't take long."

Samuel grabbed his hat and coat and hustled out the door with his guests. They all piled into Tom Stanley's Dodge, with Solomon scrunched-up on top of Father Art for the short ride. Not a word was said, as all the passengers were anticipating this unusual event. The Dodge rolled slowly on the flat New Jersey street and stopped after a perfect ninety-degree turn onto Redberry Lane. Moe was calm, but Father Art, Father Marleski, and Tom Stanley were tense. They had never witnessed a healing before and they wondered to themselves as to what Solomon actually did.

When the car stopped, everybody got out and started down the skinny sidewalk to Samuel's aunt's house. It was a typical one-story, New Jersey bungalow with white aluminum siding and awful green metal awnings supported by fake wrought iron railing.

When they got to the door, Samuel used his key and opened the door, calling out his aunt's name as he entered.

"Aunt Sophie? Aunt Sophie are you here?" He walked in with slow deliberate steps, never knowing what condition he might find her in. The rest of the procession of men followed.

"She must still be sleeping," Samuel said as he walked toward her bedroom.

There was a single line: Samuel, Solomon, Moe, Father Art, Father Marleski, and then Tom Stanley, as they walked through the narrow entrance hallway. The small house was unusually warm and musty, and creaked from aged hardwood floors. The group continued to follow Samuel and ended up in the cramped bedroom and cringed at the smell of urine and soaked linens. Moe stopped and turned back, pity and sorrow showing on his face.

"Why does she live alone?" Father Marleski asked Samuel. "She definitely needs help."

"She won't go. She asked me to make sure she dies in her bed, and to never let her daughter put her away in a home. I've honored her wish. I take care of her."

"You're a saint," Marleski said as he and Father Art went over to the lady along with Samuel and checked her condition to make sure she was at least still alive.

"Let's get her up," Art said. "Get her to the bathroom, and cleaned up."

The three men had the patience of missionaries as they attended to their duties. They got the aunt out of bed, stripped her of her wet, stinking clothes, and into the bathroom where Moe had already started running hot water in the tub.

"Whas the matter?" she mumbled waking out of a groggy sleep. "Who are you?"

"Friends are here, Aunt Sophie. We're gonna help you."

"Did you feed my parakeet?" she asked, with a paper-thin hoarse voice. Her practically lifeless skinny arm pointed toward the living room.

"Yes, Aunt. All taken care of, gave her the favorite food, too." Samuel whistled a high pitch bird routine to let his aunt hear her imaginary bird.

The priests looked at each other and showed signs of compassion in their expressions as they helped her into the bathroom. Moe and Samuel then undressed her and put her in the tub. Her condition was pitiful. A seventy-five year old woman, white hair, chalk-white, unhealthy looking skin, shriveled, and draped over a bony skeleton. Her eye sockets were deep, almost black, and ran into dark bags. She actually looked close to death, but to Samuel she was his lifeblood. She looked at her nephew and smiled as they lowered her into the hot water.

"Too late, Shummy," she said. "Uh-ohhh, peed. Uh-ohh, peed."

"I know, Aunt," he answered back in a sympathetic way. "Tomorrow I'll get here earlier."

Solomon looked at Samuel, the two priests, Tom Stanley and motioned for them to move away from the doorway of the small bathroom. Only he and Moe were able to fit in there with the old woman. Solomon took off his coat and hat, handed it to Samuel, stood by the sink, looked straight into the small mirror with cold stone grey eyes and breathed in a basketful of air for strength and composure. He looked at Samuel and the priests and closed the door with the stoic calm of a marble statue.

The anxious moments for the priests of witnessing a healing would not be. Only Moe who had witnessed it many times before, and who was deeply trusted by Solomon would be there to help.

Solomon went over to the old lady, stared at what looked like a corpse to him, and knelt down next to her. He rolled up his white shirtsleeves and leaned his body forward to her, but making sure that Moe was holding her legs firmly for support. The water was still running at her feet as she soaked and mumbled phrases in Yiddish that made no sense to Solomon. He continued to get closer to her. Moe held her in the tub and Solomon leaned over and put his hands on her head.

She moaned her Yiddish phrases louder. Solomon put his hands on her face and she groaned; it started as a whispy-raspy staccato chatter and then went into a deeper vibration.

Solomon leaned his head back as he was losing his balance over the tub. Moe still held the woman from sliding in the tub as she bellowed out more Yiddish sayings.

Solomon placed one bandaged hand on the back of her head and chanted more Yiddish. She started answering back, almost making sense now. It was a rhythmic chanting, back and forth between Aunt Sophie, and Solomon, with Moe joining in occasionally. Moe and Solomon controlled their volume, but Aunt Sophie was erratic. Her religious tones were increasing in speed, as her rantings got louder.

Outside the door Samuel was grabbing onto Father Marleski's arm, and being held back from forcing himself into the bathroom. There was torture on his face, his eyes were strained, and his lips drawn thin. Tears rolled down his cheeks.

"I don't want her to die," Samuel said with a choking cry. "She's all I have. I know she's sick, but she's all I have. Don't let her die. I love her so much."

Marleski hugged Samuel who was losing control, weeping and coughing for air.

"She's not going to die, Sam."

Inside the bathroom the moans grew louder. Solomon's body was shaking as he held his hands on Sophie's head, then on the front of her face. The blood behind Solomon's gauze bandages was oozing more freely. She moaned another horrible scream and a smear of Solomon's blood covered the right side of her face like cheap makeup. The movements of the old lady became more animated and spastic. Her arms were thrashing in the water and her head was wailing from side to side. Her mouth was spitting coarse saliva and she gasped hard for air. Then one last horrible scream from the woman and Solomon collapsed on top of Moe causing Moe to holler out for help.

"Sammy," Moe hollered. "Sammy."

The door was pushed open and Father Marleski took two quick steps with his long legs and grabbed Solomon up like a bag of laundry and carried him back out through the skinny door to the living room. He laid Solomon down on the ancient, dusty corduroy couch while Father Art ran to the kitchen to wet down some dishtowels with cold water.

Water was splashing as Art hurried himself back to Solomon and applied the towels while Father Marleski patted his face trying to get circulation back into his cheeks. He was white as hospital sheet, but the blood from his wounds was oozing fast.

"We need ice water," Marleski said and left Father Art to take care of Solomon while he dashed to the sink, grabbed a large glass bowl and opened the freezer for a tray of ice.

Samuel fell to a crouch of panic in the hall, grabbing his face with his hands. He collapsed from fright and was lying in a sprawled position. Tom Stanley jumped over Samuel and went into the bathroom to help Moe who was holding the old woman trying to keep her from drowning. Samuel was crying so hard he was shaking and could barely speak. Moe kept scolding him in Yiddish to get control of himself because he couldn't hear if the old lady was still breathing. Her legs had buckled and she went limp, sliding into the full tub of water and dropping her face under the water.

Father Marleski gave Art the bowl of water and ice tray and rushed to the bathroom to help Tom and Moe. Tom grabbed the old lady under the armpits and lifted her up. He repeated the process in a slow rhythm as a resuscitation technique. Marleski jumped in next to Tom and both of them were struggling to lift the skinny woman out of the drowning water.

She began coughing, spitting, and moving her head by herself.

"Don't pull her out of the tub yet," Father Marleski said to Tom Stanley. "This warm water will help her. Let's let her soak in here for a while. The warm water will keep her from going deeper into shock."

"Got it," Stanley said. "You can go help Father Art. Moe and I can take care of her now."

Moe nodded his head as he supported Aunt Sophie's knees and watched her focus her eyes on the helping men.

She was gaining consciousness now and didn't panic with the crowd of men around her. She knew they were there to help.

"Shummy," she called out to her nephew. "I'm hungry."

Marleski looked at Father Art and nodded his head and grinned. "That's a great sign. I'll see what we can fix up for her."

Outside the bathroom door, Samuel was still in a state of shock lying flat on his back with his hands joined together in a shaking and thankful gesture to heaven hearing his aunt's plea for food. Father Marleski grabbed both of Samuel's legs and lifted them up so they were firmly planted about two feet high on the wall, letting the blood go back to his head.

The old woman was becoming more lucid. "Shummy, I peed. Shummy, you good boy. Don't let Maddy take me away."

Samuel was scared and thrilled at the same time. He heard her cries about Maddy and forced himself to gain control. It had been years since she ever mentioned her daughter Madeline's name. Samuel grew angry with himself for his cowardice. He lifted his legs off the wall and high into the air to kick start himself into some action. Everybody else was helping but him. He rolled over, hollered out loud to relieve the stress and emotion in his blood, and swore at his cowardly behavior.

He went into the bathroom shoving Tom Stanley aside as he reached into the tub, getting soaking wet from his chest up and grabbed his aunt and hugged her.

"I'll take care of you, Aunt Sophie. Maddy won't put you away. I promise."

She reached her arm up and draped it over his head and let him hug her. He was crying tears of relief as he looked at her, but she was smiling and weaving as she still sat in the tub splashing her skinny white arm in the warm water.

Back in the living room the two priests were reviving Solomon. Art noticed that the blood from his hands was oozing more than normal and the gauze bandages were soaked. He unrolled the messy bandages dropping them onto an old stack of newspapers by the couch, and placed a kitchen towel soaked in the ice water over the wounds to slow the bleeding.

"Does this happen, often?" Marleski asked Solomon who was coming to.

"No, this was pretty bad. Either I'm very weak or she was very sick. Sometimes, I can heal them and very little happens; like when those Cuban people were coming to me at night while I was lying there in the bed at St. Gabriel's."

Father Art and Father Marleski stared at each other while Solomon talked. They didn't witness the healings at St. Gabriel's and they wished they had. Their looks were a nonverbal commitment to each other to remember every word this man said. Someday the two priests would talk about it at length. But who would believe them? They would only be able to talk to each other.

Solomon was looking at Marleski, and trying to revive himself like a prizefighter getting off the canvas for another round of punches. He noticed the heavy concern on the priests' faces as they stared at his hands, and he could not resist one of his little jokes.

"You know what, Padre?" Solomon said, as the priests attended to his wounds. "These tough old Jewish broads are just too demanding."

The two priests marveled at this man's personality. He was giving everything inside himself to help somebody terribly unfortunate, almost killed himself for his patient, and was able to make jokes about it.

An hour had passed and Solomon was up and moving around. Moe and Samuel were feeding the old lady and conversing with her in her Yiddish, praising each mouthful of food she consumed. Father Marleski was careful to let the Jewish men set their own pace for leaving the old lady's home, and waited for the signal from Solomon.

No words were exchanged, Solomon simply rolled his sleeves down on his shirt, put on his black suit jacket, took his hat in his hand and nodded his head.

Father Art and Tom Stanley went into the bedroom, changed the sheets, changed the plastic protecting cover over the mattress, aired out the bedroom and returned to the kitchen to notify the other men they were ready.

As if on cue, the travelers all rose and started for the door.

"How can I thank you?" Samuel said, addressing Solomon.

"She'll be very tired for several days," Solomon said. "Just give her plenty of rest and pour the food into her. In less than a week she'll be a new woman. Her disease might not be totally gone, but pray for her and she will have a better life for now."

Samuel couldn't hold back the tears or the coughing cry. He didn't want to. The crying was a great emotional release, tearing the burden of extensive worry from his mind.

Father Art re-dressed Solomon's hands with thin strips of bandages he made from two kitchen towels, and held the strips tight with some white adhesive tape he found in Aunt Sophie's cabinet drawers. Solomon was regaining his strength in a remarkably fast pace. He was getting back to his old self, making quick jokes for the priests and kidding Tom Stanley about letting him drive.

"The car belongs to the paper," Stanley said. "If it gets wrecked and there isn't a good reason, then I pay for it."

"I can see it now," Solomon said, raising his bandaged hands in front of him indicating a grand marquis. "Old Jewish guy with heavy bandages on his hands wrecks reporter's car because he can't see over the steering wheel."

"It'll never fly," Father Marleski said. "Nobody would ever believe it. Besides, the headline is too long."

Solomon called out something in Yiddish to the old lady sitting at the kitchen table. Samuel and Moe laughed while the gentiles looked on in ignorance. Samuel gave his cousin Moe a large hug, Solomon a smaller hug, but still with deep sincerity, and shook the hands of the rest of the men.

"It's time to go," Father Marleski said. "We have a big date in DC, and we can't be late." He then turned to Tom Stanley and whispered as he pulled his suit jacket on.

"Tom we need to make a stop at a pay phone soon. I want to find out how the nuns at St. Gabriel's made out with those crooked cops."

Tom shook his head and jingled the car keys in his hand with an anxious, "let's get going" motion.

The men left the small bungalow and headed for Stanley's Dodge parked out front. Samuel stood at the doorway with tears rolling down his cheeks like liquid marbles. The old lady sat at the kitchen table, munching on a healthy-sized Jewish salami sandwich, and staring with an amazed and puzzled look at an empty, but perfectly adorned birdcage.

Chapter Twelve

The crew of five loaded into the Dodge and headed for the freeway. It would be a while before they reached their destination of Washington, D.C., so they planned on making the most of the long trip. Stanley cruised along and looked for a pay phone as he drove.

"Over there," Marleski said. "By that Seven-Eleven."

Stanley pulled around and into the small shopping center and up close to the store. Father Marleski got out, checked his pockets, realized he was short of change, and went directly into the store.

Tom Stanley waited for a moment as if looking for somebody to come along and reached over and grabbed one of the two phones standing by the side door of the store.

"I need to make a collect call, please, to New York City." Stanley chirped out his boss's phone number with the speed of a rambling parrot, and waited only a few quick moments until somebody at the News answered.

"Yes, operator, I'll take the call."

"Go ahead, Sir."

"Herb? Herb, it's Tom."

"I know who it is. Where the hell you been? Drinking again?"

Tom leaned into the protective covering of the booth, making sure to turn his back to his friends in the car and whispered to his boss.

"Herb, you know I've been off the stuff for months. Listen, Herb. I'm onto something."

"Yeah, yeah, big shot, you're always onto something. Always going to get the big story."

"Look, Herb, I can't talk long. Check into something for me will you? There's somebody at the Justice Department in DC who is very sick and believes in miracles. Find out for me who it is and I'll call you tomorrow."

"I don't know why the hell I listen to you, Tommy. Maybe it's because I'm still crazy about your mom, but for some damn reason I'll do it. Justice Department you say?"

134

"Yeah. Real sick, probably cancer or something."

"Where does the miracle part come in?"

"Herb, if a Catholic is real sick and he wants a miracle, or the miracle is the only thing left, what does he do?" Tom Stanley asked, as he cupped the mouthpiece of the phone making sure the guys in the car couldn't hear him.

"He goes to Lourdes. He goes out there to the airport, gets on a French airline and goes to Lourdes."

"Find out if anybody in Justice or whatever department, a big shot though, has something planned for Lourdes. Oh and one more thing. Eldron Burt is kicking more Jews' asses and I think he was the one who dumped that Jew guy in the river."

"No kidding. Everybody in New York knows it, but give me proof, hotshot. Get me pictures. I'll put it on the front page. Get me a recording, get me some damned tangible evidence and you get a raise."

"Thanks, Herb. You're a gem."

"Yeah, I'm a gem alright," Herb said as he harrumphed at his young protégé and hung up the phone with a damning slam.

Stanley turned around, faced the car and continued to talk after Herb hung up and as Father Marleski closed in on the other payphone next to him. Stanley raised his voice a little to make sure that everyone near him could hear what he was saying. Father Marleski wanted to start his phone call but was distracted by what Stanley was telling his boss.

"Bay of Pigs, Herb? Of course. I told you didn't I. Who wrote the very first report on it? Yep, that's right, Herb. Sure I'll be back. Just taking a few days off to do some research in DC. Yep, I'll call you tomorrow." Stanley took his receiver and quite dramatically placed it into the phone cradle, making sure the good priest noticed the exaggerated flair.

"Problems in Paradise?" Marleski asked, as he rolled the quarters in his right hand.

"Not at all, Padre. My boss loves me. He's just afraid I'm going to leave and go to the *Times*."

Marleski looked straight at the reporter, thinking that he was making it all up. He broke into a priestly forgiving smile and pulled his eyes away from Stanley, picked up the receiver and began dialing numbers.

There were several clungs and dings after an operator told him it would be two dollars and fifty cents for three minutes. Marleski obliged and Stanley reached into his own pockets looking for quarters in case the priest ran short.

"St. Gabriel's," a pleasant woman answered.

"Sister Mary Beth Acree, please. I'm calling long distance."

"One moment," the sweet young woman with a Spanish accent said.

It was longer than a moment and Father Marleski began fidgeting with his extra quarters. He lined them up on the small pulpit-like shelf under the phone.

The priest shuffled his feet and looked skyward appearing to be calm and cool, counting the seconds as if they were large rocks falling from the sky.

Stanley, nervous from his encounter with his boss, shuffled his weight from one leg to the other and held both arms close to his chest.

"What was that Bay of Pigs thing all about?" Marleski asked Stanley while he waited for somebody to answer the phone.

"Oh, remember I told you about the Kennedys? They planned it, then they botched it, then they blamed it on the Cuban Freedom fighters for being inexperienced. The truth is the CIA gave them some support, but it was a stupid plan. They attacked from the wrong end of the island. Castro knew exactly what they were going to do, but it was the White House plan."

"Well I remember seeing it in your paper, but you didn't tell me you dug up all that stuff. You knew all of that?" the priest asked.

"Well, you were all beat up that day, remember?"

"Yeah, I guess you're right," the priest said.

"Don't say anything bad about my good president," Solomon said, as he overhead the two men talking. "I like him. He's really good for the Jews."

Stanley was a bit red-faced from the verbal attack.

"I thought you were just a beat reporter, robberies, burglaries, old widows getting evicted and that sort of stuff," Marleski said.

"Oh I do that, too, just to keep me sharp, but I really do a lot of political stuff."

The priest stared at Stanley and was impressed. Stanley's dissertation of the Bay of Pigs reminded him of a student who wrote a great term paper even though he didn't look like he was paying attention in class.

His stare at the reporter's eyes was broken when the nun came on the phone.

"This is Sister Anna. Can I help you?"

Marleski chuckled at hearing a familiar voice on the phone. "Sister Anna, Father Marleski here. I just wanted to call back and see how everybody is doing. You know about those two crooked cops you drugged that night."

"Oh, Mister Rodriquez, it's nice for you to call and check on your grandmother."

"No, no, Anna. This is Dennis Marleski, remember me? I was just there a couple days ago. Came in with Mister Weinstein, the Jewish guy who had the stomach problem and the bleeding hands."

The tone in Marleski voice was more confusion than panic.

" Mister Rodriquez, would you prefer that I talk to you in Spanish?"

"What? Anna, what the heck?"

"Okay, I'll speak slowly. I'm sorry you don't hear so well."

Marleski wheeled around and motioned to Art.

"Come here. We got troubles."

Father Art obediently jumped out of the front seat of the car and over to the pay phone. Father Marleski held the phone out so both of them could hear here.

"Go ahead, Sister Anna, but please speak slowly."

The nun began speaking in Spanish, but still spoke in semi-riddles, which clued the priests to the trouble.

"Your grandmother is in guarded condition," the nun said. "She has a couple of people attending to her right now. That troubling illness she had a couple days ago has been taken care of, but she has a new problem that has come up to take its place."

"Is there somebody standing next to you, Sister?" Father Marleski asked.

"Si, signor."

"Is he a cop?"

"Si. Several."

"Are they on the path of the two detectives?"

"Si." She continued in Spanish. "They found out because every night there was a big line of poor sick people outside waiting to see the holy man who heals them. The word got out and the police followed."

"Who you talking to?" the man standing next to the nun said in an exasperated tone.

"I am talking to Mister Rodriquez, he is calling long distance to inquire about his grandmother.

"Well, make it quick," the cop demanded. "I have a lot more questions to ask you about the old Jewish guy."

The nun obeyed the cop and finished up with the priest in Spanish. "Mister Rodriquez. There is nothing you can do for her. She is in good hands, but you must get your uncle far away in case it is contagious. The sickness is closing in."

There was finality to the click when Sister Anna closed the line.

Father Art and Father Marleski stared at each other. They understood her basic Spanish clearly enough, and also overheard the tough talk of the cops. Marleski paused for a second and realized that Tom Stanley was reading the diminished signs of confidence on his face. He continued to talk to Art in Spanish, hoping that Stanley didn't understand.

"We can't let these guys know," Father Marleski said. "It would be devastating to them."

Father Art answered him back in Spanish. "You're right."

"Hey, what's going on?" Moe asked. "You guys the League of Nations or what? What's with the Spanish? Hey, don't keep it to yourself. What gives?"

Marleski and Art went back to the car and got into the front seat while Stanley hustled around and got behind the wheel.

"Seems like you're a big hit with the Spanish people, Solomon. They have a line of people at St. Gabriel's every night looking for you. You could be the best thing for medicine since Jonas Salk."

Solomon smiled. "Yeah, just like Jonas Salk, another great Jewish guy." His bushy mustache twitched upward and could barely hide his infectious smile. He looked at Marleski, then Father Art, and then Moe, with his warm-grey Jewish eyes.

"Stanley, how are you going to tell your boss about this one?" Solomon asked. "If he didn't believe you on the Bay of Pigs, can you imagine what he's going to do to you on this one?"

Marleski leaned his weary head back and rested it on the edge of the seat. He needed to keep the spirits of the whole group upbeat, even though he knew the dirty cops were closing in on them. He would have to hurry the mission. He closed his eyes and tried to drink in the entire experience he had been through. He tried hard to interpret what the Spanish nun had said and desperately wanted to compare her warnings with Art to make sure they heard the same thing, but couldn't chance it just yet.

The nervousness in his body was fighting his own thoughts and he hoped the rocking of the Dodge would lull him off to sleep. He started to doze off when Father Art nudged him.

Father Marleski lifted his head and looked at Art. Father Art did a little direction flow with his eyes toward Tom Stanley behind the wheel. Father Art noticed something. Stanley was wetting his lips and swallowing, but in an unconscious manner. He kept up this strange behavior, and then began rubbing his lips with his right hand. It was disoriented behavior, to be sure, but nothing that Art or Marleski hadn't seen before at the soup kitchens where they volunteered.

"You know what I think we all need," Marleski said.

"What's that?" Stanley answered.

"When we get to DC, we're going to stop at a beer store, one of those specialty places, and I'm going to buy a case of that good German beer that Solomon likes. We're going to take it into the Boyle's house and have one hell of a good time tonight."

There was more whooping and hollering out of that Dodge than there was in all of Europe the day World War II ended.

"Yes, sir, Padre. Let's get Lieberstrassen this time. Okay?"

"Anything you want, Solly."

Tom Stanley smiled, licked his lips a little longer and pushed on the gas a little harder. The rear end of the Dodge Coronet picked up; the exhaust shot out another jolt of smoke and the five travelers were speeding on their way to DC.

The trip was dull and boring for everyone, and several attempts were made to liven it up. Conversations ranging from New York politics, city traffic, poorly prepared students and the price of gasoline all died after short discussions. Father Marleski insisted on talking about anything but the problem at hand and continued to strike the right vein. Soon it seemed as if each person took a turn giving reports of themselves and their lives. Some of the stories resembled, "what I did last summer on my vacation", but with a much more intense feeling.

Somehow, Moe asked Father Art how he became interested in anatomy as a specialty field, and it started the complete histories of everyone in the car.

He was surprised to find out that Father Art was a medic in the Army during the war, kicking off his interest in medicine and anatomy. The details of how he would sew guys up in battle and get them back to the field hospitals was an inspiring tribute to the quiet, but dedicated man.

"I was finishing up pre-med school, after the war, when the lightning bolt knocked me off my lab stool and informed me to go to the seminary. I finished pre-med, but never looked back from there."

Then it was Father Marleski's turn. "I was in my third year of college when I left school and joined the marines. Actually, four of my classmates and I did it on the same day, on a dare. Just went into the dean's office filled out a small piece of paper, told him we would be back after the war, shook his hand and left for the Pennsylvania station to be shipped off to become a fighting marine of World War II."

"Incredible," Stanley said, as he steered the car, but took quick glances over and sized up the two priests, soaking in the contrast of then and now. "This is incredible to imagine where you were then and what you are today."

Stanley was killing himself inside that he didn't have a tape recorder under the seat. This was a terrific story. How would he ever be able to remember all of these things to make it to the front page?

"Yep, I fought the Japanese on the islands in the forties," Father Marleski said. "And later, when I became a priest, my first parish assignment was in a Japanese neighborhood on the West Coast. Talk about a shocker. I had nightmares every night that one of those sweet old ladies, who came to see me after Mass everyday, was carrying a machete under her dress."

The two old guys in the back laughed at the way Marleski delivered his story.

"Hell, fighting the Japs was terrible I'm sure," Solomon said. "But we had Germans stick knives under our throats, and threaten to kill us and take our tongues. Here look at this," Solomon said, opening up his shirt and showing the long horizontal scar on his neck, and the vertical scar on his chest.

"It goes from here, to here," he pointed with his aging crooked index finger from the bottom of one ear to the other, then from the top of his ribs to his heart.

"I bled like a pig and they thought I was dead."

"That's nothing," Art said. "Look at this." He lifted up his white hair on the back of his head. A section as large as a child's hand revealed no live scalp, just scarred tissue that once held promise.

Art was a bit miffed at the Jewish guys and wouldn't be outdone. "Dennis show them your knife wound."

"No, Art, forget it; c'mon this is silly, we've gone far enough."

"No let's see it," Moe said, knowing he was agitating, but hopefully in a friendly way. "I don't believe you."

"It's there," Father Marleski said. "I just don't like to show it to anybody."

"I think you're just saying that," Solomon said.

Father Marleski knew that the others in the car weren't going to be satisfied until he produced a real macho-man's scar.

"Okay, Tommy," he said, with a sigh of resignation, "Pull over. I'll show them my scar."

Tom Stanley the ever-obedient servant did as he was told and pulled over to the berm of the road. Father Marleski got out, removed his jacket, handed it to Father Art, tugged away at his shirt and pulled it out of his pants, undid his belt and zipper and revealed the nastiest looking scar they had ever seen.

A gruesome dark brown line in the shape of a long "L" that went from under his right rib cage, across the center of his belly and down to the left hip.

"Spring 1945, 3rd Marine Division, Iwo Jima, thirty-six days of pure hell," the priest said.

"Holy hell," Solomon said. "That's bad."

Tom Stanley was dying for a camera.

There was a moment of silence for the severity of the wound as all the people in the car just stared at it, while Father Marleski stood there patiently holding up his white shirt until he was sure they had seen enough. He didn't want to hear that he had to do it again anytime soon.

It was an awkward silence. Four grown men parked on the berm of a highway looking at another grown man showing off his scar-torn belly. The silence lasted only a fraction longer, when a slight objection broke the air.

"But," Solomon continued, with a raspy tone, just above a whisper voice, and raising his bandaged hands reverently in the air, and shaking his head. "I've seen worse. If a German did that to you he would have gone all the way around your belly. You're lucky it was a Jap and he stopped halfway."

Father Art and Father Marleski broke into an uproarious laughter.

"If you two guys had witnessed the crucifixion," Marleski said. "You probably would have told Christ he was lucky that Roman soldiers did it to him in the springtime instead of the Germans doing it in the winter."

Father Art was rolling in the front seat from the silliness of the whole thing of 'my wound is worse than yours'.

"That's nothing," Moe said. "I can top that."

He got out of the car with a serious and resolute look; he stood next to the priest, and faced his friends in the car. The whole crew, including his life-long friend Solomon, was curious as to what he would do. Solomon was shaking his head in wonder, his old friend had never told him about any other wartime wound.

Moe stood next to Marleski, making sure everybody noticed the comparison of the large priest to the small five foot-four man. Then he made crisp animated movements in taking his jacket off, to heighten the effect, and handed it to Solomon, as if it were a religious ritual. Then Moe pulled up his shirt just as Marleski did, folded it into his T-shirt to hold it up, unfastened his worn black belt, dropped his pants and his boxer shorts down to his ankles and stood there like a Jewish-Roman soldier in a museum.

He looked a ridiculous sight, as motorists who whizzed by did not believe what they were seeing: an old Jewish man, greying beard and mustache, with his shirt pulled up and his very private essentials being bared to all.

"It was ten below zero," Moe started his story, still standing there half-naked. "A German guard, a Gestapo, ordered me to stand outside in the freezing cold, naked, for five hours, while he threw water on my thing. Look at it. It shriveled up that night to half its length and never came back to its regular size again."

The roars and laughs could be heard all the way to Mount Rushmore as all the men crowded back into the car. The Jewish guy certainly broke the whole crew up with his crazy and zany humor. He was a mixture for the experts; serious one moment, outrageously funny the next.

Stanley was amazed at the diversity of the stories these men were delivering. He kept framing headlines in his mind of what this story would be like when it finally came out in the *Daily News*. He plotted in his mind how he would build a tape recorder into the dashboard of the Dodge, activated by a switch of his foot. If an opportunity like this ever happened again, he wanted to be ready for it.

He was interrupted from his deep thought of trying to figure out what section of the *Daily News* his boss would put the story about these men, when Solomon and Moe were able to settle down from their laughing. They started telling serious stories about their experiences of escaping the Germans during the war, getting to Israel, and then to the United States.

"We carried gold coins in a brown, re-sealed can of C-rations marked 'lima beans'. We knew the Germans hated the salty beans and would let us keep them, making fun of us as we huddled them close to our bodies. We played the part of the stupid humble servant for them it kept us alive, and let us sneak some money out of Germany to fight them back."

"Yeah, we had lima beans on the top, lima beans on the bottom, and thousands of dollars in gold coins in the middle, soaking in lima bean juices," Moe said. "It was a disgusting smell when we finally opened the can."

"Amazing," Stanley said as he turned around and looked at the two back seat passengers. They were short, old, and eccentric looking to him in their typical Jewish wardrobe and black hats, but they were brilliant.

The squirrel-like characteristics learned by these two men during the war, were still with them now. Solomon had sewn many thousands of dollars worth of diamonds in his suit jacket, but he carried it around as casually as that squirrel sitting in a treetop nest sitting on his acorns.

The two priests and two Jewish guys kept picking on each other. Stanley wasn't paying attention to them because he was lost in his own thoughts. He shook his head in amazement at his predicament. He had one of the greatest cast of characters that any Broadway producer would die for, but he knew it would be a story nobody could ever believe without some really hard concrete proof.

"Pictures," he thought to himself. "Pictures don't lie. I've got to get the Leica out of the trunk and back into action." He was daydreaming and directing the shot in his own mind, a true Bonnie and Clyde layout. He'd put the two old guys in front of the car, with Solomon's hands extended forward. Then he'd have Father Art and Father Marleski on both sides of these guys pointing to Solomon's magical saintly wounds. He'd set the camera on the hood of another car, put it on time exposure and jump into the shot. He would be a hero. His boss would give him front-page exposure, maybe give him a big bonus to pay off an old IRS fine, his friends would love him again, and best of all, maybe this great story would save his sorry ass from being fired.

There had to be a way for him to pull this off and still keep Marleski's confidence. Maybe he would have to sneak the pictures while the old man was sleeping. Maybe, but how?

Chapter Thirteen

It was early evening when the Dodge pulled through the DC traffic and ended up in Georgetown. Both Father Art and Father Marleski were quite familiar with the city, having completed several courses at the famous school during their doctorate days.

"Down there, Tom." Marleski pointed as they traveled south on Wisconsin. "Turn left on Q Street and go down to 31st."

Tom hunched forward with a half-lean and drove with an easy cautious manner watching the cross traffic as Father Dennis pointed left then right.

"We're getting closer, Tom, slow down a bit. Yeah I guess that's it right about there. The big house with the English brown brick and ivy on the front."

Tom pulled up next to the house and leaned forward toward the windshield trying to get a better view. He hunched closer on the steering wheel, turning left with two turns of the wheel toward a narrow driveway. He came to a complete stop when a tall, middle-aged black man in a houseman's grey uniform waved to him with a white towel. Tom turned the Dodge toward his direction and went into the entryway as the black wrought iron gates opened almost magically by the power of a long electric arm.

"Wow," Art said. "I knew the guy would be important, but this place is First Class."

The level cobblestone driveway winded easily past the front entrance to the three-story Jeffersonian brick home. A mansion to say the least, Art thought: large impressive double-doors in front with perfect architectural symmetry throughout.

"This place sure is nice. But I hope he has something to eat," Solomon said. "I've had this tremendous appetite all day."

Father Marleski didn't speak, but was concerned to hear Solomon complain about his stomach again, a sure sign that he needed a longer stay at St. Gabriel's hospital.

The black houseman held up an opened hand to Tom in understandable sign language to stop. Tom pulled up close to him and rolled down his

144

window.

"You the people from New York that's coming to see Mister Boyle?"

"Yes we are," Tom said.

"Pull around the back of the house, please," the servant said waving the towel in perfect toreador style. "And I'll come help with the bags."

Tom nodded his head and let the idle of the engine coax the car about eighty feet toward the back of the house, and stopped when he reached a comfortable parking place.

As the guests were getting out of the sedan and stretching their legs, a black Doberman came flying out of the house, down the long stretch of grey wooden steps, made a pacing clubhouse turn around the car, and right to Solomon's hands. He sniffed at the old man and zeroed in on the blood, when Solomon pulled back with immediate fright.

"Enos, stop that," a voice called from behind a screen door in the back of the house.

The dog didn't listen to the master but focused his eyes on Solomon's face while he lifted himself up onto Solomon's chest with his front legs, while pulling at the blood stained bandages with his shark-like teeth.

"Enos, dammit. Stop it."

Solomon was petrified as he pulled his hands in front of him for protection, but trying to hold the muscular Doberman off at the same time.

An older white male, about sixty-five, came running out of the house in an awkward pace, running after the dog. He ran past the two priests, fought to hold his balance on the cobblestone drive, and without hesitation grabbed for the Doberman. He reached up toward Solomon's face, pulled the Doberman by its heavy leather collar and yanked him unceremoniously down to the ground.

"Don't ever do that," he said to the dog and smacked him with an open hand on the right side of his muscular body.

The dog cowered as if it had been beaten before for a similar routine.

"Back in the house." He smacked the dog again and it shot to the back door like a dart.

"Gentlemen, I'm really sorry. Name's Charlie Boyle," he extended his hand in a friendly greeting. "I'll be your host for the next several days."

Mister Boyle looked at Solomon who was still in the defensive mode, still holding his hands in front of his face for protection.

"Please, forgive me. I should have locked him in the cellar. Let's go in the house. I'll make sure nothing like this happens again."

The priests, two Jewish men and Tom Stanley all introduced themselves to their host, grabbed their bags along with the help of Leonard the houseman, and headed for the back porch.

Solomon was wary about going in, but Charlie Boyle continued to assure him that the dog would never be a problem again. The look on Charlie's face was of tremendous concern he knew he was entrusted to take care of these special guests, and was highly embarrassed that it had such a terrible start.

Leonard grabbed a couple bags, Charlie grabbed Solomon's and they all headed for the welcome of the back door.

Inside the house, they were greeted by an ebullient, old, heavy-set, black woman working in the kitchen, and humming in perfect harmony to some Negro spiritual music on the radio. She was busy cutting vegetables for a large salad and preparing an evening meal for her new guests.

"Welcome, welcome, welcome," she sang out. "I hope you boys are hungry, because I sure did put on the feed bag."

"This is Cecila," Charlie said. "If you're not careful she'll feed you to death. Ohhhh, and yes, we did find a kosher restaurant and they brought food over for Solomon and Moe."

Her outgoing personality made the visitors feel comfortable immediately. Solomon took a couple whiffs of the flavors in the large, turn-of-the-century kitchen, and broke into a huge grin. He reached for a chair and sat down making himself at home at the kitchen table. The two priests and Moe were not surprised at his eagerness to start eating, and didn't discourage him from picking at the large bowl of chocolate chip cookies elegantly arranged in a crystal bowl.

"My, you sure are hungry, honey. When was the last time that you ate?"

"These priests have been starving me," he said to her, pleading his case to a sympathetic jury. "Something about fasting for Easter."

The old lady looked at him, while the priests were shaking their heads. She smiled so large that she displayed the unusual gap in her teeth, and convinced him with her body language that she didn't have the slightest idea what he was talking about.

The greetings lasted only a short while, Charlie being a rather fastidious host and offering them the comfort of the living room. The Doberman, not totally convinced that Solomon was not a rare steak to be enjoyed on the living room carpet, was obedient to his master and lay down with his paws stretched out in front of him, and his head resting between them. He eyed his new friends, but kept licking his mouth with his long tongue as the smell of

Solomon's blood penetrated his sensitive nostrils.

After dinner, the dog settled down and went to the basement for the evening, giving Solomon and Moe great relief. Moe was concerned because he looked just like Solomon and didn't want the dog to make any mistakes during the night.

"Let's have a brandy, gentlemen, and we can talk," Mister Boyle said as the visitors stretched themselves out on the plush furniture. Heavy, high back winged chairs covered in red leather, overstuffed sofas, and several coffee tables were perfectly arranged in this room that was reminiscent of one of the cover shots of Better Homes and Gardens.

Not only brandy was offered, but also huge Cuban cigars were passed around. Tom Stanley took one, as did Solomon and Mister Boyle.

"Nothing smells like a Cuban cigar," Moe said. "In our building where we work in New York, you can tell what floor has the most money by the smell of the cigars. Our floor is almost all Cuban cigars. Bernstein's floor, ooy, I don't have to tell you. I think they smoke ropes. They stink so bad."

Solomon was sitting in the biggest, fluffiest chair in the room, content with digesting the welcome kosher meal prepared for him and Moe. He was leaning back, feet crossed and shoes off, puffing on his cigar, but never touched the brandy. Marleski made sure of that.

"So you have to tell me, old man," Boyle said, in a friendly manner leaning over and patting Solomon on the knee. "How did you get this special gift?"

Solomon let out with a small puff of smoke and eyed Boyle with an objective stare. "It's a long story, but I hope you haven't told too many people we were coming."

"Nope, just special people here who have to know."

"Good, we have to keep it that way. Any publicity could ruin it for everybody."

"Who's the big man, Mister Boyle?" Marleski asked

"Don't know, Father. I'm just the middle guy in this whole thing. I was asked by a friend in the Justice Department to put you guys up until it was the right time. Could be tonight. Could be tomorrow, but definitely within three days. Somebody obviously can't do without this Mister Weinstein."

The sun was at its lowest point in the sky before falling off completely, when Tom Stanley excused himself and went back out to the car. He fumbled with his keys a bit and opened the trunk with a rusty-squeaking noise. Inside the trunk were several mismanaged cardboard boxes of old newspapers, yellow tablets, an old suit that never made it to the cleaners, lots of junk mail

147

that he insisted on saving, and then a beat up leather bag containing his Leica camera. He was upset that there wasn't any fresh film in the bag, but checked the film window in the back of the camera.

"Sixteen shots left," he whispered. "Enough shots to tell the story." He looked around to make sure there were no servants peeking out of windows, and pulled the camera out of the bag. He checked the focus, turning the lens to infinity, set the exposure, aimed the lens at the back of the house, and click.

"No that's no good," he said to himself. "Anybody could have taken this shot. There's no proof it's my story." He backed away to the farthest part of the yard and snapped another shot, but this time the massive house in the layout was accompanied by the back of his big Dodge, perfectly showing his license plate.

"Of course you're a genius, Tom Stanley," the reporter said, referring to himself in the third person. "Old Herbie is going to wet his pants when he gets the whole thing: story, details, pictures. Gotta get a couple shots of the Jewish guys, though. Especially just lounging around smoking cigars. Great human interest; a holy man who smokes cigars and drinks beer. Good God! Am I great or what?"

Stanley closed the trunk lid with the ease of a burglar and walked quietly to the steps of the back porch. He noticed the old lady in the kitchen still working away and humming to "Jesus, Thou Art Mine", when he raised the 35mm and snapped off a shot with the speed of a western gunfighter. He walked around the long, wooden, wrap-around porch and found himself outside the library. He noticed Solomon still sitting there, puffing away on that huge cigar, and rubbing his stocking feet against each other to stir the circulation.

There was a crack in the lace curtain wide enough for the lens to focus through. He waited for a second, the old man puffed out and dropped the cigar away from his face. Click. Quick-draw-Stanley did it again. Then there was Charlie Boyle holding a family picture out to the two priests for their examination of Boyle's heritage. Tom lifted the camera again. Click. He was delighted. The candid shots were just what he needed.

He didn't know who Boyle was, but he obviously had great wealth and was tied to somebody high up in the administration. He couldn't wait to dig into this guy's life to find out more.

"Hey, Tom, what are you doing out there?" Father Marleski asked.

"Oh just looking at this house. Great architecture."

He rolled the camera to the side of his body and headed back for the safety of his car, dropping the camera in the bag and closed the trunk. There would be time for more pictures later, he assured himself. Can't blow it now. He was heading for the house again when he was distracted by the creaking of the electric arm opening up the heavy black metal gates.

The car behind the gate was barely visible as it also was black and only the sparse area of chrome on the grill was showing forth until the gate was almost fully opened.

An extra long Mercury, with black tinted windows and a silly-looking whip antenna on the trunk, pulled onto the cobblestone driveway. Stanley opened the trunk again and slid his camera out of the bag and into his hand. He pulled his old crumpled suit jacket out and covered the camera, leaving only the lens exposed. He knew something was going down with this black limo, and he waited by his car to see. The limo stopped by the front entrance and all four doors opened. Out came a group of four professional looking men: clean shaven, white shirts, skinny red or blue ties, and polished shoes.

"Can't be cops," Tom said quietly. "Necks are too skinny. Can't be hoods. They all have glasses and briefcases. Gotta be lawyers or something like that."

The driver of the limo pressed a button near the front door of his car and the metal gate closed with a squeaking, clunking sound.

Tom acted without thinking, raised his arm slightly, with his suit jacket concealing the body of the camera, and clicked. Whoever they were, they would be in the *Daily News* in less than a week.

"Gotcha," Tom said. "Whoever the hell you are, I got you."

Tom debated about trying to get the camera inside the house to take more pictures, but decided it was too risky, putting it back into the trunk and returning to the house with a nonchalant attitude.

The four suits were what Tom thought: government men from the Justice Department. He made a mental note of the way they were dressed, uniform precision that made them look more like a singing group from the fifties, than government lawyers from the sixties. The similarity of the black pinstripes, wing tips, and black horned-rimmed glasses was nauseating to Tom.

When he walked into the library, the government men were as business-like as granite blocks on a cold windy day. Standing straight, showing no emotion, briefcases and yellow tablets efficiently ready, the lawyers started grilling Solomon about his life's story. Where was he from? What did he do? Was this stigmata thing for real? How did he get it? Did he have any weird diseases?

Solomon was getting visibly upset at the third degree.

"Look, there is this bastard cop in New York City who ruined my life, because as the president of the diamond brokers, I decided we would never make another payoff to a cop. He swore he would get even with me and he has. He somehow created a criminal record for me and reported it to the Justice Department making it impossible for me to get a passport approval. My wife and boys are in Tel Aviv. I want to go see them desperately."

His speech was delivered to stone statues.

"What do you think about America?" A skinny-necked suit asked Solomon. "Have you ever been a member of a Communist party?"

"Get serious, guys," Father Marleski chimed in as he left his place by the mantel and went over to the group of government stiffs. He raised his voice partly for shock value and partly because he was disturbed with the repetition of the government inquisition. "The man is here to help somebody at the top of the hierarchy," Marleski said. "He hasn't done anything wrong and you know it. He's supposed to get a clean passport in return for a favor. We've been through all of this over the phone days ago. Where's your boss? What's his name? Barnes?"

"We're just doing our job, Father."

"Well you know the deal, quit stalling. Line up who we're supposed to see so this man can get on with his life."

The head of the four suits looked at Marleski and wanted a verbal contracted battle but decided to make a phone call instead. He huddled with his three other cronies in the hallway and talked to his supervisor on the phone. There was a long and secret discussion among the four with plenty of whispering, pacing back and forth and hand gesturing. After the absurdly pretentious meeting in the hall, the men hung up the phone and came back to the library.

"Okay, tomorrow is the day," the senior government man said, standing stiff as a stone military statue, with his briefcase in front of him. "Get a good night's sleep. We'll come and get you about noon, take you to the destination, have you complete your assignment, and then bring you back here. Wear a dark suit, a white shirt and a tie. You better be able to really heal people. And does your twin also heal people."

"We aren't twins," Moe said, sitting in a red leather chair next to his look-alike friend. "But most gentiles make the same mistake."

Without saying much more, the government men shook Boyle's hand, packed up their briefcases and left the house by the front door. Leonard the houseman, left the library with the tray of brandy and glasses, and returned to the kitchen. Tom Stanley tip-toed out the back door, down to his car, into the trunk of his car, grabbed the Leica, focused for infinity, held it under the crook of his arm and snapped another quick shot. He captured the group of lawyers as they huddled by the front of their car before they piled in.

"Damn, I've got to get this film to New York," Tom said to himself. "This is front page stuff. A Pulitzer Prize."

Inside the house the mood was morbid. Father Marleski was having second thoughts about committing Solomon to this deal. He knew it was the only deal the old man could get, but still it seemed like a lousy one.

"Solly, you don't have to go through with this. You want me to work something else out?"

Solomon looked at Moe for a second opinion. Moe gave the nodding of his head and Solomon let out with another puff of smoke.

"Padre, I want to meet this guy, if he really wants me this much he must believe. That's what I'm supposed to do. Time's running out for me. I don't have much more healing left in me. It seems that every time I heal somebody I get weaker. Let's take this shot. It's the only thing I have left."

Father Marleski stared at Solomon, both of them realized that Solomon was dying and desperate to get back to see his wife and boys.

The small talk continued late into the evening for the men. Solomon was the first to zonk out, dropping his head to his chin and let out with a wispy snore. Moe and Father Art helped him up to his bedroom on the second floor and Father Marleski, Charlie Boyle, and Tom Stanley stayed in the library and discussed politics, baseball and religion.

"Mind if I help myself to a brandy?" Stanley asked Boyle.

"Not at all. Clean glasses are in the kitchen."

Stanley excused himself and went into the other room; the craving in his belly for liquor was calling for two days. As he got closer to pouring the drink, his hand shook with excitement, his tongue began to swell like a child ready for a dish of ice cream. He swallowed hard to remove the salty taste in his mouth before tasting the liquor.

He made a clumsy effort of opening the kitchen cabinet door and pulled out a wide-bottomed, bell-shaped, brandy snifter. Huge by any standards, but his experience told him the bigger the glass, the better the flavor. It didn't take long. He pulled off the cork, poured a healthy portion, never swirled the glass as he should have, but lifted it and quaffed the brandy, spilling half of it down his neck. He should have scolded himself for his sloppiness, but reached for the bottle again and repeated the exercise, letting out with a big gasp of air he was holding in his lungs. The alcohol had an immediate effect on him, it burned his esophagus on the way down, but the rush to his bloodstream was satisfying. He pulled out a kitchen chair, sat down, and smiled at the name Napoleon VSOP.

"Very Special Old Preserve," he said. "Well you sure are preserving me now. If I live long enough to see what happens to these two Jewish guys and these priests I'm going to buy the biggest bottle of you I can find. He poured another glass and stole a look back to the library where Father Marleski and Charlie Boyle were still gabbing away.

"Say, Tom," he said to himself in a ridiculously orthodox English accent. "Would you like another spot of this famous brandy?"

"Oh no I couldn't. Save some for the starving children in China," he answered himself.

"But please, Tom. You're such a great guy and a Pulitzer Prize reporter, too. Please have another." He was moving his head back and forth in a silly animated English schoolteacher way.

"If you insist." He lifted his glass, held his pinky finger out in a rather gentlemanly manner, and dramatically poured the brandy to his lips. He repeated the absurd behavior several more times until the fumes of the expensive brandy filled his brain and the brandy itself babied his blood. He became bowling ball heavy and fell to the kitchen table with a resounding thud.

The loud bang onto the oversized Formica table startled Father Marleski out of his comfortable leather chair and forced him to run into the kitchen to check on his friend. He eyed the half-empty bottle of brandy, the spilled glass onto the table, and the wide opened mouth of the exhausted journalist.

"Well, my good friend," the priest said. "I think you've had a tough enough day. How about if I carry you up to your room so you can get a good night's sleep."

The motionless reporter almost seemed dead, but the husky Marleski lifted him off the chair, picked him up, draped him over his shoulder and carried him up the stairs to the bedroom. Marleski sat his inebriated friend on the edge of the bed, pulled off his shoes and then watched as Tom precariously fell backwards, with arms sprawling onto the expensive Early American antique comforter. The priest smiled a bit, then frowned at the sadness of the lonely man, turned off the light and left the room.

Father Marleski went back to the library to finish up his conversation with his well-educated host, Charlie Boyle, who talked to the priest for another fifteen minutes. The major area of discussion was the rare, but unwanted gift that Solomon had, and they wore out the hypothetical situations of what they would do if the gift were extended to them.

Tomorrow would be the day, they insisted, as they broke up the conclave for the evening and headed for bed. Solomon would be taken to a secret hideaway, administer to the wealthy or public figure, heal that special person, get the clean passport that he needed, and be on his way to Tel Aviv.

Father Marleski passed a thought of finality to himself, as he walked up the elegant winding staircase to the second floor. After this episode, maybe he could get back to a more normal way of life. "But," he said to himself. "Maybe this is my normal way of life. Why me, Lord?" He walked a few more steps and thought again about the young woman in New York selling the flowers with the elephant legs. If he had this gift of healing, he would make her his first try. Or would it be someone else? Would it be Samuel's old aunt? What if Eldron Burt were dying and begged Marleski for a healing. Would he do it? Could he do it?

"Why me, Lord. Why me?"

Chapter Fourteen

The mid-morning sun was warming a small gathering of Eldron Burt's assistants who were standing in the asphalt driveway next to St. Gabriel's Hospital. The group of professional cops gathered outside and was discussing the next options in their investigation. It didn't take Burt's assistants long to realize that he was really missing, not just for a day or two of womanizing and drinking, but really missing. They were convinced that something sinister had happened to him.

Andrew "Andy Boy" Maloney was next in command and relished the unbridled authority now bestowed upon him. He would be as ruthless as his boss, because he was a product of the Pavlovian type theory: act as you were trained, copy what authority you know. Rough tough, no rules, and no regulations, enforcers doing what they wanted to do. Kick ass, never take names and never leave any evidence or witnesses.

Maloney was convinced that Burt was kidnapped or met with foul play, especially after hearing about the threats from the locals and knowing how tough old *il bastardo* was to them. He ordered his troops to backtrack everything they did in the last several days to uncover clues. They had closed in on St. Gabriel's but couldn't loosen the tongues or wedge out the slightest word from the fervent nuns or doctors.

"We need to find something else," Maloney said, as he led his subordinates out of the hospital. "Where do we go next?"

The cop who had been keeping watch at Moe's apartment chimed in. "What about Moe's wife? Moe never showed up again. Maybe he and the old man skipped town with the money. Maybe we can get something out of her."

Maloney looked at the older detective. "Oh, that's brilliant, Evans. Why didn't you think of that when the phantom caller told you to go to Harlem to see Burt?"

"Well, it sounded like a real cop."

"Well it sounded like a real cop," Maloney said mocking the man. "Who knew you were there?"

154

"A couple people in our department."

"Who else?"

"I don't know."

"You don't know," he mimicked again. Maloney walked back and forth rubbing his hand over his head. He had been promoted quickly up the chain in Special Squad, even though he was only thirty-five. Burt liked his college-educated brains and often called on Maloney to solve detailed problems for the boss. Analytical, and methodical, that was Maloney. He paced like a caged tiger as he talked.

"Okay, here's what we're going to do," Maloney said, using his index finger as a magic marker while he laid out the next several chess moves on the hood of his Chevy.

"Evans, you and Eddy get over to Fordham and see if there's any gossip about where the priests went."

Evans and Eddy Baker jumped into their car and headed for the college without second-guessing the new young boss.

"Homer, you and Morgan get over to that deli. What's it called? Yeah, Morty's deli, where Burt had that fight with those priests. They gotta know something."

"What about you, Mister Maloney?"

"Me? I'm going to pay a visit to an old Jewish lady who is going to tell me all about her husband and his best friend, the Jewish guy with all the money. Everybody check in at headquarters at noon, and no later," he hollered as the meeting broke up.

The three cars took off and headed in three different directions, cinders flying, smoke swirling and rubber screeching sounds being heard for a whole block as they pulled away in their black sedans.

Detective Maloney was determined to break this case wide open, find his boss, and become a superhero. Eldron Burt, the boss of the Special Squad, never told Maloney how much money he extorted every month from the Jewish Diamond Brokers. All Maloney knew was that his cut was $200 per month. He never guessed what Burt's cut was, but he never asked, figuring that someday Burt would simply let him run the entire scam. If Burt were missing or dead, then Maloney would have to take over, but he didn't know enough about the total details to do it.

He knew that Solomon Weinstein was the person elected to make the deals with Burt and only he could pay out the money. He also knew that Moe Kessler was his best friend, and that Moe's wife was the only person around

155

to talk.

Maloney made it over the bridge, pushing slower cars out of his way with a sophisticated tap of his siren. He wasn't as brash or rude as his boss was with a car. He tapped his siren, old Burt would lean on the damn thing until people grabbed their ears in surrender.

He checked the address written on the top of his clipboard and pulled over close to the apartment building on Flatbush.

"Observation is the first rule of psychology," he muttered to himself, as he closed the door to his Chevy and walked around. He was out of place, an Irish boy, gentile, in a blue business suit and large brimmed, light grey felt hat, walking around this section of Brooklyn. He looked peculiar to the residents of the area, but sauntered around and studied the people on the street, the shops, the customers in the butcher shops, and the garbage trucks hauling away the mounds of chicken feet and feathers.

He strolled in front of Moe's apartment building, leaned against the wall near the front door, folded his arms and waited for something to happen. Fifteen minutes went by and nothing moved or stimulated his devious mind. Undaunted, he walked around the large red brick apartment building and found himself in a back alley, looking up at an erector set of fire escapes and laundry. He waited again; knowing with a detective's cynical instinct that eventually some clue had to be nearby.

"I feel it," he said, echoing his egotistical belief by the scraping of his foot on the dirty, garbage stained asphalt. "If I'm going to find Moe, I have to think like Moe. I'm married to this lady for many years. I don't just leave her and run off with my friend. I'm an old and faithful man. I have habits I can't break, I have to let her know how I am. So what do I do? I can't call because the cops have the phone tapped, so I call somebody else I guess, and that's how I let her know."

Maloney was analytical again, and antsy with his obsession. "I would get word to her by the back alley because the front alley is being watched by the cops. So I call a neighbor and send a signal with the laundry hanging out. That's it," Maloney chuckled to himself. "The laundry, just like Indians and smoke signals, these crafty Jews use laundry signals. A red blanket means something dangerous, a green shirt means something else, purple socks means meet me somewhere special."

He lined his back up against Moe's apartment building and surveyed the other buildings straight ahead of him. What he observed was another matter, a jumble of the worst messages man could send, even prehistoric man: white sheets, white pillowcases, white socks, white underwear, black dresses, black socks.

"What the hell kind of a signal is that?" he said, as he stared longer, looking left and right, when his thoughts were broken by a noisy window being lifted on the second floor; and a man's voice was calling out.

"Masha," Yitzhak called out in an excited tone. "Masha."

Maloney standing directly under the fire escape wasn't visible to Yitzhak, but raised his head up and casually focused on the man.

The kitchen window to Moe's apartment went up with a metal scratching noise and made Maloney pay closer attention.

"What, Yitzhak?"

"I got news," he said.

"You got news?" she said raising her voice in a pleasant manner.

Yitzhak wanted to make sure she understood. "You know, news from Moshe."

Maloney practically broke his neck spinning his body past a garbage can to get closer to Yitzhak's voice.

"Shhh," she said raising a finger to her lips. "You can't say it's from Moshe, just say what the news is?"

"Moshe said that 'the sun is shining.'"

"Thank you, Yitzhak. Tell me again when something else happens, but don't start out by saying it's from Moshe."

Yitzhak totally puzzled, smiled, saluted her and closed his window.

She waved back, left her window opened and went back to her chores in the dining room.

"Observation," Maloney whispered to himself. "All you have to do is observe and you can be a genius like me."

Maloney grabbed a couple sturdy wooden boxes, built a platform for himself, stood up on the boxes and reached for the extension ladder on the fire escape. It was above his fingertips. He squatted down as far as he could and sprung straight up, barely catching the edge of the black ladder with his fingertips and pulling it straight down with a squeaking, crunching noise as it hit the boxes. He froze, hoping nobody heard his clumsiness. He waited, nobody responded. Up the ladder he went, onto the permanent metal rails and up to the second floor, just outside Masha's kitchen.

He paused for a moment leaning his back against the red brick structure to get his breath back, then tapped on her window.

No response. He waited for a minute more and tapped again.

"Is that you, Yitzhak?"

She went into the kitchen and saw Maloney scrunching his way off the fire escape and onto the kitchen floor.

"Who are you?" she stammered.

"Please, ma'am. I'm here to help you." He reached inside his fancy blue suit jacket and flashed his badge to her. "I'm detective Maloney."

"I don't want no more cops," she said. "I'm sick of cops. I don't know nothing." The sudden fright made her fidget with her sheet white hair, pushing the loose strands back to the tight bun.

"Mrs. Kessler, please, I'm here to help. Moe's in a lot of trouble. He needs help."

She looked at him, wanted to believe him, but still had her doubts.

"How can you prove you want to help?" she said.

"My great grandmother was Jewish."

"You don't look Jewish," she said, folding her arms across her chest, reinforcing her doubts.

"Look, the crooked cops are after Moe and his friend Solomon. We have to find them before they do. Where did they go?"

"Don't know," the old lady said, still defiant.

Maloney wouldn't give up. "Okay," he said, letting out a heavy breath of frustration. "You leave me no choice. I'm taking you into headquarters where you'll be safe."

Masha sank with fear. "I will not leave my home," she demanded, slamming her foot on the kitchen floor. I will stay here. Bad cops, good cops, I hate you all. I will stay here."

"Sorry, but this must be done, turn around," he said, as he grabbed her skinny white wrists in a smooth and often practiced motion, handcuffing her hands behind her back.

Masha was scared to death and realized screaming for help wouldn't work. "The Nazis couldn't kill me. What makes you think you can?" she said. Her voice becoming shaky, and nervously hoarse.

Maloney became irritated, dragged the reluctant old lady down the hall and locked her in the bathroom. "If you scream out, I'll shoot you." He pounded an angry fist on the door.

Masha was frozen with fear but dared not show it. Her experience with bullies taught her to be strong and never cower to their demands.

Maloney made sure she wouldn't move from the temporary jail and went about sweeping the house for clues. As any good detective would do, he started with the bedroom. He became disillusioned in a hurry when he realized that Hassidic Jews, other than handling diamonds at work, live a terribly Spartan life. Simple clothes, no frills, simple furniture, only a few large drawers, special linens, some very special religious ornaments and cloths, many pictures of Jewish people during religious events, but little else.

"Where did they go?" he kept asking himself. "She knows. I've got to get it out of her." He continued ransacking the house. He became as impatient as a young groom, pulling out drawers and turning them over. He continued his search through the dining room, the small back bedroom and then the hall closet, where he stumbled upon the ugly pink hatbox in the hall closet.

"Uh-huh. What's this?"

With the cocky thumbs of a blacksmith, he pulled open the box and examined the contents, tearing away the frilly tissue paper. He discovered a treasure of Jewish paperwork.

"Looks like bonds. Jewish bonds," he said. He didn't understand the denominations, but figured it must be a significant amount from the detail of the expensive paper and printing, and the way they were wrapped.

"I could cash these in. Maybe they're worth a lot of money. Burt would never know. Who's gonna tell him? The old lady?" Maloney laughed to himself.

He paused only for a moment to let his analytical mind come up with a better idea. He scrambled further through the box, found more Jewish papers and stumbled upon Masha's passport. He looked further and was not surprised that he didn't find Moe's.

"Okay, old lady. I got you all figured out."

Maloney dropped the box to the floor, held all the bonds and special Jewish papers in his hand and went back to the bathroom. He opened the door and saw the old lady leaning against the sink, arms twisted and cuffed behind her.

"Okay, Masha Kessler," he said reading from her passport. He dropped it to the ground and held an official looking paper, probably a birth certificate, or something to do with a religious occasion in his left hand and pulled out his Zippo lighter in his right. He flicked the flame on and put it close to the paper.

"Where's Moe?" he said looking straight at her.

She looked away from him, tears rolling down her cheeks, mutterings of a religious prayer coming out of her mouth.

The flame got closer and caught the paper on fire.

He waited for a reaction from her, dropped the paper to the linoleum floor, causing a brownish smoke to flare up.

He took the next paper, one of the Jewish bonds in his hand and repeated the process. She never budged, just kept praying and letting the tears roll down her cheeks.

"How come your passport is here, but his isn't?"

She was relentless. He got closer to her. "What if I set your dress on fire? Then what?" He walked next to her and flicked the lighter again. "That pretty, simple black dress, looks like polyester to me, would burn up like a dry pine tree in the Jewish desert."

"I told them to give you the money," she said, choking her words with fear. "But Solomon won't budge."

"Ohhhh, now we're getting somewhere? Tell me where Solomon is and I'll let you go and I'll let Moe go. I just want Solomon," he said with a syrupy sickening voice. "I won't burn anymore papers, or bonds, or you."

"Promise?" she said in a military stoic tone.

"Promise," he said with a perfect choir boy smile, while he raised his hand as if taking an oath.

She fretted about her choice, but decided she didn't have much to bargain with. "Solomon went to Washington DC, to see somebody high-up about getting a passport to Israel.

"Israel? When?"

"Don't know, they wouldn't tell me."

"Where are they staying? "

She shrugged her shoulders and cried heavily for betraying her lifelong faithful husband. The same husband who braved the knives and guns of the Nazis. She shook her head with her hands still cuffed behind her as she looked away from the cop in shame. Her pure white skin now reddened from shame and anguish.

"Okay, somewhere in DC." He walked next to her and flicked the lighter next to her hair. "You gotta do better than that."

She raised her head skyward hoping for a last minute intercession from heaven. "Justice Department," she said barely getting the words out.

"Oh my God, this is going to be easier than I thought." He drew even closer to her, his lips were next to her smooth angered red face, about to kiss her cheek. "I'll just call my friend in the witness protection unit, and you'll have your Moshe back here faster than you blink."

Maloney reared his head back and laughed, with the evilness of the villain who tied the maiden to the railroad tracks.

"Witness protection? I don't know what that means," she said.

Maloney looked at her in a pathetic way, realizing she told all she knew. He debated taking all the Jewish papers and bonds, hoping to find a better clue in them, or making a quick profit for himself, but threw them on the floor in a last effort to scare something more out of the old lady.

She never budged toward him, but turned her face toward the bathtub.

Maloney backed out of the bathroom, closed the door, ran to the kitchen and escaped back down the fire escape.

Masha stood in the bathroom sobbing hard and choking for air. It was at least five minutes before she allowed herself to stomp on the smoking papers on the floor. She danced on them with her plain black low heel shoes, making sure there was no more smoke or flames. The anger inside her fueled her action. She hollered at herself for her weakness of giving in to the detective. She fussed with the cuffs behind her back and rubbed against the doorknob, twisting it until it opened. Like a freed rabbit she ran for the kitchen window and hollered out to her friend.

"Yitzhak. Yitzhak. Yitzhak." she screamed his name until he poked his head out onto the fire escape.

"What is it, Masha?" he said, chomping on a handful of crackers.

"Please, I need your help."

Yitzhak dropped his box of crackers, bounded out onto the fire escape and into her apartment. He was horrified when he saw her handcuffed.

"Masha, what happened?"

"Quickly, Yitzhak, we must get in touch with Moshe. He and Solomon are in a lot of trouble. Did he give you a phone number where he was staying?"

Yitzhak felt useless. He had a hard time thinking and acting. "Yes, I wrote it down on the kitchen wall, next to the phone, but we'll call later. Now, we must get these cuffs off you, but how?"

"Take me down to Heimie's. He can cut them off."

Yitzhak listened and followed Masha's directions carefully. For all the stress she had undertaken she still managed to think clearly enough to act rationally.

"What's that smell?" Yitzhak asked.

"The bathroom, the bonds, get the bonds off the floor, Yitzhak," she screamed.

Yitzhak was a nervous wreck. He listened, he acted, but he wasn't sure actually what he was doing. After he bundled the mess of papers off the floor, he piled them nicely on the kitchen table, then reached over and helped

161

Masha again.

He was fumbling at everything he touched. First the papers, then her, then he checked her cuffs again trying in his limited way to remove them.

"No, Yitzhak, downstairs. Help me to the door. We must get to Heimie's, now."

Out the front door they went, down the ancient stone steps with heavy black metal railings, out to the street, to the corner and hurried up the few steps to Heimie's butcher shop.

At first, the butcher was amused, thinking the cuffs were a practical joke. It only took seconds of looking at Masha's impassioned face to realize she was really in distress.

Words weren't necessary. She turned her back to him and motioned for him to get to work. He never hesitated, sharpened what thin saw blade he could find to do the job and started sawing.

"Yitzhak, go to Irving's and get a hacksaw. Hurry," Heimie ordered. "This meat saw will never do it."

Yitzhak obeyed, rushing his heavyset body out of the twelve-foot high door and down the few steps to Irving's hardware store a few small stores away.

Within minutes, a small militia of Jewish volunteers from the hardware store and butcher shop busied themselves on the metal handcuffs. Masha cried as the men tortured her hands to cut them free.

"When will the stupidity stop?" she asked the small crowd. "When will we be free from these monsters? First Hitler, now the bastard cops."

It was a hectic half an hour until the cuffs were released from Masha's hands. The butcher continually begged forgiveness for cutting her hands and wrists with his clumsy and nervous actions. It wasn't until Irving pushed Heimie aside and took over the duty of using the sawing wire that the cuffs were torn free. Heimie was tearful as he wrapped the old lad's wrists with white butcher rags and hundreds of quick prayers for healing.

"There will be time for that later," Masha said. "Quick we must get in touch with Moshe before he walks into the trap."

The troop of older Jewish friends all left the butcher shop and ran for Yitzhak's apartment. Back through the skinny cold hallway, up the ancient stone steps to the second floor. Masha was the oldest of the group, but she was the most fit. Her slim, but sturdy body had negotiated these steps so many times over the years, that she actually enjoyed the challenge of running them to keep in shape. She got to Yitzhak's apartment on the second floor and was barely breathing hard. The door was locked and she waited for Yitzhak.

"Damn it, it's locked," Yitzhak said. "I came through your apartment remember?"

Masha was upset. She scampered down the steps again, ran next door to her apartment, up the identical set of steps, into her apartment, rushed through to the kitchen, deftly out onto her fire escape, turned right, went ten steps and swung herself over to Yitzhak's fire escape.

Into his window she went and straight for the front door of his apartment, where the group of older men was standing and waiting for her. Without a lengthy conversation, Yitzhak ran for the kitchen phone and still breathless pointed to the number on the wall. He hesitated because there must have been at least one hundred numbers written there.

Yitzhak studied, pointed to a number shook his head "no", pointed to another.

"DC," she screamed at him. "Let's first look at the area code for DC."

"Oh yes, of course," he said back with little confidence. "Uhhh-here. Here it is. Yes, this is it, I'm sure."

Masha grabbed the phone but had trouble reading the number without her reading glasses. "Irving, Heimie, somebody read this number for me, please." Her voice was shaky but she still was more in control than any of the men.

"I'll dial it," Heimie said as he grabbed the phone and spun the rotary dial with his thick, blood-stained, index finger.

The phone rang maybe five times.

"No answer," Heimie said.

"Give me," Masha said. She took the receiver from him and put it in her right hand, holding the white towel on her bleeding wrist with the other. "C'mon," she said, bouncing up and down to help the horrible impatience of waiting.

It rang more.

"Please, somebody answer, please," she cried in pain.

Click. "Boyle residence, Leonard, speaking."

" Mister Leonard, I'm calling from New York City. Is a Mister Moshe Kessler there, please? It is important that I talk to him."

"One moment," Leonard said, in mechanical, soldier like dialogue.

Masha could hear the phone being placed down on a hardwood surface. There were vibrations of sounds near the phone, clearly Leonard's footsteps on a marble or slate floor. He walked away and there was a deafening silence.

Masha waited for what seemed an eternity of minutes. She viewed terrorist scenes in her subconscious, and moved around in the kitchen, pacing to remove the anxiety in her stomach.

"Please, Mister, please," she begged to an empty receiver on the other end of the line. She strained her ears to try to hear something, but all was still as quiet as a mushroom mine at midnight.

"What's going on?" Irving asked Masha.

She waved at him with an irritated motion to be quiet so she could hear any movement at all.

The footsteps on the hard marble came closer to the phone. Leonard picked it up as if it were a bugle announcing the entrance of the troubadours.

"I'm sorry, ma'am. But the four of them left with a group of men from the Justice Department. They will be back sometime this afternoon. May I take a message for him?"

"Oh no," Masha screamed. "It's too late. Get him back. Tell him it's raining."

Terribly confused, Leonard held the receiver away from his face and stared at it as if the woman on the other end were surely insane. He paused and rejoined the conversation. "With all due respect, ma'am, it is clear today and quite sunny."

"Please get this message to him, 'It is raining.'"

"I will not argue with you, ma'am. When I see him I'll tell him."

"You said 'four of them', who are they?"

"Two Jewish guys and two priests. Just Mister Stanley is here."

"Who is Mister Stanley?" she asked.

"He came with them yesterday, but he had a rough night last night and now he's just sitting in the kitchen drinking black coffee."

She lit up. " Mister Leonard, let me speak to him."

Leonard put the phone down again and went to the kitchen. Minutes later, Tom Stanley picked up the phone.

He sounded horrible. His voice was rough and he had a miserable hammer-pounding headache.

"Hello," he whispered.

"Who is this?" the over-excited Masha hollered into the phone.

Stanley pulled the phone away from his head. "Please, lady, not so loud. My head is killing me."

" Mister Stanley do you know my Moshe?"

"Who?"

"Moe Kessler," Heimie screamed into the phone.

"Yeah, I know him. He'll be back later."

"Mister Stanley," Masha said. "Please get in touch with him. He and Solomon are in terrible trouble."

"Like what?" Stanley asked trying to clear his head from the throbbing.

"The dirty cops found out where they're going and they're after them. Tell him, 'it's raining', he'll know what to do."

Stanley pulled the phone away from his ear and held it above the cradle for about ten seconds and then dropped it. He looked back to the kitchen and saw Leonard guarding the cabinets where the brandy had been locked up. One drink, he thought to himself. Just one little drink.

He went back into the kitchen and stood eye-to-eye with Leonard.

"Something tells me you want another drink, Tom. But something else tells me you have a damned important assignment in front of you."

Stanley eyed the liquor cabinet again. And Leonard got closer to him one more time.

"Don't even think about it," Leonard said. "Not for one damned second."

Chapter Fifteen

Stanley stood for one more second looking at Leonard then backed away and headed into action. He rumbled out of the kitchen, headed for his bedroom and grabbed some clothes, hustled back down the steps and stopped Leonard in the hallway.

"Where did they go?" he asked the houseman.

Leonard stood as stiff as his grey uniform with the buttoned up white shirt.

"Sir the limo with the government guys came and hustled them off to the X.O."

"X.O.? What the hell's an X.O.?" Stanley asked.

"Why it's the Executive Office building, Mister Stanley."

"Across from the White House?"

"Yes, sir. That's where they went."

"God, it's a damn trap. I got to get to him. Where's Mister Boyle?"

"In his study, sir."

Stanley rushed out of the hallway, shirt half off, shoes on but not tied, hair a mess, no shave, and wrinkled pants, and burst into Boyle's study.

" Mister Boyle, I need your help. The old men are in a lot of trouble."

"What?" Boyle answered back with an incredulous tone.

"I can't explain now, but I really need your help, please."

The quiet, sedate, Mr. Boyle wasn't one for excitement. He was a well-to-do retired executive who didn't get involved with too much excitement, except for Democratic political campaigns and fund raisings.

Stanley rushed around the house as if he knew what he was doing, but he made it up as he went along. He realized that by running around he would think of something brilliant to do, and maybe at the same time burn up some of the alcohol in his system.

"We have to catch up with them before the crooks do," he kept repeating to himself.

He rushed into the bedroom where Solomon and Moe were staying and hoped that by being there he would get a great inspiration. He saw some clothes laid out on the freshly made beds and two suitcases. Stanley was convinced the two guys wouldn't be able to return to the mansion to grab their belongings. They would be arrested, or worse, and have all of the money and possessions confiscated by the dirty cops.

Stanley acted first and thought later, he hollered down the steps for a helper.

"Leonard, c'mon up here and help me."

Both Leonard and Mr. Boyle with question marks on their brows reacted rather than argued with him. Leonard ran up the steps and listened to his guest.

"Help me pack these things," he said. "We have to catch up with the old men."

With the efficiency of his station, Leonard packed suits, shirts, socks, and underwear neatly into two bags. Stanley checked other things in the smaller bag and made sure that the paper bricks of money were there and intact.

It only took minutes and the two of them were back down the steps and standing in the hallway where Mr. Boyle was ready to go with his coat on.

"Let's go," he said, and the three of them rushed out the back door, down the grey wooden steps and hustled for the grey Lincoln sitting in the garage.

With a little less speed than the New York City cops, they fired up the engine and raced for the already swinging black metal gate to the entrance.

They were about to fly out of the driveway when Stanley screamed, "Wait."

Mr. Boyle slammed on the brakes and everyone one of them almost flew out through the windshield.

"Jesus, Tom, don't scream like that. What's the matter?"

"Wait," he demanded, as he opened the car door and raced for the back porch again. Seconds later the Doberman shot out of the screen door like a black rocket, heading straight for the opened door of the Lincoln.

"Damn it," Leonard said. "He let the dog out."

Then Stanley came jumping out of the back door with a large box of Ritz crackers, his yellow legal reporter's pad, a thick black magic marker from Cecilia's kitchen, and followed the dog straight for the car.

"We need the dog," Stanley said as he jumped into the back seat and slammed the door.

Neither Boyle nor Leonard protested, but followed Stanley's lead. The brand new 1961 Lincoln pulled out like a supercharged tank. Boyle struggled with the waddling left and right as he pushed for all the power the car would give. The huge 400 cubic inch V-8 moaned as it practically pushed other cars aside, racing to find the extra-long black Mercury of the Justice Department.

"Take the shortcut," Leonard said to his boss. "I'll show you."

Leonard pointed and hollered directions, while Stanley tried to make friends with the staring and militarily rigid, Enos the Doberman.

"Here, boy. Let's make friends," Stanley said, as he pried open a wax paper seal on the Ritz crackers, feeding the dog to become his friend. "I need you, Enos. Do you understand? I need you."

Enos showed his shark like teeth and steel black eyes to the reporter. If it wasn't a steak, he wasn't eating. Stanley grabbed Solomon's bag. Surely there would have to be some tiny trace of blood in those clothes. He forced the aging zipper and opened the bag pushing it closer to the canine.

Stanley was thrilled with himself as the Doberman shoved his long snout inside the leather suitcase and licked the edges of his lips with his long wet tongue.

"Down, there," Leonard yelled. "Go south on 28."

The Lincoln made a squalling noise as it rounded the bend.

"Floor it."

"Floor it?" Boyle said objecting.

"Floor it. The black ass Mercury was flying when it left. You need to haul ass if we're going to catch them."

The reluctant, and always perfectly correct Charlie Boyle was terrified to break the law, even though he knew his new friends were in for a terrible shock. He pondered the possibility of the embarrassing situation of two Orthodox Jewish guys, who were his guests, being arrested. The thought of the disgrace and humiliation forced him into action. He floored it, getting to M Street, pulling a hard left, going through two red lights and heading south on Pennsylvania.

"Now that's what I call, 'hauling ass'," Stanley said.

The Doberman pulled his nose out of the suitcase only long enough to eye Stanley and growl.

"Easy, boy," he whispered. "We're almost there."

Mr. Boyle was flirting with disaster as he leaned way over the double yellow line, passing cars and blowing his horn. Leonard was facing straight ahead, sitting in the passenger seat, but by now, he had his eyes closed. Boyle knew where to go from here. As a regular visitor to the central area of DC, he knew all the twists and turns leading down to Executive Office Building. Past 21st, 20th, 19th, and closing in on 17th, they came to the building.

A traffic cop near the building forced them away from the VIP area, signaling for them to go south on 17th, but Boyle refused. He turned left and upset the cop.

"We need to find that limo," Boyle said. "But too damn many of these cars look just like it."

"Go around," the guard ordered.

Boyle disobeyed, shouting out of his window. "I got business at the X.O."

"Then turn left and go find a place over there."

"Damn this is going to put us near the White House," Boyle said. "I'm going to try to park."

"Keep going," Stanley said. "We'll park near the White House and walk. Time is wasting."

Charlie Boyle wasn't in any mood to argue. He drove, he parked and he let out with a huge sigh of relief when he turned the car off.

Five DC cops came running after the Lincoln for entering a VIP area without the right license plate.

" Mister Boyle, tell Enos to find Solomon."

"What?" the old man said as he leaned into the back seat. He was shocked. Stanley had taken the fat magic marker and written a short cryptic message on a yellow sheet of paper and stuck it under Enos's thick leather collar.

Mr. Boyle grabbed at his chest to stop the hyperventilating. Stanley couldn't wait any longer. He grabbed one of Solomon's shirts stuffed it to the Doberman's nose, opened the back door and hollered at the dog.

"Go find, Solomon, boy. Go find him."

The dog shot out of the back of the Lincoln leaving Leonard and Charlie Boyle stuck in their seats.

"Let's go," Stanley said as he rushed out of the car with two bags, and the Ritz cracker box.

Leonard and Boyle looked at each other.

"What the hell is going on?" Charlie asked Leonard in a totally foggy state.

"Beats the hell out of me," Leonard said. "But that damn dog ain't going to no X.O. He going to the White House, Mister Boyle."

"I'll be damned, he is."

"Hey, you guys," the cops hollered out as they pulled their guns from their holsters. "Get your hands up."

Stanley ran as fast as he could with his terrible hangover trying to catch up to the Doberman. It was a useless attempt but he followed his trail. One of the cops ran after Stanley and the Doberman, but the reporter and the canine had too much of a head start.

The dog ran faster than any greyhound, directly to the center gate on Pennsylvania Avenue. Rarely opened except for VIPs, the gate was opened today for some special occasion. Parked directly outside of the gate was the extra long black Mercury of the Justice guys.

Stanley was exhausted as he made it near the gate, only to watch the Doberman fly by the inattentive security cop and straight to the front door of the White House. A marine guarding the front door in his dress blues, without flinching an eye, opened the door for the dog and let him run in.

"What the hell," Stanley said, as he closed in on the security guard at the gate."

"Sir, tourists, have to use the West entrance, but you're too early for a tour.

"I'm with that dog, the Doberman."

"Oh that's the attorney general's dog," the security guard said as he held Stanley up with both of his hands. "One of his dogs anyway. The guy has about a hundred kids and about fifty different dogs."

Stanley leaned over at his waist and grabbed for some air. He looked back to the grey Lincoln halfway down the block and saw his two friends still being held at bay with the DC cops holding guns on them. Boyle looked at Stanley and pointed to the North entrance to the White House as if to ask, 'did the dog go in there?'.

"All we can do now is wait," Stanley said.

It was an impressive setting for the two Jewish guys and two priests. They were thrilled to be at the White House, especially sitting in the famous hallway with the thick red carpet and the massive low-slung chandeliers.

All four of them were ushered to a sitting area outside of the Oval Office. They looked at each other, smiled, shook their heads in amazement at the entire situation and whispered their thoughts.

"Who would have ever thought, Padre," Solomon said.

"Never in a million years," Marleski answered.

Father Art was too nervous to sit and paced back and forth. All of them kept looking at the secretary outside the president's office waiting for a signal to go in.

Everyone was becoming increasingly nervous.

"Padre, I gotta go to the bathroom."

Father Marleski quietly got up off his Early-American sitting bench and went over to the woman.

"Excuse me, ma'am, but he has to go to the bathroom."

She whispered back in church-like fashion. "He'll have to use the attorney general's bathroom. Three doors down and to the left." She leaned closer to the priest. "Make sure he lifts the seat."

Father Marleski dutifully acknowledged by nodding his head and started to back away.

She motioned for him to come closer again, she looked at the Oval office door making sure it was closed and continued talking.

"The vice-president always uses the attorney general's bathroom when he comes over, but he never lifts the seat. It makes the attorney general madder than hell, if you'll excuse the expression. So make sure he lifts the seat."

Father Marleski was thrilled to be included in such a cryptic international secret. He was impressed that this woman had taken him so closely into her confidence.

The three men walked down the hall with the reverence of being in church: Moe, Solomon and Father Marleski. Three doors down and to the left, there it was, the attorney general's White House office. A quick dash and Solomon was the first in, Moe and the priest waited.

"Look at all these pictures," Moe said, touching one picture after another. "All these Kennedys, all these places, all these kids."

Father Marleski kept an ear out for the president's secretary to call them, or for the attorney general to suddenly arrive and shoo them away. The priest was attracted to one picture in particular sitting in the back of a menagerie of photos. A typical K-mart type frame holding a colored shot of the president, the attorney general and their wives, all with arms around each other, in a casual manner, with a joyous smile. Father Marleski looked around and decided that a souvenir would be just what Solomon needed for his trip. A picture of a bunch of beautiful Irish men and women with frumpish hair, large white teeth and lots and lots of kids.

He looked around to make sure nobody was coming into the office and then pulled the picture out of its frame, reached over and picked up one of the many pens sitting in a pewter mug on Bobby Kennedy's desk and proceeded to sign a neat note to Solomon. The smile on Father Marleski's face was so large he had to rub his cheeks to keep them from hurting.

Each man took a turn to use the bathroom, each making doubly sure that the seat was lifted and no splashes were made, and then returned to their sitting area near the Oval office when they were finished.

Father Marleski reached into his suit jacket pocket and pulled the photo out and with a smooth motion, stuck it into Solomon's suit jacket pocket without his knowledge.

When the men got back to their waiting seats, they were surprised to see sitting across from them a very large man, nicely dressed in an expensive blue suit, but wearing brown cowboy boots. His balding, straight grey hair framed his incredibly huge ears. He exhibited a heavy Texas accent as he talked.

"You boys, been waiting long?" the vice-president asked.

"No, Sir," Father Art said, and at the same time wondering if they should be standing at attention when the Texan talked or sitting with legs uncrossed.

"I hope you boys don't mind if I go in before you. We've got some damn business about Cuba going on right now. It sure is messy."

"Certainly," Father Marleski said.

The Texan continued, with an overtly crooked smile. He loved an audience, no matter how small. "You gonna hit the president up for a contribution or something? The Jewish-Catholic League maybe?" He laughed, and leaned over, his massive hands holding on to the edge of the authentic Early American bench.

The door to the Oval Office opened and the attorney general came out. He finished his last thought to the president as he held the edge of the door in his hand.

"Whatever, happens, Jack, deny it. It's the Freedom Fighters' word against ours. Who do you think the people are going to believe? Let's keep it that way."

He finished his short speech, closed the door and headed to the president's secretary's desk. He brushed his hair twice with his left hand and straightened up and buttoned his suit jacket. He leaned over the desk and talked to the president's secretary. He dropped the volume of his voice.

"Mrs. Lincoln, clear the president's calendar this afternoon from 3:00 to 3:30. He has an important meeting with that special intern Mimi. I'll have the secret service clear the floor. I'm sure you can take a break at that time. Alright?"

"Yes, sir. That'll be fine." She looked at the attorney general with a straight face, but never focused on him.

"The president says it's very important," Bobby repeated. "Oh yes, and we don't need the vice-president right now, but the holy people can go in."

He turned around and faced the priests. "Father Dennis, Father Art, Rabbi Solomon, Rabbi Moshe, nice to meet you. The president is waiting for you, but we can give you only five minutes. Alright?"

"Thank you, Sir," Solomon said. "We won't need that much time."

The vice-president stood up.

"What the hell do you mean, 'we don't need the vice-president right now'? What the hell does that mean? Do you realize that if anything ever happened to the president I would have to step in and become the new president?"

He didn't hide his anger. "Someday, you Kennedys are going to have to realize this ain't no dictatorship. You need me and the Congress to get done what you need to have done." He stuck his long index finger out to the attorney general. "Someday, Mister Boston-baked-bean-Harvard lawyer, you and this old rough-assed Texas schoolteacher are going to have it out, and I bet I'm the one who will end up the winner. I should be involved in these meetings on Cuba. When you get your ass in a wringer about it, then I bet you'll turn to the old wizened owl of politics, and ask me to figure a way out of the mess you made. And you know what? I'm gonna tell all of you smart-ass-Harvard-white-boys to go to hell."

The vice-president dropped his finger from Bobby's chest and threw his hands in the air in disgust and walked back towards the long hall, away from the Oval Office.

The attorney general slammed his hands to his hips and just waited until the big man stormed down the hall before he left the waiting area to the Oval Office and back to his own office. He combed his hair with his left hand again.

"I guess we're next," Father Marleski said. "Let's go and get this over with."

All four of them walked slowly into the Oval Office.

There he was, the president, sitting in the middle of the office in his famous rocking chair, smoking a long and wonderfully perfumed Cuban cigar, reading some classified papers.

Solomon got to within five feet of the man, when he felt his knees shaking. Moe stood by his side. The two priests were on either side of the Jewish men. The president continued reading, even though he knew there was somebody in front of him. They waited until he had finished, then he looked up. A plastic smile spread across his face. Those large Kennedy white teeth shined out as his smile got larger. His tanned face belied the fact that he suffered from any type of illness. His cheeks, patted with cheap powder makeup, seemed flat and dull as he smiled and greeted his guests.

"Mister President, how are you today?" Father Marleski asked.

The president continued smiling "What is this, gentlemen?" he asked.

"This is the man that you asked for," the priest said. "Mister Barnes arranged it? Holy Water?"

The president stared longer at the priests and then at the two Jewish guys.

"But who are they? Twin Jewish guys?" he asked pointing to the Hassidic Jews.

Father Marleski was stymied. He was sure that Barnes had explained to everyone necessary including the attorney general.

"Well, which one of you is the man I need to talk to?" he asked.

"He is," they all said, and pointed to Solomon.

"He's supposed to perform some special duties for you, Sir."

"And why do I need all the rest of you?"

"We'll wait outside, Sir, if you wish."

"That's a good idea," the president said, and waved a slight hand indicating they should return to the sitting room in the hall.

Only Solomon was left with the president as the door closed. He continued to survey the scene of the Oval Office. It was just as the pictures showed it on TV. Solomon dropped his jaw as he viewed the room. The huge beige rug with the massive blue presidential seal, a loving picture on the wall of the first lady in a pink fluffy gown, the large dark brown presidential desk, basking in the sunlight from the windows behind it, and the man himself sitting in that comfortable Brumby homemade rocker.

"You're a great president, Mister President," Solomon said, the words barely coming out. He tried to clear his throat. "The best since Roosevelt. Probably the best ever." Solomon fumbled with his hat, holding it in front of him like an altar boy holding a candle.

"Thank you, Rabbi. Now how do we go about this special gift of yours."

"I never cured anybody of Addison's disease before, sir. But it really doesn't make any difference."

"You know?"

"Yes, sir," Solomon said.

"Well then you know about the pain I'm experiencing and the damage to the adrenal system."

"Yes, sir," Solomon repeated.

Solomon stood before the most important man in the world. The Hassidic Jew attending to the first Irish Catholic president the United States ever had.

"You know, I was thinking about going to Lourdes, but this will save me a trip, right? Besides, if I go to Lourdes everybody will wonder why I'm there and then there will be a thousand cameras, and…well this is much better."

"Yes, sir," Solomon said, in a half trance, and knelt down in front of the president who was still sitting in his rocking chair. The Healer carefully removed his gloves by pulling at the fingertips with his teeth. He placed his gloves on the ceremonial rug under the president's feet, and began to place his hands on the president's legs.

"Whoa, wait a minute," the president said looking at the gauze-bandaged hands of Solomon. "What are you going to do?"

"This is how I heal people," the surprised and humiliated Jewish man said with a servant-like response.

Kennedy stood up, with hands forward in protest.

"Well, I gotta have the secret service guys check this out first. You look like you have blood or something on your hands."

Solomon was stunned. "Yes, it is, but I thought you knew."

The president went over to the intercom.

"Bobby, you know anything about this Jewish Healer guy?"

"Yeah, Jack, he's cleared. Listen, Jack, just talked to McNamara. We need to do something to discredit the Cubans. We're getting a lot of heat in the papers."

"We'll talk about that later, Bobby. First I need to know about this guy in my office. Maybe you better get in here." He clicked the intercom off and went back to Solomon. He stood there eyeing the old man while he puffed on his cigar. No words were spoken, but he kept giving Solomon the third degree.

"You can't tell anybody about this, Rabbi. You understand that, don't you?"

Solomon just nodded his head. He was so astonished that he actually had spent two minutes with the president that his vocal chords had tightened up. "Yes," he eeked out.

"I mean nobody. Not doctors or lawyers and especially not anybody to do with the newspapers, or God forbid, any of those Republicans."

Solomon nodded again as he was still kneeling in front of Kennedy's rocker. Kennedy was unsteady about the whole thing, but anxious for a miracle.

He sat back into his rocker, but did so with a wary eye on the old man. He wondered if the Secret Service had checked him out enough. Should he call somebody in just in case? No way. The possibility of one of the Secret

Service knowing what he was about to try could mean the end of his political life.

The president eyed Solomon and stared at the kneeling Jewish guy. Their eyes locked and Solomon wondered what the president was thinking. Solomon felt a pang of guilt kicking him in the stomach, was he really exchanging his gift of healing for the right of free passage?

He looked back down to the president's legs and moved the edges of his fingers closer to the president's knees. The president still held himself away from Solomon.

"Mr. President, it's alright. You just have to believe. It's the main part of this. Please, Mister President, let me try it."

The president was still cautious and held his opened hand to Solomon. He wanted to make sure and he wanted Bobby there to assure him.

"Just wait one minute, Rabbi. I gotta think this through." The president looked to the door again and hollered.

"Bobby, where the hell are you?"

Solomon couldn't stand it. He was quivering. His hands, those miracle hands, if they could just touch the legs of his hero he could heal him. He thought to just reach out and grab the president's leg and hold on long enough for his powers to work. Would they work? Solomon thought to himself. Does he have the faith. Let me do it, he said to himself again. Just do it. What can he do? He can't kill me.

"Bobby," the president called out again as he stepped away from the rocker leaving Solomon groping at an empty chair.

The door flew open and the huge Doberman came pouncing in and jumped on the old man with a fury.

"Get away from me you stupid mutt," Solomon hollered at the dog. "Help me, somebody. Help me, help me."

The president hollered out into the hallway. "Bobby, one of your dogs is in here. C'mon over here and get him will you? He's just about to kill this old Jewish guy."

The dog never growled, but fastened his hungry jaws on Solomon's hands.

Father Marleski, Father Art and Moe came running into the Oval office behind the powerful black rocket and realized he was after Solomon's bloody hands again.

"Lord, help us" Father Marleski hollered as he grabbed the dog by the throat and put his own life in danger. He struggled with the dog and fought his stubbornness, sticking his hand next to Enos' teeth.

"Bobby, get in here. Get this damn dog out of here," the president hollered.

"Jack, I didn't bring a dog today," Bobby said as he came running to the Oval office. "Must belong to somebody else."

Father Art grabbed for the center of the dog, Father Marleski held his face and front shoulders and Moe held his kicking hind feet.

Solomon fought off his panic and sprung to his feet, grabbing his gloves from the floor as he jumped up. He covered his bloody hands with the gloves hoping it would deter the dog.

"What's this?" Father Marleski said, as he grabbed the yellow note from the dog's collar.

He squeezed the dog with one hand and unfolded the yellow sheet with the other.

"Moe, it's raining. Call Masha," the priest said, reading from the note.

The president pushed a special red panic button near his desk and five Secret Service men came flying into his office with guns drawn.

"Freeze," they demanded, holding forty-fives and small machine guns pointed at the holy men.

The Doberman jumped out of the arms of the priest and shot like a jet down the hall and back toward the front door.

"Don't shoot," the priest demanded. "He won't hurt anybody. He's Boyle's dog."

Bobby turned around and scolded the head of the Secret Service for allowing this to happen in the first place.

"It's raining!" Moe said to Solomon in almost a sacred voice. "Solly we gotta go."

Solomon looked at Moe, then the president and then all of the Secret Service men.

"But I haven't finished," he said. He looked at the president. "I have to finish," he demanded.

"Maybe another time," the president said, and motioned with the back of his hand for the Secret Service men to clear the office.

"What about my passport?" Solomon asked with wide eyes of disbelief, trying to get the Secret Service guys from pushing him out of the office. "I came all this way to get my passport."

"See Mister Barnes about that," Bobby said. "Now if you'll excuse us?"

The bodyguards cleared the office in a matter of seconds. Down the hall they led the religious men and to the security desk near the front door.

Solomon insisted, looking back as he was led away.

"What about my passport?" he kept asking in a pitiful voice. He could feel the chance of freedom dropping out of his body with every step away from the White House.

"C'mon Solly, let's go," Moe said as he helped his friend along.

They were near the front door where they saw Enos the Doberman, calm, relaxed, and ready to lead them somewhere else. They followed him out the front door, and were led unceremoniously by the bodyguards to the front gate, where Tom Stanley, and Leonard were waiting patiently.

"He found you," Stanley said in a happy surprised voice.

"He found us, but he cost me my life," Solomon said. "They threw us out. How am I going to get my passport?"

"I'll talk to Barnes," Marleski said. "He's got to understand. Remember we made no promises."

"Solomon I talked to Masha," Stanley said. "The gooney birds know where you are. They're coming for you. You gotta go now. That's why I brought your bags."

"Is all my stuff in it?" Solomon asked, referring to the money.

"Yes, and just to help you along, here's a cracker box to be used instead of a C-ration can."

"Got it," Solomon said.

"Where to now?" Moe asked.

"We can't go back to Boyle's house

"Hey, wait a minute," Father Marleski said. "I've got a great idea."

Chapter Sixteen

Solomon and Moe were on their way to National Airport, but in different cars. Father Marleski and Solomon flagged down a taxi, near the North entrance to the White House. Following behind the cab in the Lincoln were Father Art, Tom Stanley, Charlie Boyle, Leonard, Moe, and the dog.

"What gives?" the cabbie asked.

"Just follow that Lincoln," Father Marleski said. "We'll tell you the rest when we get close to the airport."

Traffic was moderate going to the airport, and Solomon kept tugging at his suit jacket, making sure the diamonds that Samuel had sewn in were still there. He fussed with his bags, and cleared about half the Ritz box, dropping waxed paper cylinders of crackers on the floor of the cab, and shoved money in the middle. The thin cardboard sides were cracking and the center of the box had a huge bulge.

"What are you going to do with all of that," the priest asked, holding his hand over his mouth as a privacy screen from the cabbie.

"My people can use it in the kibbutz," Solomon said. "They need medical supplies, and we're going to build a dispensary."

Father Marleski was touched. With all of Solomon's troubles and pain he could have been selfish about the money, but he thought of everybody else first.

Solomon checked on the diamonds again, that were sewn in the hem of the jacket.

"Don't worry, Solly," the priest said, with a compassionate smile. "I saw Samuel sew those things in. He was very meticulous."

Solomon listened and smiled, but he was still nervous and hoped that Marleski's plan could be pulled off.

The cabbie followed the Lincoln, but kept looking back in his mirror for any new instructions. "Hey, Rabbi, why do you wear those gloves in May? Is it a religious thing or something? Can't show your hands in public?" The cabbie was serious. "Hey, I know. Like maybe you got that special disease that affects them Jewish people?"

"Special disease?" Moe asked.

"Yeah, I read about it in one of those newspapers, you know the one that told about that lady who gave birth to that Australian monkey? Yeah, anyway, I read that Jewish people get this special disease. They get real cold and have to have their hands wrapped all the time."

Solomon did a slow turn and looked at Father Marleski, who was making a slow turn to look at Solomon. Each man raised his hands, shrugged his shoulders and looked at the cabbie to see if he was for real.

Solomon was so nervous he fussed with everything near him.

"I'm going to see Millie," he said to the priest. "I'm going to see my boys." The tears ran freely from Solomon's weary eyes and washed down his now skinny cheeks.

Father Marleski threw a huge arm around his friend and gave him one of his patented hugs that just about squeezed the air out of the old man.

"Some night when I'm sitting there around the fireplace with my feet up on a warm stole, reading my boring newspaper, I'm going to be thinking about you, Sollie. And I'm going to say to myself, 'gee, Marleski, you didn't even get killed tonight.'"

The two men laughed hard as they shook hands with a hearty gesture and expressed to each other their lifelong friendship without saying a word.

Solly looked ahead through the windshield of the cab and spotted his friend Moe looking out the back window waving and crying.

Solomon broke down and cried harder and Marleski held an arm around him tighter.

"It has to be done, my friend. You have no other choice," Marleski said.

As the Lincoln pulled up to the El Al airlines, Father Marleski and Solomon hunched down in the back seat so they couldn't be seen.

"Okay, cabbie, go straight ahead, all the way to Alitalia."

The cabbie looked in his mirror saw an empty backseat and eased on the brakes.

"Hey, where'd you guys go?" he asked.

"Just keep going," Solomon said, as he and Marleski were huddled down.

"Man, you guys are weird," the cabbie said.

Father Marleski picked his head up just long enough to make sure the Lincoln pulled over and Moe, Father Art, and Tom Stanley headed for the El Al ticket counter.

"Pull in front of that limo just up ahead there, cabbie," the priest said.

Marleski was peeking above the seat. "Yeah, that's good. Okay, Sollie, are you ready to make a run for it?"

"I'm ready, Padre. Just tell me when."

"Should be just a couple minutes."

Moe and Father Art sauntered up to the long line at the El Al ticket counter with Father Art's bag in his hand. Moe and Father Art tried to be nonchalant, but they were also trying their best to attract attention at the same time, but the people they wanted to be watching them weren't.

They shuffled their feet a bit with nervousness.

"I'm going to be late," Moe said, with a voice that was less than a whisper.

"You'll be okay," Father Art said making sure he was talking just as loud as his friend was.

Several people focused in on them and their rather unordinary volume for a regular conversation.

"What if I miss the plane to Tel Aviv?" Moe asked Art, again with a tone louder than normal.

"Then you'll have to buy your own plane and fly it yourself."

The loud talking didn't take long, Art thought. They especially caught the eyes and ears of two dapper dressed men standing near the counter who started toward them.

"Here, they come," Father Art whispered, as he pulled on the brim of his hat and turned his head slightly downward. "Are you ready to run?"

"On your command," Moe said, as he handed the bag to the younger man.

The suspicious looking goons quickened their pace as they came toward the two religious men, pushing other customers aside they came closer still.

"When I say, 'go', just go," Art said.

"I'm ready," Moe said back.

"Five, four, three two, one, let's go," Art said, and the two men took off for the front door, pushing people aside as they ran, and right toward Tom Stanley who was standing watch by the front entrance.

"C'mon, Tommy, give us some cover so we can get out of here," Moe said.

Moe and Father Art headed for the open door of the airport, did a quick right turn, headed for the curb while holding their hats on their heads as they ran, and darted straight for the open back door of the Lincoln. Tom Stanley waited by the front entrance, and threw his famous body block at the two cops to slow them down. All three of them hit the ground with several other passengers; spilling bags and scraping knees in the fight.

Tom wrestled with the two goons and wanted to make a quick break for it, but one of the cops tied him up in an arm lock. Leonard saw Tom in trouble and was about to come to his rescue when the Doberman came flying out of the car and headed over into the fight.

"No, Enos," Charlie Boyle hollered, but it was too late. The Doberman made a long leap at the cop who had Tom Stanley and grabbed at his arm, causing the cops to drop the to the ground for protection.

"Get back here, Enos," Charlie hollered. He whistled for the dog with his special shrilling sound and the dog backed off the two men and ran to the car, diving through an open window.

"Let's go," Charlie said. "Let's hope they follow us."

"Oh, no," Art said. "They're running after us instead of getting a car and chasing us. Where's Tommy going?"

"He's headed for the parking lot. He's trying to totally confuse them. They're supposed to follow us."

"Damn it. I'm going," Charlie said. "If these cops are so stupid they don't have a car nearby, how can Solomon get away? If we don't go now they'll think we're supposed to be caught."

The cops stopped chasing Tom to the parking lot and came after the Lincoln. Charlie waited until the cops had their pistols drawn, watched as they pointed the weapons, and floored the Lincoln, leaving a long streak of rubber at the National Airport curb.

The two cops stopped in their tracks, aimed to fire, thought better of it and headed back to the curb, jumping into their own car and raced after the Lincoln.

Father Marleski and Solomon picked their heads up in the back seat of the cab, paid the cabbie with one of Marleski's one hundred dollar bills, never looked for change, grabbed a couple bags for Solomon and shot for the ticket counter at Alitalia.

Solomon grinned a horrible, huge smile as he came out of the back of the taxi. He was still grinning and laughing as Marleski helped him carry his bags.

They both surveyed the scene near the north entrance and went directly to the open ticket counter at the Italian Airlines.

"Yes, Sir, Rabbi, may I help you?" the ticket agent said without looking up.

"One ticket for Rome and then Tel Aviv," Solomon answered.

"You can take a direct flight on the Israeli airline," the helpful man said.

"Yes, I know, but I really want to try the Italian airline this time," Solomon said. "I heard you have great food."

"Yes, sir we do. Do you have reservations?" the ticket clerk asked.

"No, but I heard you always have room on Alitalia. Isn't that your slogan?"

"All I have is First Class," the man said with a distinct accent.

"How much?"

"Five hundred and twenty seven dollars, Rabbi."

Solomon reached into his front pocket and had a hard time trying to pull the money out with his gloved hands.

"Here," the priest said, as he fished into Solomon's pockets, pulled out a wad of bills, and laid the money on the counter.

"Is that one way or round trip?" Solomon asked.

"Round trip, sir."

Solomon looked at the priest, and then the ticket agent. "But I only need it one way. How much for one way?" Solomon asked.

The clerk stared at Solomon

"I need to see a passport," the clerk said.

Solomon reached into his suit jacket pocket and pulled out a passport giving it to the clerk.

The clerk stared at it for a moment, eyed Solomon, eyed the priest and started writing the ticket, with a rather indifferent attitude.

"Well, here's why you need a round trip ticket," the clerk began to explain. "When you get to Rome, the officials will detain you for hours, thinking you are a troublemaker because you are going only one way. I'm just saving you the trouble. A round trip ticket saves you the grief. If you don't come back, you can get a refund."

"So give me a round trip ticket already," Solomon said.

"Yessir, and here you are, Mister," the clerk said as he eyed the passport again. " Mister Moshe Kessler. Did I pronounce that right?"

"That's right," Solomon said. " Mister Kessler. Mister Moshe Kessler." The smile on Solomon's face was broad enough to push his bushy mustache almost up to his eyes. "Thank you, young man. I'll dance at your wedding."

The ticket clerk smiled at the two likeable religious guys and reached for the larger of Solomon's bags, checking it all the way through to Tel Aviv. Solomon kept the smaller suitcase, an old black leather one, somewhat bigger than an overnight bag, but still stuffed with clothes and items that he held close enough to his side to become part of his skin.

"Gate sixteen at four-thirty PM. You'll have to go through customs first before you board, Rabbi."

"Let's go, Padre," Solomon said to Marleski.

The two men walked toward the gate with Solomon pushing his normal walking pace. Solomon was so eager to get on the plane, that he began praying in Yiddish, with the priest answering his chants in Latin, with quick bursts, and each nodding his head to the religious beat.

"Gate sixteen," he said in Yiddish. "It's going to take me home."

"Remember, Sol, keep your hands covered as much as you can."

They reached the entrance to the gate and Father Marleski stood back as Solomon entered.

"Bags up here, Buddy," a burly black guy said to Solomon.

Solomon looked back at Marleski and had an unusual fresh look of confidence. His smile was clear. He was going home.

"Got any illegal contraband on you, Mister?" the customs agent asked.

"No," Solomon answered. "What's a contraband?"

"Got anything to declare?"

"No."

The customs man grabbed the bag and threw it with the grace of a chimpanzee.

"Hey, Chuck," the customs agent hollered to his helper. "Check this one out. Something's fishy here. Guy wears leather gloves in May."

"Okay, buddy come over here and open this bag."

Marleski went as close as he could to the gate in case Solomon needed his help. Solomon went forward and his confidence of getting home had just vanished. The guard zipped the bag opened and dumped the contents of Solomon's tightly packed clothes and special items on the exam table.

Out came all of Solomon's sacred stuff: shaving kit, white shirts, underwear, T-shirts, socks, and a large block of hundred dollar bills, about the size of a half a loaf of bread, wrapped with heavy-duty brown butcher paper and cheap rubber bands.

"Whooooaaa. Well, what's this," the obnoxious agent asked as he held the block of bills in his hand.

"It's my total life savings," Solomon answered with a perfectly practiced tone. I need an operation, and they don't take Blue Cross, or checks in Tel Aviv. Only good old fashioned American or Jewish cash."

"Oh, yeah, like I'm gonna believe that, pal. Okay, let's get the truth. Get the supervisor over here. I think you're going to jail, buddy. Don't you know you're only allowed to take a limited amount of money out of the country?

You a drug dealer or something?"

Solomon was sweating as he stared at both of his investigators, turned to Father Marleski for help, and then looked down at his hands. Was it possible that the crooked cops notified all of the airlines about him leaving? He hesitated for a moment, wondering if he should run, but his legs told him otherwise. He hesitated for a while, then began to whimper and pull at the fingertips of his gloves with his teeth. He made his movements jerky and noisy for effect.

"What do you got there?" the guard asked with his gruff tone.

Solomon didn't speak, but laid the gloves down and began unwrapping the white gauze bandages. He let the gauze pile up on top of the unceremonious heap of clothes dumped by the agent. As he got closer to his naked hands the eyes of the agents began to focus on his actions. They weren't sure what they were seeing, but had to let their official curiosity be satisfied.

The gauze got thinner down to only about three layers when one of the agents freaked out.

"Stop, man. Is that blood? I can see you got some damn disease or something, what is it?"

"You mean you didn't read about it in the Enquirer?" Father Marleski said as he came up behind Solomon. "Even the cabbie who brought us here knows about the rare disease that attacks Jewish men."

"Man, don't take the rest of those bandages off."

"Okay," Solomon said. "You don't want to look? Everybody else wants to look," he said, and he held up his palms toward the small crowd around him, hoping to embarrass his interviewers who held their hands in front of them as an artificial screen from the grotesque sight. The gauze was hanging like a worn popcorn stringer on a Christmas tree, but still partly covering the wounds.

"No man, it ain't necessary. Just tell us about the money. How much is here?"

"I don't know, they told me I could be in the hospital for months. Probably need about ten thousand."

"Look, Mister, uhh what's your name?"

"Kessler. Moe Kessler."

"Okay look, Mister Kessler, we gotta talk to our supervisors about this. You have any other papers on you? You might have to be quarantined."

Father Marleski reached into Solomon's inside suit jacket pocket and pulled out the souvenir photo that Father Marleski had secretly smuggled in there. Solomon was amazed that he had it, causing the agent to also stare at it.

"Hey, Chuck, look at this picture," the agent said to the man who was rifling Solomon's bag. "It's the president, and the attorney general, and their wives. It's real."

Solomon looked over to Marleski and realized who put the photo there. "Of course it's real," Solomon said, looking back at the guard. "I'm a very good friend of both of them."

"God, Chuck. If we stop this guy from getting through, we could be in big trouble. You know how the boss hates to get into trouble with any of this political stuff. Remember the time we stopped that Sorenson fella. Man did we catch hell."

"Yeah, sorry, Mister whatever your name is, here let us help you repack your bag. Damn you don't look like somebody who knows the president like real good friends."

"Looks are deceiving," Solomon said.

The two customs men jumped into action, packing the white shirts, underwear, shaving kit, and then the sacred picture of the Kennedys. They handed his passport back to him and knocked the picture out of his hand. When the agent bent down to pick it up for Solomon he studied it further.

"Hey, wait a minute, Mister It says 'to my good friend, Solomon'. Your name is Moshe."

Solomon and Marleski froze with panic. These guards weren't stupid afterall, they thought. Solomon could fake out the Gestapo, but some stupid security cops at the airport would be his undoing.

"Actually," Solomon stuttered. "The first lady always calls me Solomon. The president picked up on it. He always said I help him make very wise decisions. For instance, I'll remember your names and give some suggestions to the attorney general on why you should be made sergeants or something, instead of baggage checkers."

"Yessir, Mister. My name is Pookich." He was smiling with a stupid looking puffy cheek look.

"And mine's Dernicky," the other one said as he handed Solomon his unwrapped brick of hundred dollar bills.

"Oh, believe me, I'll remember those names, don't even have to write them down," Solomon said. "Hey, you want some Ritz Crackers?" he extended the box forward to the inspectors.

The guards thought about sticking their hands in the same box with a man who was bleeding to death.

"No thank you," they said.

Solomon fumbled with the block of money and hanging gauze at the same time, but put the block safely back into his suitcase. The gauze was still dragging on the clothes as he peeled about five old one hundred-dollar bills off the top of the stack, crumpled the bills up like paper balls, and dropped them on the floor. The eyes of the agents followed the paper balls and Chuck covered them neatly in one swift motion with his foot. Blood on Ritz Crackers they would never touch? But, blood on a bunch of hundred dollar bills? That was worth taking a chance for.

"Make sure you don't tell anybody about this," Father Marleski said to the two agents, with an official whisper, and an unofficial wink of the eye. "The Rabbi here and the president both like their privacy."

"We understand, sir. Your plane is over there, gate sixteen. Let me help you with your bag."

"Thank you," Solomon said, as he wound up his gauze bandages, grabbed his small suitcase, his prized box of crackers with about fifty thousand dollars in it, and headed for the first class section of the plane. He paused just for a moment and turned back to his old friend Father Marleski.

Solomon stood there, tears rolling down his now sunken cheeks as he stared at his friend for the last time.

"See you in heaven, Padre."

"God Bless you, Rabbi," Marleski said back.

"I'm really not going to live much longer am I, Padre?"

Marleski didn't answer with words, but with a religious smile letting him know that more important things waited for him.

"I just want to know one thing, Padre. Why? Why did the Lord pick me?"

Marleski put his hand on Solomon for the last time.

"Solly, everyone of us in life are given a special assignment, but we never know why."

Solomon looked at his friend and tears fell freely from his squinting eyes. "I could have healed that Kennedy guy. Why didn't he let me touch him? I could have healed him, Padre. I know it. Did you see how sick he was? The flesh on his neck was dark and loose. His eyes were just staring straight ahead begging for my help. I know it, Padre. I know it."

"God bless you, Solly," Marleski said.

The old Jewish man smiled hard at his friend, tears rolling down his once cheerful cheeks, hugged Father Marleski and started back toward the plane. He walked with his usual short stroke steps down the gateway, handed his ticket to the pretty Italian stewardess with the silky black hair and smiled.

"You know why I decided to fly on the Italian plane?" he asked her.

"No, Rabbi," she said with a friendly accent.

"They advertise in the magazine that they got that good, cold, Italian beer on board. When you fly the Jewish airlines, you know what? All they serve you is coffee, tea or juice. When I get to Israel I'll have plenty of time for juice, but tonight, it's cold Italian beer."

Solomon waved to his comrade Marleski, who was still standing there by the pillar, and threw a fumbling kiss with his shaking hand to the rest of the airport in a final gesture for leaving America. He turned toward the opened door of the airplane, lifted his head and walked forward. He reached his hand out to the captain waiting at the door. He smiled harder, but the tears never stopped falling down his cheeks. He could feel the warm air from the hot sands of the Israeli desert calling him to his lasting freedom.